Jane Isaac studied creative writing with The Writers Bureau and the London School of Journalism. She was runner-up 'Writer of the Year 2013' with The Writers Bureau. Jane lives in rural Northamptonshire with her husband, daughter and dog, Bollo.

Jane's debut novel *An Unfamiliar Murder* was nominated as best mystery in the 'eFestival of Words Best of the Independent eBook awards'.

The Truth Will Out

Jane Isaac

Legend Press Ltd, The Old Fire Station, 140 Tabernacle Street,
London, EC2A 4SD
info@legend-paperbooks.co.uk | www.legendpress.co.uk

 British Library Cataloguing in Publication Data available.

Print ISBN 978-1-9098785-5-6
Ebook ISBN 978-1-9098785-6-3

Set in Times
Cover design by Gudrun Jobst www.yotedesign.com
Printed in the United Kingdom by TJ International

Acknowledgements

There are many people who helped nurture this novel to fruition. Firstly, I must thank David at Rutland Minis for listening with good humour when you received that Wednesday morning phone call early last year, asking about storage space in the door panel of a Mini. Your knowledge and advice was much appreciated and any deviation or errors in the book are purely my own.

Thanks also to my good friend and retired Detective Superintendent, Glyn Timmins, who gave me so much time and insight into senior policing. The next lunch is definitely on me.

I was very fortunate to have the ear of Dr Jenny McGillion who gave valuable advice and insight on the psychological background of one of the characters. Thank you for your time and frankness.

To my four beta readers: Susan Harris Dorsey, Rebecca Bradley, Kev Wooldridge and Kate Anderson. Your feedback was very valuable, certainly improved the story and helped to make it what it is today.

Gratitude goes to Lauren Parsons, Tom Chalmers, Lucy Chamberlain and all the lovely team at Legend Press for believing in the novel, taking it off their slush pile and being so supportive throughout the publication process.

I am blessed with wonderful friends and family whose input and support has helped tremendously along the way: Dionne Lister, Bernadette Davies, Emma Thompson, Peter Arnold, Stephanie Daniels, Jean Bouch and Derek Archer.

Most of all, I wish to thank David and Ella - for absolutely everything.

To Derek and Penny, two of life's special people.

Chapter **One**

Eva Carradine's foot tapped a staccato rhythm as she sat back in her chair and waited for her computer to connect. Green velvet curtains shrouded the window beside her. An umbrella lamp and gas fire combined with the light of her laptop to produce a soft hue in the room, just enough for her to view the buttons on her keyboard.

Naomi's face appeared on the screen in front of her. No pleasantries were exchanged. No gestures made. "I can't do this anymore."

Eva's stomach fisted. She stared at her friend's crumpled face. "Naomi, don't... We said we wouldn't talk about this. We promised." The image on her laptop flickered as Naomi reached across and took a glug from a glass of red. Crisp classical notes rose and fell in the background. "How was work?"

Naomi shook her head. "Hopeless. I can't concentrate." Her glass clattered as it hit the hard surface.

Eva flinched. "You need to get a grip." She took a deep breath, "Everything's going to be okay."

"What if it's not?"

Suddenly Naomi turned. For a split second she halted, her head inclined.

"Naomi, what is it?"

She whisked back to face Eva. "There's somebody in the house… "

The gloved hand appeared from nowhere. It stretched across Naomi's mouth gripping her head back tightly, pulling her skin taut across her cheekbones.

Eva stared at the computer screen in horror. "Naomi?"

Naomi was pulled away, out of view. Eva heard crashing noises as blurred movements flashed across the screen. Urgent voices were muffled by the tranquil sound of Beethoven's 6th, still playing distantly in the background. It was surreal, almost in slow motion, as if it were taking place underwater.

Eva's throat constricted. She leant in closer. "Naomi!"

A flash in the distance. Somebody approached the screen. The hand. It loomed towards her…

As it drew nearer, Eva felt the paralysis of fear take over. Just as the hand reached her, she scooted back, adrenalin igniting every muscle in her body with a sudden kick of energy. She fell over her chair, sending a coffee mug and a pile of magazines crashing to the floor in her scramble to get as far away as possible. A movement flashed over the Skype box on the screen before it went blank.

Naomi! A sharp pain spiked Eva's lower back. She pressed her hand to it.

What should she do? Call an ambulance? The police? No! Not the police. Definitely, not the police…

***

Ten minutes later, Eva opened her front door and glanced nervously up and down the street. A light carpet of snow covered everything in sight; an icy draft pinched at every bare patch of skin. She rushed past the maple out front, whipping its branches angrily against the relentless wind. By the time she had secured her case, locked her front door and reached the comfort of the driver's seat, her teeth were chattering incessantly.

Eva wiped a palm across her forehead, pushing strands of hair out of her face. In desperation, she pulled her mobile phone out of her pocket and dialled Naomi's number for the umpteenth time. The phone rang out – one, two, three – when it reached six and the answer phone kicked in, the muscles in Eva's hands were trembling violently.

She glanced at the clock. The ambulance would be there by now. Eva yearned to see Naomi, make sure she was okay. But going over there could mean… A shiver skittered down her spine. She dialled another number, cursing as it switched to voicemail, leaving a desperate message. Come on, Jules. He had to be there. He promised.

Eva drew a shaky breath and ignited the engine. It was going to be a very long night.

Chapter **Two**

Detective Chief Inspector Helen Lavery rubbed her forehead and forced herself to take another look at the photograph of sixteen-year-old Kieran Harvey that filled her computer screen. His buckled frame was closed into a foetal position, a hand stretched towards the curb, beautiful blond hair soaked in blood.

She clicked a button and brought up another image next to it. Leon Stratton looked younger than his seventeen years, his lithe body contorted on the tarmac, arm wedged unnaturally under his body, a gaping hole in the centre of his chest.

Helen's stomach knotted every time she looked at them. Kieran reminded her of Matthew whilst Leon's dark hair and skinny body looked just like Robert. Her own boys - just a few years younger than these dead shells.

She turned the photos around on the screen, as if looking at them from another angle would offer up some new clue they hadn't already discovered. Their backgrounds suggested a link, but no murder weapon had been discovered. Both shootings occurred within a month of each other, a year ago in Roxten. Yet, despite huge police efforts, they still hadn't been able to produce a credible suspect for either crime.

Helen massaged the back of her neck. She hated homicide cold case review; the burning sense of injustice got underneath her skin and slunk about like a worm trying to find its way out.

The press had cranked up the pressure. They pounced on the shooting of fifteen-year-old Germaine Long in nearby London two weeks earlier, claiming that the UK was developing an escalating culture of gang related gun crime.

In an effort to placate, the Home Secretary had declared that incidents involving firearms in the UK were at their lowest for twenty years. But, like a cornered wasp, the press fought hard, whipping the public into a frenzy and forcing the newly elected Police Commissioners to focus on every unsolved firearms incident. They wanted results and fast.

She looked back at the photos and considered the linking factors. Both boys shared previous records for assault and possession of cannabis. Intelligence indicated that both were linked to a group who called themselves the 'East Side Boys', which, it was suspected, were responsible for a significant amount of acquisitive crime in Roxten. She switched to the map on her laptop.

Once a quaint village on Hampton's periphery, Roxten was swallowed into the midland's city during the 1970s when migrants flooded into the town as it expanded to accommodate London overspill. A contemporary architect was commissioned to design several new cutting edge estates to make maximum use of the space available. Housing estates grandly named 'The Royal Albert' and 'The Queen Victoria', which later became known generically as 'the rabbit warren', were comprised of numerous alleys and back entrances making them particularly difficult to police.

When austerity tightened the screws during the depression of the 1980s, a cloud of darkness descended on Roxten and the rabbit warren, now the less salubrious area, was dragged into a pit of gloom.

Helen yawned. The rabbit warren was where both boys had lived, where both murders had been committed. And, after working Roxten for a year as an immediate response sergeant during her ten-year career, she knew more than anybody that getting evidence out of residents of the rabbit warren was near on impossible.

She stretched out her arms, glanced at the clock. Twenty past eight. Her eyes brushed a photo in a rustic frame on the corner of the desk. As she picked it up and fingered the outline of her late husband, a familiar longing flooded her chest. Briefly, she allowed herself to wonder how different her life would have been if he hadn't died so suddenly ten years ago. She wouldn't be squirreled in her study, working her evenings away before curling up to watch the late news and venturing off to bed, alone.

The buzz of her mobile interrupted her thoughts.

"Ma'am, this is Inspector Staples in the control room. We have the body of a young woman at eight Brooke Street, Hampton. Cause of death is gunshot wounds to the chest."

***

Brooke Street was located off Hampton High Street in the centre of the city. Red-bricked terraces lined the curbside with front doors that opened directly onto narrow strips of pavement. By the time Helen arrived it was a hive of activity. Police cars parked at angles blocked off either end, an ambulance sat in situ, filling the middle of the road. Uniformed officers swarmed around neighbouring terraces, assiduously searching out witnesses and taking statements. In spite of the inclement weather, the pavement was littered with nosey residents desperately trying to get a handle on what was happening. Helen even recognised a few members of the local press and raised her eyes to the heavens. It didn't take long for the vultures to descend.

She slipped through the rubberneckers and made her way

up to number eight through a cloud of cotton wool puffs. The earlier rain had turned to snow, thick flakes falling like feathers from the sky. It was hard to believe it was the middle of March; the clocks would be going forward in a couple of weeks.

Helen nodded and flashed her badge at the uniformed officer at the entrance to number eight. He was stamping his feet, blowing into his hands in an effort to keep warm. She pitied his position, recalling being ordered to guard a crime scene once as a probationer. By the time relief arrived, she had been bored out of her brain and desperate for the toilet.

She paused briefly to gown herself up and sign into the crime scene log, then moved into the house. Immediately the smell of burnt carbon tainted her nose, like the smell that lingers in the air on fireworks night. Shards of glass crunched under her feet as she crossed the threshold and glanced around, trying to look past the devastation. The lounge resembled a war zone. The cream silk curtains were spattered with blood. Soft, black cushions were scattered around the room haphazardly. A black fur rug lay scrunched up in a corner. She could see that the glass beneath her feet had largely belonged to a mirror that lay in pieces on the shiny laminate flooring, in front of the fireplace. Only a rosewood piano, gleaming under the lights on the far wall seemed to have escaped.

Her eyes rested on the body of a young woman, crumpled on the floor next to an old desk and an upturned chair in the corner. Tumbled over her face and shoulders were vibrant locks of ginger hair, mingled with congealed blood. A spray of red covered the wall behind her.

Crime scene investigators moved about busily like an army of white clothed ants. She nodded to a few of them, then headed straight across to the body and crouched down to take a closer look. Beneath the strands of hair that partially obscured the face were green, glassy eyes. In spite of the purple patches across her cheek and the split in her lip she could see that this had once been a very attractive lady. And so young. Helen felt a pang in her chest.

The victim's legs were curled up, her right arm flung out to the side. She wore black jeans and a loose vest top, which bore two bullet holes in the centre; a few patches around the bottom and one of the shoulder straps, the only clue to its original lime green colour.

Helen became aware of a close presence and looked up to see Sergeant Sean Pemberton tower over her. Almost as wide as he was tall, his bald head glowed under the bright lighting.

He lifted his head in greeting, "Ma'am," he said, an underlying growl exposing his Yorkshire roots.

Helen stood, barely reaching his shoulder. "Hi, Sean."

After working on an incident with Sean Pemberton last year, she'd fought to acquire his services to fill a permanent DS post in the Homicide and Serious Crime Squad. Pemberton was a seasoned, no nonsense detective whose approach to policing reminded her of her late father, James Lavery, who had managed murder investigations for fifteen years before his retirement.

"Thanks for getting everything set up here." She gave a sideways nod. "What do we know about the victim?"

He turned a page of the notebook in his hand. "Naomi Spence. According to a neighbour across the road she'd lived here a couple of years. Hospitality graduate, worked at Memington Hall hotel as an events planner. Not known to us. Likely cause of death would be the gunshot wounds to the chest, although by the looks of her she put up a pretty good fight. PC Havant was first on scene. Used to be with firearms. He reckons the size of the bullet holes are consistent with a small calibre hand gun."

Helen scanned the body. "There are two bullet wounds to the front, but only one exited, so at least two rounds were discharged," Pemberton said. "It's possible the other is lodged in there somewhere but the autopsy will confirm that. Can't find the shells."

She followed his arm and her eyes rested on a bullet lodged into the skirting board, which somebody was meticulously photographing from different angles. "Okay, make sure you get that off to ballistics as soon as," Helen said. She lowered her voice to continue, "See if you can speak to that mate of yours in the testing lab and pull some strings?"

He nodded. "Sure."

"Any sign of a break in?" she asked, her voice resuming its normal level.

"It doesn't look like it, we've checked front and rear. Both were locked when uniform arrived. They had to force entry themselves."

"So we think she may have known her attacker?"

"In the absence of another route… " He wrinkled his nose and nodded. "Wouldn't have been difficult to let themselves out. There's only an old Yale lock on the front door."

"What about keys?" she asked. It wouldn't be the first time an assailant made off in the victim's car.

Pemberton smiled knowingly. "Two sets hanging up in the kitchen. Car keys too," he said, second guessing her next question. "Looks like she owned the red Fiesta parked up the road."

Helen looked back at the body. "Any suspects?"

"Not at this point. The informant was female. She phoned an ambulance from a mobile number. Pay as you go, not registered so we can't trace it. Didn't identify herself. She'd left the scene by the time we arrived."

"Strange." Helen looked around the room. This didn't fit the usual profile of a female murderer. Although women accounted for around a quarter of UK murders each year, they usually lacked the gratuitous violence adopted by male killers. And they rarely used firearms. She looked back at the bruising across Naomi's arm and face. "Any witnesses?"

"Not as yet. I've got uniform started on house to house, so hopefully that'll dig up something soon."

"Good." Helen swept her eyes across the room again. Whoever did this steamrollered through the victim's lounge, then fired two bullets. They certainly weren't discreet in their actions. "Anything missing?"

"Doesn't look like it. Odd though. They've turned the whole house upside down looking for something."

Looking for something… Helen could see the flat-screen television and DVD player were still in situ. A Wii games console lay on its side on the floor.

"What about her handbag?" she said.

"We found that in the cupboard under the stairs." Pemberton pointed towards the hallway. "Twenty pounds in cash, along with a few coppers, credit cards, all there." He hesitated. "No mobile phone though."

So, this wasn't a burglary gone wrong, Helen thought. The offender was looking for something specific, something worth killing for.

She looked down, glimpsed something on the floor and bent down to examine it. The frame was broken, the edge torn, but it was definitely a picture of the victim, with the same flaming hair pulled back from her face with sunglasses. She had her arm around a blond girl. They were both in jeans and bright fleece tops, smiling broadly. Both girls looked in their early twenties. The photo oozed youth, vitality, opportunity.

She looked back at the body. "What about time of death?"

"Pathologist's best guess is between six and eight o'clock at this stage."

"He's already been?" Helen flashed her eyes to the door.

"You just missed him. Dr Gooding arrived same time as me, about eight forty."

"Great." She rolled her eyes. Out of the two pathologists that covered their area, Gooding was the least thorough. And he hated being on call. They were unlikely to get anything solid out of him until the morning. She turned and called across the room, "Alan, okay if I take a look around?"

Alan Jones was the CSI supervisor, a slim, bespectacled man with sharp, pointy features. He was bent over the bullet in the skirting board, examining the surrounding area. He glanced sideways. "Yes, but stay on the white paper. We've taken some preliminary photos, but they've been all over the house." He sniffed. "Looks like we'll be here for days."

"Okay." She gave Pemberton a quick nod and wandered out through the hallway into the kitchen alone.

Many of the cupboard doors were open. Broken dishes, pans and tins of food spilled out onto the floor. Again, Helen tried to look past the devastation. The galley style kitchen was partially fitted with pine veneer cupboards. It looked like somebody had run out of money to finish it off. A folding table sat in the far corner with two collapsible chairs leant against it. No dishes in the sink, no coffee cups on the side. Two wine glasses sat on the drainer.

She rubbed her purple, gloved hands together. The pungent aroma of red wine filled the air. A drawer hung out containing appliance instructions. Another drawer that looked as though it had been derailed in the search contained a messy host of mobile phone chargers. A third, an array of new birthday cards.

Helen made her way up the steep stairs, carefully keeping her feet to the metre wide strip of white paper rolled over the carpet, her knees aching as she reached the landing. She counted three rooms on the first floor. She bypassed the bathroom and headed for the spare bedroom. The pink floral duvet and pillows were pulled off the bed and the empty drawer beneath sat askew with blankets, throws and spare pillows strewn across the floor.

She moved into the main bedroom. Books had been swept from the bookshelf and jumpers, t-shirts, underwear from a nearby chest of drawers filled the floor. She opened the closet. At the bottom, shoes had been tipped out of boxes and sat haphazardly on top of one another. Helen looked up to see dresses, suits and casual wear hanging neatly from their rail. The stark contrast between the orderly hung clothes and the disarray of shoes surprised Helen. She stared at them for a moment, her eyes working from one to another. The arrangement of the clothes was the real Naomi, before someone had blasted through her home in their search.

As she stared at the hangers she thought about her own wardrobe, packed tightly, about three quarters of the clothes never seeing the light of day - either they didn't fit her anymore, or she hadn't found the time to sort them out. But Naomi was tidy, ordered. No doubt the rest of the house usually followed the same suit.

Helen sighed and remembered her own mother nagging at her when she was a child. 'A tidy house is a tidy mind,' she used to say. Well Naomi Spence had a very tidy mind. So what went wrong?

She headed back towards the top of the stairs and entered the bathroom. Towels spilled out of the linen cupboard in the corner. The contents of the medicine cabinet filled the white sink, door still ajar. Even the top to the toilet cistern had been removed.

Speckles of white on the windowsill caught her eye. Helen leant forward, focusing on the area. There were more grains, white in colour.

She turned to the door and shouted for Pemberton.

Within seconds he had taken the stairs, two at a time, and was standing next to her. "What is it, ma'am?"

"What does that look like to you?" She pointed at the

grains of powder.

He bent down to take a closer look. "Are we thinking cocaine? It's definitely the remnants of a line of something."

"Ask CSI to come up here and bag it up, will you? I think we might have a victim with a habit."

As Pemberton disappeared, Helen chewed the side of her mouth. She was just wondering if the killer could have been searching for drugs, when she heard a faint noise. Her body stiffened to listen. Nothing. Just as Pemberton walked back in, it came again. She tried to place it. Pemberton moved towards the windowsill and she grabbed his arm to hold him still. He looked at her curiously, opened his mouth to speak, but she shook her head to silence him. It seemed to be coming from the landing. She let go of his arm and followed her ears out there, eyes darting about, searching for the source. "What was that?"

"What?"

There it was again. A faint tap. A scratch. She stopped.

"It's just CSI… "

"It's coming from up there." Her eyes rested on the loft hatch. The cover sat crooked. She narrowed her eyes to focus on a few small tufts of fibreglass that poked through the hole. When she looked down she could see more wisps littering the floor beneath.

"It's been disturbed recently," she said quietly.

They both stood still and listened to the intermittent rustling that grew louder and softer, then louder again. It was a strain to hear it at times, with all the noise from downstairs.

"Something's up there. Let's take a look." She grabbed a chair from Naomi's bedroom and placed it underneath the hatch.

Pemberton met her gaze. He continued in a hushed tone, "You're not suggesting…?"

"More likely a mouse or rat."

"Can't stand rats." He shook his shoulders.

Helen snorted, smiling fleetingly at how a bear of a man like Pemberton could be frightened of such a small creature. Rats weren't her favourite animals either, something to do with the tails, but it wasn't the possibility of facing a rat that bothered her right now. Whatever the killer was looking for could be hidden up there.

"Hold up." Pemberton said. He reached out his arm to stop her as she tried to board the chair. "You're never going to see, even if you stand on that."

She looked at him and raised a brow.

He rolled his eyes and pulled a small Maglite torch out of his pocket. "I can't believe I'm doing this."

The chair wobbled as he climbed on. Helen had to clasp it with both hands to keep it steady. He lifted the hatch slowly, and raised his head through the open space. A raw draft wafted through the gap. All was quiet. She watched him shine the torch.

"Well, well, well… " he said.

"What is it?"

Suddenly there was a fluttering noise. It grew urgent and louder until within a split second, Pemberton had toppled off the chair and onto the floor. Helen just managed to duck out of the way in time.

The whole house shook under Pemberton's weight.

She gaped at him for a moment, letting out a sigh of relief when he raised his head and rubbed the back of it. "Sean, are you okay?"

He squirmed around on the floor for a bit, twisted his back this way and that then swung his feet around to a seated position. "No harm done. Good job it was a soft landing."

She stared at him and the thin carpet beneath.

"Believe me," he continued, grinning. "When you're this size, it's always a soft landing."

"Everyone alright up there?" Alan shouted from below.

"Yes, thank you," she called back. "Sergeant Pemberton's just testing out the floorboards."

"Make sure you keep to the white paper!" Steve called back.

Pemberton pulled a face as he shuffled back onto the paper. She watched him rub the base of his back. "Sure you're okay?"

"Fine."

They turned their attention to the source of the noise. A small blackbird fluttered around their heads in panic. "Must have been looking for a warm place to roost, away from the snow," he said. "Come in through a gap in the roof tiles, I bet, and got stuck."

She pressed her lips together. "Anyway," she looked back up at the hatch, "what did you see up there?"

He rubbed his back some more, but when he met her gaze she could see a twinkle of recognition in his eye. "I think we need to get the ladders in and take a closer look."

***

Eva screwed up her eyes to focus on the road as she drove north, the soft snowflakes almost mesmerising her as they floated into the windscreen. Naomi. Why hadn't she responded to her calls, her messages? Unless she couldn't. A hard lump expanded in her throat as her mind switched back to last Friday, the day this nightmare began.

It was the end of their week's holiday. They were driving through France, en route to the ferry port, breaking the journey intermittently to photograph pleasant views, ancient churches, old farmhouses.

They stopped for lunch in a little town on the top of a hill, an hour north of Paris. It was a bright spring day, the sky a milky blue. Neither of them spoke French apart from the odd word and she recalled her chagrin at not being able to read the menu or converse with the locals. When she was young, her mother and stepfather had taken language courses before their annual holidays. It was one of her stepfather's pet peeves and she could still hear his words now, 'If a visitor to another country makes an effort to speak a little of the language they will be treated with respect by the locals.' He would have been very disappointed.

She remembered their apprehension at what they'd chosen to eat. Afterwards they howled with laughter when *croque-monsieur* turned out to be a toasted cheese and ham sandwich. It was a rare moment of real belly laughter. Tears flooded Naomi's eyes and ran down her cheeks. Eva's breath caught in her throat. The merriment continued back in the car afterwards as they drove down the road to the petrol station.

Naomi refuelled the car and Eva leant back in her seat. She wound the window halfway and stretched her hands to the roof, enjoying the rush of fresh air on her face. As Naomi rejoined her, she ignited the engine and tried to wind the window lever. It wouldn't budge.

She pressed harder. It moved an inch and then faltered. This was a special edition Mini, only 20,000 miles on the clock. The shiny blue paintwork and Paul Smith interior were in excellent condition. She pushed again and heard a single clunk.

"Oh, great!" Naomi said. "That's all we need!"

Eva sighed as they both jumped out. Naomi was right to be frustrated. This was a car they were delivering to the UK for a friend, a bargain struck in return for a free holiday. He would not be pleased if it was delivered with a faulty window. They both played with the winder to no avail. Eva tried to prise the door panel apart, flinching and jumping back as she caught her nail.

They stared at each other. "We can't leave it like this," Naomi said.

Eva scanned their surroundings. They were in the middle of the small French town. Opposite was a patisserie with a colourful window display, flanked by a boulangerie on one side, a coiffure on the other. She turned and glimpsed a garage, set back from the road, a single grey car parked out front. She couldn't read the sign but it had to be worth a try.

They drove across and parked next to what they now recognised as an old grey Peugeot outside. Although the workshop door was open, it looked deserted. They left the car and stepped over pools of dried oil in the entrance into a dimly lit garage. The walls were lined with cans containing lubricants and ancient-looking tools. A strong smell of diesel hung in the air.

"Hello?" Naomi called out. Her voice echoed back at her. The girls glanced across at each other, bewildered. Eva had just decided to give up and retreat to the car when she heard a scraping noise and spied a body rolling out from beneath the single Renault parked at the far end, bright torch in hand.

They crossed the garage and towered over the olive skinned man who stood to face them. Smears of grease covered his blue overalls, oil marks were set into the crows' feet around his eyes. He spoke in a deep French accent and both girls stared at him, momentarily baffled. Eva pointed to the Mini and the French man followed as they walked across to it. With a series of strange noises and actions she showed him the window.

He nodded and moved into the workshop. When he returned he held a screwdriver and jemmy. He pointed at the lever and nodded in approval. Eva imagined that he didn't get many modern cars with electric windows in here. In fact, she couldn't imagine he got many cars in here at all. The girls stared as he unscrewed five screws and prised at the panel.

The process took less than three minutes.

The panel wobbled as he lifted it away, and then he gasped. Eva jolted forward. Tucked into the door casing were several brown parcels, tightly wrapped in shrink-wrap, bound in the centre with duct tape.

The world closed in around Eva. She was aware of the French man's presence. Excited words spilled out of his mouth, his arms waved about animatedly. Naomi clutched her arm…

A car swerved in front, snapping Eva's attention to the present and forcing her to brake. In normal circumstances she would curse the driver. But not right now. Right now, she was still reeling from the memories of last Friday. Tears welled up in her eyes. How could their lives change irrevocably in the course of one day? And now this. She lifted a hand from the steering wheel and raked her fingers through her long blond hair. Not for the first time, did she wish they hadn't taken that holiday.

Chapter Three

Helen glanced around the room at her sparse team. With Hamptonshire being a small force, she was often pressured to lend detectives out to sub-divisions to assist with local operations. But at least, with the current pressure to solve the cold cases, she had the comfort of most of her own team back with her at the moment, even if wide scale reductions in the policing budget had reduced her civilian support by half. And, as it was the closest office to the crime scene, they would be able to adapt their own offices at Hampton Headquarters where computers, phone lines and white boards were already set up into an incident room. At times like these you had to be thankful for small mercies.

"Right then, everyone," she said winding up her briefing, "what motivates somebody to climb through the open loft space to gain access to a property, ransack the house, fight the occupant and then kill her?"

Following Pemberton's discovery, a thorough search of the terrace revealed that somebody had broken into the back of an empty house, three doors down. They had crawled through the open loft space that linked the adjoining properties and dropped down onto Naomi's landing using her extendable, folding ladder; carefully folding it back as they left.

"Why creep through loft space? Why not break a back

window?" Rosa Dark, a petite detective in her mid-twenties with short dark hair, olive skin and an attractive face asked as she looked up keenly from her pile of notes.

Pemberton shrugged a single shoulder from his position at the back of the room, "Element of surprise."

"They could have skulked about upstairs for ages without her knowledge," Dark said. "Maybe they'd even searched first?"

Helen thought back to Naomi's house: the drawers pulled out, the bookshelves emptied. She shook her head. "The state of the victim's house indicates a frenzied search. They made no attempt to keep quiet. The victim would have heard them, gone to investigate." She hesitated for a moment, percolating her thoughts. "And the tussle between the victim and the killer was restricted to the lounge. We're pretty sure of that."

"So, it looks like they searched the house after she was killed?" Helen followed the voice to DC Steve Spencer, a short slender man perched on the edge of a desk in the corner. Spencer's time as a detective preceded Helen's ten-year career in the police service.

"I think we'll work on that premise for the moment," she said. Helen felt the onset of a shiver and fought to suppress it. The idea of Naomi locking her doors and checking her windows before settling down for the evening, unaware that a killer lurked upstairs waiting to pounce, made her skin crawl.

"They must have known her habits, been aware that the house down the road was empty, that the loft space of that terrace was open," Pemberton said. "A lot of terrace attics are bricked up, isolating each house these days. Often it's a stipulation for house insurance."

"I agree," Helen said. "They knew the area, were armed, prepared that she may be home. A well planned attack." The room was silent. "We also need to find out what the killer was so persistently looking for."

Helen's mind turned to number two Brooke Street, where

the killer accessed through a broken window. An immediate search of the garden had discovered a couple of footprints in the smattering of snow. These were quickly measured and photographed. They suggested that the killer escaped over the fence, their prints joining a plethora of others on the main pavement beyond. As she shared this information, something puzzled her - CSI estimated the footprints were size eleven. The informant was female, but surely few women could claim such a shoe size?

"We've sealed off the house three doors down. It appears to be empty, but we'll need to contact the landlord, find out who has keys and get details of previous tenants that may know about the open loft space."

"Right," Helen continued. "Let's find out everything we can about Naomi Spence." She raised her eyes to the clock. Ten thirty. "We'll focus initially on where she had been today. Had she been to work? Who are her friends there? Who would she confide in? What time did she leave? What sort of mood was she in? I want to know her every movement right up until we were called out this evening. Memington Hall is a hotel so there should be somebody there around the clock."

"Sergeant Pemberton and I are off to deliver the bad news to the family." Helen watched a sea of shoulders relax around her as relief flooded the room. Usually delegated to the lower ranks, the death message was a part of the job dreaded by all officers. But, in a major investigation, Helen preferred to do it herself. People's reactions could bring a lot to the case. They may say something, often an inadvertent comment, which may lead the investigation in a certain direction. Also, as most victims are killed by somebody they know or somebody close to them, they may provide an insight into Naomi's social life and family background. And Helen didn't believe in delegating a job she wouldn't do herself.

Helen watched them retreat to their desks and begin the

laborious task of piecing together Naomi's final hours. With her inspector absent on long-term sick leave, it never ceased to impress or amaze Helen how much they all pulled together to get the job done. She moved back to her own office: a cubicle in the far corner, with a window that overlooked the car park at the rear of the building. White venetian blinds sat open at the other window that looked out into the incident room. She could see Pemberton outlining their current priorities on a whiteboard, Spencer pinning up the first tranche of photographs.

As she grabbed her coat and bag and headed back out into the main office, a thought rushed into her mind. She turned to Spencer, "Get me a copy of the informant's phone call to the control room, will you? I want to know whose voice is on that call."

***

Over the years, Helen had faced many different reactions to the death message. Some people collapsed dramatically into floods of tears, crushed by the news. Others are numbed, unable to comprehend the incomprehensible. Some are even physically sick. Occasionally people get angry, aggressive even - she'd never forgotten an elderly mother who slapped her across the cheek when she'd told her that her son had died in a car crash. There were those who displayed active disbelief, accusing her of lying to them, 'I only spoke to her an hour ago' or, 'it couldn't possibly be him', while others strangely accepted the news as if they were being told that they had just failed their driving test, and later it hits them like a bolt of lightning.

As she delivered the news to Naomi's parents, Helen watched the colour slowly drain from Olivia Spence's face before she stumbled, body trembling, legs buckling beneath her. Everyone rushed forward. Her husband, aided by Pemberton, managed to catch her just in time and manoeuvre her into a nearby armchair. For several minutes, Olivia sat motionless, head dipped. Henry Spence positioned himself on the arm beside her and clasped her hand in his.

"I'm so very sorry," Helen said, after giving them a few minutes. The words were inadequate and she knew it.

Naomi's parents sat in silence. Pemberton retreated to the kitchen. A sweet smell lingered in the room. Helen followed it to a vase of pink roses mingled with white spray carnations on the dresser. Beside it was a photo of Naomi in mortar board and gown, a smile stretched from ear to ear. The only resemblance this photo bore to the corpse at Brooke Street was a mass of ginger hair.

Olivia Spence lifted her head as Pemberton returned to the room with two mugs of what Helen guessed were very sweet, milky tea to calm the initial shock. The white hair that framed Olivia's face was cut very short and with her striking green eyes, clear complexion and petite nose, Helen could see where her daughter's beauty had derived.

Olivia's hand trembled as she instinctively brushed a fleck of dust from her navy trousers and straightened the striped scarf that decorated her white jumper. She opened her mouth as she reached for the mug but no words came out. Instead she nodded, despair etched into her face.

Henry Spence took his tea and stood, rocking on his feet in between sips. He was a small man, less than five and a half feet tall Helen guessed. The buttons of his blue shirt gaped slightly to reveal an overhanging stomach. His face looked completely empty, as though he would never be truly happy again.

"I'm sorry, but I have to ask you this," Helen said gently. "Do you know of anyone who may have wanted to hurt Naomi?"

Olivia shook her head. Henry stared into space and said nothing.

Helen looked around the lounge room of their detached family home. There were endless photos of the three of them: one on top of the television having a meal together in a restaurant; a family portrait on the wall behind the sofa with Naomi seated between them; another on the bookcase of Naomi in school uniform, strands of hair falling messily across her face. Helen estimated that the Spence's were probably in their early sixties, so Naomi would have arrived later in life and by the looks of things very much cherished. Everything screamed of a close family, one that had been shattered in the course of a single evening.

Her eyes rested on a photo of Naomi seated at a grand piano in a black strapless gown, red curly hair piled on top of her head, fingers poised over the keys. It reminded her of the piano at Brooke Street, now a crime scene. So far, house to house enquiries had proved fruitless. Naomi's immediate neighbours on both sides were out at the time of the incident and those that were indoors were tucked up in front of fires, windows and doors tightly shut, cutting out the brutal weather beyond. Her nearest neighbour at home was an elderly man in his nineties who lived alone, a couple of doors up. The officer that interviewed him wasn't surprised he hadn't heard anything. Apparently you'd need a miracle to hear anything over the sound of his television.

CSI had drafted in extra staff to comb the attic but the discovery felt like a stone in her shoe that she couldn't push out. The more she thought about it the more she realised that the use of the loft space was ingenious. It reduced the chance of being seen by witnesses, allowed for a quick and easy escape route if disturbed, and, as Pemberton suggested, afforded the element of surprise. But then, why the fight? Shootings were usually fairly clean killings. The killer doesn't have to get close to their victim. The fight didn't make sense. Just like the female informant.

Helen looked back at the Spences. They'd finished their tea. They looked tired although she guessed sleep wouldn't offer much respite to them tonight, or in the forthcoming days and weeks. She stood. "Is there anyone we can call? Someone close perhaps?"

Henry stayed very still for a second. Sweat glistened on the bald patch on the top of his head. "No, thank you."

"Okay. We will need someone to formally identify Naomi."

"Could it be a mistake, be someone else?" Olivia suddenly found her voice. She looked up, her eyes holding onto to the tiniest thread of hope.

Helen shook her head. "We found her driving licence photo card at the property. I'm sorry. It will just be a formality."

Olivia's face folded.

"It's all his fault," Henry mumbled, through tight teeth.

His wife shook her head, placed a shaky hand on his arm, but he brushed it away. "We should have stopped it. She was fine before she met him."

Helen watched him for a moment. He continued to rock, backwards and forwards, on the balls of his feet, his gaze averted. There was something behind the sadness in his eyes. "Is there something you would like to tell us, Mr Spence?" she eventually asked.

"Paton," he said, "Jules Paton." He choked the name out. And when he started he couldn't seem to stop. He launched into a tirade of abuse about Naomi's ex-boyfriend.

Much of what he said was incoherent drivel. He punched the words out, one after the other, like a toy that had been wound up and couldn't stop until it ran out of energy. As Pemberton furiously scribbled away, Helen managed to glean that Jules Paton was Naomi's ex-boyfriend, a married man, although separated from his wife and two children and several years Naomi's senior.

Henry Spence talked about a relationship that lasted two years, a destructive relationship where Jules had introduced Naomi to cocaine. His nostrils flared when he described his bright young daughter's delight at getting the job at Memington Hall, doing really well, made for great things. Until she met him.

"Oh, in the early days he impressed us all," he continued, "describing himself as a 'business man' who worked in the motor industry and played the stock market in his spare time. He flashed cash, impressed Naomi with his black BMW, treated her to meals in expensive restaurants, took her to posh hotels." The nostrils flared again. "Then later, he started to control her, knock her about."

Olivia gasped. "Henry, we don't know that!"

"What about that black eye last summer?"

"She said she had an accident, fell at work."

"And the bruises on her arms?"

Helen watched Olivia look away and put her face in her hands. She waited a moment, then sat forward. "What did Naomi say about the bruises?" she asked.

"She always stuck up for him, had an answer for everything. But we weren't born yesterday. She was changing - changing from a confident, intelligent woman into a frightened, lost soul and was completely reliant on him. Only after he'd sunk all her savings into funding their joint habit, did he drop her two months ago when the bank account was finally empty."

Henry Spence collapsed into the armchair behind him. It was as if somebody had opened a valve and released all the air from his lungs.

Helen gave him a moment. "Are you saying that you think Jules Paton killed your daughter?"

He took a while to respond. Finally, he looked across at her. "If he didn't do it himself, then he got her mixed up in something she couldn't get out of." He lifted his hand, jabbed a sausage finger at her. "Either way, it's got something to do with him."

She watched as he turned away in despair. So, Naomi had dated a man they didn't approve of, a man that had drawn a wedge between them. She looked back around the room at the numerous photos of Naomi with her parents. Undoubtedly, this would be difficult for her parents to accept. But that didn't give Jules Paton a motive for murder.

There were the abuse allegations. Surely, if they had been that bad they would have been recorded, although she couldn't rely on that. She thought back to the body in Brooke Street and Pemberton's words, 'It looks as though she put up a good fight.' Victims of domestic violence rarely fought back, afraid of a heavier beating or worse - severe mental intimidation.

Could this be the rage of a jealous ex-lover? But why the house search? And what about the drugs? Could Naomi have developed an addiction she couldn't fund? Did she upset somebody? Fail to pay her debts?

She gave him another moment to compose himself, before continuing gently, "You say that they separated two months ago?"

Henry nodded.

"Has Naomi seen or heard from him during this time?"

"How would I know? She wouldn't tell us even if she did."

Helen fixed her eyes on Henry Spence. Perhaps these were the desperate words of a grieving father who had never approved of his dead daughter's boyfriend. Or maybe he was grasping at straws, or looking to plant blame. But, she couldn't afford to ignore any lead at this stage. "Do you have an address for Mr Paton?"

Henry nodded and approached the dresser, searching through the drawer until he lifted out a black, leather address book. He leafed through the pages and stopped abruptly, thrusting the open book towards her. "That's the last address we have. He might have moved. We didn't exactly maintain contact."

She passed the book to Pemberton who jotted down the details.

"Thank you. How had Naomi seemed in herself, these past two months?"

"Barely comes round these days," he mumbled.

"When did you last see her?"

"I spoke to her on the phone last Sunday."

Helen turned, surprised to hear Olivia Spence's brittle voice.

"She sounded," Olivia hesitated for a moment, "okay. A bit tired, maybe." Her voice disappeared into the room as despair crept back across her face. The same despair that would be making many visits over the next few hours, days, months.

Helen paused for a moment. She turned to Henry. "Did she report any abusive incidents to the police?"

He shook his head. "No idea."

Helen gazed at Olivia. Her eyes had sunken into her sallow face, the effects of the last hour sucking the very life from within her. After making arrangements for them to visit the mortuary in the morning, and taking down a list of Naomi's friends and close associations she stood to leave.

Helen was walking back to the car, Henry just closing the door, when she remembered something and turned back. "I'm sorry, may I just ask one more thing?"

Henry pulled the door back. He gave a tired nod.

"Did Naomi have a mobile phone?"

***

By the time Helen reached the car, Pemberton was settled in the driving seat, deep in conversation on the phone.

Helen waved to interrupt, relayed Naomi's mobile number and requested a check on her call record. Then, waiting for Pemberton to finish, she settled herself into the passenger seat and glimpsed the dashboard clock. Two minutes past twelve. She lent her elbow on the windowsill, rested her head back. Her eyes were dry, head heavy.

Pemberton shut off his phone. "That's interesting."

"What have you got?"

"Nothing on Naomi. Not even any intelligence. If she had a social habit, she kept it fairly well under wraps. And no reports of abuse either."

"What about Paton?"

"No record as such, apart from a caution a few years ago for possession of cannabis, but plenty of Intel."

"Well, spit it out Sean."

Pemberton turned to face her. "He's been associated with cocaine supply. Spotted in several places where we think exchanges have been made. A couple of sources have said he deals. But he's never been charged, and the last entry was… " He glanced down at his notebook, "last November." He pushed the corners of his mouth down. "I guess he's been quiet for a while."

Helen pushed out a sigh and watched the white puff balls disperse into the air around her.

"Spencer has been out to Memington Hall," Pemberton said, changing the subject. "The receptionist said Naomi had a late appointment with a bride to be - a Miss Taylor. She saw her leave just after seven. She remembered it clearly because she was doing the late shift and only started at six."

"Did she speak to anyone at Memington before she finished?"

"No. Most of the day staff had gone home and the receptionist said she was on the phone when Naomi finished. Naomi just put her head around the door and gave her a wave."

"Any CCTV?"

"Yes, he watched the tape but it just shows her leaving by the rear entrance and going straight to her car. I'd estimate her car journey home only takes about fifteen minutes, especially at that time of night. And we know that her Fiesta was parked in Brooke Street, just a few doors up from her house."

"So, for the moment we are thinking she drove straight home?"

Pemberton shrugged. "In the absence of any other witnesses, it looks that way."

Helen looked out into the darkness. The snow had stopped falling; the air was still. She turned Henry Spence's account over in her mind. Jules Paton was Naomi's ex-boyfriend. He dabbled in drugs, would have been familiar with the layout of her home. But the state of Naomi's home didn't suggest a crime of passion. The intelligence suggested no history of violence or firearms and no police record to speak of. And no apparent motive.

All she had were theories, sparked by the words of a desperate man. She had no evidence to suggest him as a suspect. But, what if Paton was the killer? What if he was at home now, burning his clothes and disposing of the gun?

Another thought itched at her. The two wine glasses beside the kitchen sink. Naomi's parents confirmed she lived alone. There was also the possibility he'd visited earlier that evening. He might have seen something. Or he might have information that could assist them. She reached for her seat belt. "Let's go take a drive by Mr Paton's and see if anyone's home."

***

Nate inserted the key into the lock, the same key he'd retrieved from beneath the flowerpot yesterday when she'd done the school run and taken the kids to their Monday football practice. It had taken less than an hour to get it copied and return the original.

The house was shrouded in darkness. He padded slowly across the hallway, taking short steps to avoid any squeak from his trainers on the laminate flooring, then up the carpeted stairway.

He stopped on the landing outside the first room and peered through the gap in the door. White LED lights shaped like stars gave off a soft, vanilla glow, just enough for him to see two small huddles, in two single beds. The little people were sleeping. He moved on to the master bedroom, squeezed through the gap in the door and stood there for almost a full minute, allowing his eyes to adjust to the darkness.

She was fast asleep, peaceful. He watched her a moment, then pulled the gun out of his pocket, jumped forward and placed a gloved hand firmly over her mouth. Her eyes snapped open. Her head frantically tossed from side to side. But his grip was firm. He was stronger than her and he knew it.

He used his other hand to lift the gun to her throat, turning it so that it pointed up towards the bottom of her mouth. I could kill her right now, he thought to himself. All in the pull of a trigger. Perhaps she would put up a struggle, just like the other one. He felt a sudden, warm rush at the memory. He had enjoyed that. For a split second he was sorely tempted…

Instead, he put his mouth to her ear, gently brushing it across her hair as he did so. Her whole body quivered. "I am going to say this once," he hissed. "Tell Jules to get back home, now. Then we can talk."

She nodded, as much as she could manage beneath the weight of his hand, eyes filled with terror.

"He has twenty-four hours. Or I take you all out." He glanced at the wall that separated her from the children, then back down at her. "Them first, then you. One by one."

Her body started juddering.

"I'm going to remove my hand now," he said. "Any noise, any whimper, and I shoot one of the kids."

She nodded.

He removed his hand. "If you're thinking of calling the cops, just remember I'll be watching you. All of you. How is your niece getting on at nursery these days?"

She shrank back in the bed. He surveyed her for a moment with hardened eyes, before he turned and left the room.

Nate tucked his gun in his pocket as he made his way out down the alley at the side of the house. He was sure she wouldn't call the police. She was tangled in this web as well. And where would she go for her next gram?

Nate didn't understand the craving for drugs. He'd dabbled over the years, mainly amphetamines and cannabis, but none gave him the shot of adrenalin he experienced after a kill. That was his very own hit of cocaine.

He paused, removed his gloves, formed two fists and knocked them together like a boxer. His gold sovereign rings banged together. *Clink, clink, clink.* He was THE MAN.

Chapter Four

Jules Paton lived on Granary Avenue, a quiet, tree-lined arrangement of late nineteenth century, three storey terraces on the edge of Hampton centre. Having obtained details of Jules' black BMW from the incident room, Pemberton spent a couple of minutes driving up and down, scouring the nose to tail cars that lined the curb. When the search proved ineffectual, he parked up at the nearest available space to number fifty-three.

In contrast to the other houses in the row, the curtains at Jules' house were undrawn. Darkness seeped out of the long sash windows. An old, mock Victorian light shone in the tiny, open porch of the house next door.

Helen was aware that they faced a potentially dangerous situation, possibly an armed killer. And without intelligence or evidence implicating Jules, they couldn't bring in the armed response team to assist in the arrest. Although Jules' car was missing, she was also conscious he could still be nearby - he wouldn't be the first offender to have hidden his car. She called the control room, alerting the duty inspector to their whereabouts so that back up, if needed, would be available quickly.

Helen and Pemberton exited the car to a blanket of silence. Even the gentle closing of car doors sounded like trombone notes at this late hour. The air was clear and the snow that had fallen earlier was melting rapidly; a few cotton wool coverings on tree branches, a smattering on the odd patch of grass, the only remnants of its visit. Helen looked enviously at the houses enveloped in darkness, all wrapped up for the night, the owners asleep in their beds.

"Looks pretty deserted," Pemberton said as they approached.

Helen opened the front gate into a pocket size, paved garden and peered through the window into a sitting room. Two small, dark sofas sat on a wooden floor facing a black, wrought iron fireplace. A flat-screen TV stretched across the chimney breast. A plain rug lay on the floor beneath.

Pemberton withdrew his head from the letterbox. "There's a bunch of post down there," he said. "I don't reckon he's been here in a while.

Helen glanced back through the window. The room was so tidy it looked as though it had been primed for a house viewing.

"Can I help you?"

Helen jumped at the voice. She darted round to face a short man with grey hair and inordinately long, fluffy sideburns. He jerked back, momentarily startled. The oversized fleece he wore gave him the appearance of a hobbit.

She quickly recovered herself, reached into her pocket and flashed her ID.

"Hampton Police," Pemberton said, as he proffered his own badge.

Only then did Helen notice that the man was actually standing in the garden next door, a metre high stone wall separating them. "I'm DCI Lavery and this is DS Pemberton," she said. "We were just hoping to have a word with Mr Paton."

"Jules?"

She nodded.

"He's not there, been away a few days." He flicked his head briefly towards his own front door. "The wife's feeding the cat."

Helen glanced up at the neighbouring house. Dark ivy snaked up and interlocked around the downstairs window. An empty hanging basket hung beside the porch. "You live here?"

"Yes."

"May I ask for how long?"

"Twenty years." He screwed up his eyes. "What's all this about?"

"Just some routine enquiries," she said. "How long has Mr Paton been your neighbour?"

He shrugged. "About eighteen months." He looked from one detective to another. "This sounds serious."

She ignored his comment. "I'm sorry I didn't catch your name?"

"Stuart Wilson."

"Thank you, Mr Wilson. Do you have any idea where he has gone?"

"Away for a while." He pushed his mouth down at the corners. "Didn't say where. The wife is feeding the cat until Saturday."

"Do you have a contact number for him?"

"No. All I know is the wife spoke to him before he left. You're welcome to call round and speak to her, although I doubt she'll be able to tell you any more. She'll be here in the morning."

"We'll be back in the morning then." Helen ran her eyes over his clothes. Underneath the large fleece he was wearing navy overalls.

He caught her interest. "I've just come in from work," he said. "On the late shift at Blewsons warehouse round the corner."

Helen smiled and nodded. "Thank you for your help." She

pulled a business card out of her pocket and handed it over. "If you do see or hear from Mr Paton, could you call this number?"

After taking down the Wilsons' contact details, they made their way back to the car in silence. It wasn't until they were inside, battling with seat belts over heavy overcoats, that Pemberton eventually spoke up, "Why would a man, who has gone away for a while, secretly return to his ex-girlfriend's house and crawl through the open loft space to beat and murder her?"

"The holiday could be an alibi."

"Maybe she'd met someone else?" Pemberton said. He blew into his hands and rubbed them together.

"They were separated."

"Perhaps he still harboured feelings for her?"

Helen shook her head. She didn't buy the spurned lover argument. "More like she had something, something that was worth a lot of money to him; something that was worth pulling her house to pieces to find."

"Like what?"

"I don't know. Drugs, maybe? Henry Spence suggested they were both users. She wouldn't be the first to store it in her loft. Perhaps he thought he'd help himself and when it wasn't there, got angry?" Pemberton rested his hands in his lap and stared out into the darkness as he considered this theory. "It would also explain why he beat her first," Helen added.

"How do you mean?"

"Well, why engage in combat? If you have a gun, you can kill from a distance. No need to get your hands dirty. Whoever did this had a good go at her, then practically wrecked the house looking for something."

"Must have been expecting a fair bit," Pemberton said.

"What?"

"Well you wouldn't go to that much trouble for a line of

coke, would you?"

Helen was only half listening now. Another thought was picking away at her brain: If Jules was the murderer, who was the female informant? And where was she now?

***

Hours later, Eva's feet sank into the sand. She heard a noise overhead and sat forward, raising her hand to shield her eyes from the sun. The sight of the aeroplane relaxed her shoulders. Where was it heading? Bermuda maybe, or the Bahamas? The sky was a beautiful cornflower blue, brushed clear of clouds, the sun in the corner stretched down, sinking into her welcoming skin. She angled her head and looked across at the ocean. The tide was coming in, rapidly moving up the beach with every lap. She could smell the salt. It looked clear, icy, inviting…

A peripheral sound distracted her. *Tap, tap, tap.* She blinked, shook her head and glanced around. *Tap, tap, tap.*

Eva jumped in her car seat, abruptly awakened from her dream. Her stomach dropped.

The man stood still, before he moved forward and proffered a card.

She stared at the photo on the card before raising her eyes. His light brown hair had thinned, opening his widow's peak into a half moon across the front of his head; his cheeks had sunken into hollow grooves beneath his cheekbones, but there was no doubt it was him. The card read *St Anne's Car Park Security.*

He removed the card and mimed for her to wind down the window. She wound it down slowly and stopped half way. The key was in the ignition. She quickly pressed her left foot down on the clutch, slipped the car into gear and allowed her left hand to hover over the handbrake, the right hand on the steering wheel. Any sudden movements, she thought to herself, and I'll turn the key.

"Miss?" His voice was loaded with a strong, Glaswegian drawl. "You can't sleep here." She followed his right arm which pointed to a sign about twenty metres ahead of her: *Parking for two hours maximum. No camping, no sleeping.* "This is a private car park," he continued. "There's a motel next door if you need to get some kip." He pointed to the modern, brick motel next to the fuel station.

Her mind switched back to the events of the night before. She remembered driving on an endless road for hours, following lights ahead of her that turned off periodically. But she kept going, not daring to stop. She remembered the fatigue setting in. The weariness overcame her as she had closed one eye to rest it, then the other. She couldn't allow herself to sleep. Her speed slipped to 50mph. She'd opened the window and turned up the radio.

Finally, when she'd exhausted all her reserves, she pulled into the services, intending to stop in the car park and close her eyes for five minutes before topping up with petrol and moving off again. All she needed was a power nap.

Eva swept her eyes across the dashboard to the clock. Seven thirty in the morning. She'd slept for almost six hours. A feeling of dread crept down her back as she recalled Tuesday evening's events.

"Miss?"

Eva nodded and turned over the engine. She needed to get moving, and fast.

Chapter Five

'Emergency Services. Police, fire or ambulance?'

'Ambulance.'

'Just connecting you.'

'Ambulance Service. What is your location?'

'Eight Brooke Street, Hampton.'

'May I take your name?'

'She needs an ambulance urgently.'

'Can you tell me… '

Click.

Helen pressed a button on her laptop and looked across at Phillipa Hartwell. She hadn't been at all surprised to find the manageress of Memington Hall expecting her when she arrived unannounced at nine thirty that morning. They sat in her oak panelled office where a sweet, pleasant scent filled the air from the kind of perfume that lingered when someone passed. An oil painting of a man from the eighteenth century stared at Helen from the far wall.

"Do you recognise that voice?" Helen asked.

Phillipa shook her head and blinked her long lashes with aplomb. "I'm afraid not."

Helen shut down her laptop. It wasn't surprising really. The phone line crackled throughout the recording and the caller's voice displayed no particular accent, no clear distinguishing features. The informant was, as her mother would say, 'cleanly spoken'. It could have been any one of thousands of women in the locality. And the recording lasted less than twenty seconds.

Helen watched Phillipa sit back and smooth a crease in the red shift dress that fitted neatly around her small frame. A Gucci watch peeped from beneath the sleeve of her jacket. She guessed that she was in her mid thirties, like herself, although she couldn't imagine forcing her own body into that dress every day, coiffing her hair into a similar French pleat that didn't move with her head and decorating her face in a manner resembling a beautician on a night out. These days Helen squeezed herself into size twelve trouser suits, and tied her hair back loosely. "Why don't you tell me what sort of person Naomi Spence was?" she asked.

Phillipa averted her gaze momentarily, as if she was looking for the right words. "She was well liked. Popular with the clients. Indeed my best achiever in terms of sales. We are all deeply saddened and shocked by her loss."

"What was her position?"

"Events planner. Mostly weddings, but we also do conferences and parties. I'll give you a brochure before you leave, if that would help?"

"Thank you. What about her work record?"

Phillipa laced her fingers together on the desk in front of her. "Good. She was punctual, reliable."

"Are you aware of anyone that may wish to hurt her? Perhaps an upset client?"

"Not at all. I can assure you on that front. Naomi was a professional. And my door is always open. If there had been a problem, I would have known."

Helen reflected on her meeting with Naomi's parents. Her dad's account gave the impression that Naomi was a changed character these past two years. And then there was the recent relationship break-up. She leant forward. "So, you haven't noticed a difference in her recently?"

"She did separate from her boyfriend a couple of months ago," Phillipa said, lifting her eyes. That seemed to affect her a bit."

"In what way?"

"She was quiet, withdrawn for a while. A couple of weeks ago she came to see me, to request some leave. I gave her two weeks off."

A muffled tinkle sounded in the background. Helen watched her retrieve a thin mobile from her jacket and stroke the screen. "Do excuse me for a minute."

As she stood and turned to face the window, Helen looked past her to the view beyond. A decorative, stone staircase led from the deep patio below the window up a pathway between two cleanly manicured lawns. Roman statues sat in the middle of each lawn which were edged with short, neat privet hedging, sculptured into topiary balls at each corner. The vista beyond included a bridge over a river, trees in the distance. The morning sun had fought its way through the clouds and was now bouncing off the stonework. It looked almost too perfect, like a painting in a gallery.

It couldn't have looked more different to the square of lawn and brown shed that formed the view out of Jenny Wilson's kitchen window earlier that morning. Proving less than a five minute detour from her journey, Helen had called in to see Jenny on her way to Memington Hall. Arriving just before eight thirty, a round woman with a ruddy, jowly face met her at the door. Jenny greeted Helen with an inquisitive smile, as if this were the only exciting event to occur in her life for many years. Her chest heaved as she led Helen through the narrow hallway, past the open door to the lounge where Jeremy Kyle blared out from the television and into the small kitchen at the back, where they'd sat together at a polished pine table. But any hopes of discovering a clue as to Jules Paton's location were quickly dashed. Although Jenny's account took her twenty minutes to relay, it held nothing more than what her husband had told them the night before. That Jules had gone away last Sunday and wasn't due back until this weekend.

Phillipa turned back and pocketed her phone. "Sorry about that. Where were we?"

"You granted leave."

"Ah, yes - I believe Naomi went away on holiday with a friend. To Italy I think. She returned to work on Monday."

"Do you know who she went with?"

Phillipa shook her head. "No."

"How has she been since her return?"

"I'm afraid I can't really say. I've been away at a conference the last couple of days and have only spoken to her on the phone since she's been back. But she seemed fine."

***

Nobody noticed the man in a baseball cap, skulking in Granary Avenue that morning. Nate had become accustomed to sinking into the background. He'd stood beside the flaked trunk of the plane tree opposite Paton's house and watched Helen arrive. Just like last night when he'd spied on her as she checked out Jules' place with her colleague. Everything about the detective chief inspector screamed of police. But there was a clean prettiness in her complexion. And with her softly curved frame, the long dark hair messily tied back, the crisp white shirt that stretched across her chest… Nate felt a stirring in his groin. Her tenacity was impressive. Especially since she didn't know he was there. Watching, waiting.

He fisted his hands and knocked his sovereign rings together. *Clink. Clink. Clink.*

***

Naomi's room at Memington shared the same wood panelling, latticed window, oil painting of a man in eighteenth century dress, but was half the size of the manageress'. A similar oak desk was situated in front of the window and beside it a bookcase jammed with old books that looked as if they hadn't been touched in years. In the other corner was an arrangement of French style chairs around a low table.

Helen checked her watch. She'd just taken a call from the superintendent. He wanted her back at the station and had sent Pemberton to relieve her, ringing off before she could ask why. Helen sighed. Time was tight. And Phillipa Hartwell hadn't given her much to work on. She pressed her tongue against the roof of her mouth, remembering her father's motto: 'the devil is in the detail.' He loved this quote, which formed the basis of every investigation he managed - note everything, however insignificant it may seem at the time, because you never know when you might need it.

She pulled the latex gloves out of her bag and wriggled her hands into them. Apart from an old-fashioned blotter, the top of the desk was completely clear - no desk tidy, no photographs, no in tray, no computer. She thought back to Phillipa Hartwell's office. Her desk was in the same immaculate condition. Either they didn't do any work around here, or it was all locked away somewhere.

On closer inspection, the desk was not as old as it initially appeared, more like a reproduction of an eighteenth century version. She ran her finger over it, the rubber clinging to the varnished oak. The blotter was neatly laid over a green leather inset and there were three drawers down one side. Helen opened the bottom drawer first and immediately came face to face with Naomi's workload. Hanging files contained pink envelope folders, marked with names and dates of clients. She opened one named 'Taylor - Letts Wedding 16 July' to find a timetable, a page of notes that looked like they were taken at a meeting and a spreadsheet of prices. Curious, she scanned down to the total, which read £21,653.47, and balked. It was astonishing what people spent on weddings these days.

Helen fleetingly remembered her own wedding at The George Hotel in Hampton centre, a Georgian building that had since been converted into luxury apartments. Both just out of university, their budget tight, her only indulgence was a vintage wedding dress costing just short of two hundred pounds. Her father had still been alive back then and paid for a small reception of forty close family and friends. It couldn't have cost more than two thousand, all in.

She replaced the folder, closed the drawer and opened the top one. This housed a tidy array of pens, paper clips, a ruler and highlighters. Helen moved on to the middle drawer. It squealed like a kitten's meow as she pulled it open. Two leather-bound books – one black, one a deep wine red – sat on top of a laptop. She flicked through the pages of the black book. It listed names, times, dates: Naomi's professional appointments. She turned to last Tuesday. There were two appointments listed for that day. One at 11.00am for the Shaws' and one at 6.00pm for Michaela Taylor. Both had contact numbers.

She looked through pages of addresses in the other book, and then cast it aside.

A thought struck her. She picked up the diary again and brushed back a couple of pages. Her heart sank. She was hoping for some mention of the holiday, perhaps a name of who she went with and where, but the pages were blank. Frustrated, she put it down on top of the desk. All these items would need to be bagged up, cross referenced and thoroughly examined back at the station.

Her eyes rested on the laptop still in the drawer. It seemed strange to have everything hidden away, no computers on desks, no printers in the corner.

A sudden knock turned her attention to the door. She looked up to see Sergeant Pemberton's head appear. "Sean." She beckoned him in, not at all surprised to see the manageress at his tail. "I see you've met Phillipa Hartwell?"

He nodded. "Just now."

Helen turned to face her. "This is Sergeant Pemberton. He'll be getting things organised here to interview your staff."

Phillipa stared at them both. "Right, I'll leave you to it then."

Pemberton chuckled as he closed the door. "I see she's not a fan of 'old bill' crawling all over her fine establishment."

"Doesn't look like it. Any news yet on ballistics? Forensics?"

"Just checked. CSI are still at the property, but hoping to get us a preliminary report by tomorrow morning. They were able to confirm that the powder we found in the bathroom was cocaine though."

"Is that the best they can do?"

He gave a frustrated nod. "I'll keep pushing. We've just had a call from the paramedics. When they moved the victim from the house to the morgue they found a black button tangled in her hair."

Helen widened her eyes. "Oh?"

"It's possible it belonged to a jacket the killer was wearing and became dislodged in the scuffle."

"Any distinctive features?"

"It bears the mark *Toujours.* We're looking into whether that's some kind of designer clothes brand, to try to identify the item of clothing it belonged to."

"Excellent. Keep me posted."

"Oh, and the bullet in the skirting board has been couriered to ballistics. I've spoken to my contact there and they're snowed under with the current drive on outstanding gun crime cases. But he's going to give us priority. We should hear back within a few days."

"Good. Any news on Mr Paton?"

"Nothing as yet. We've checked with all major ports and he hasn't left during the last seven days. No sightings of his car on police network cameras either. He seems to have disappeared off the face of the earth."

"Anything on the victim's phone records?"

"We've been chasing. It should be through any time. Dark's gone out to support the family and see what extra information she can glean. Spencer's working through the list of her friends to see if that throws up anything. I'll just get the guys set up here to take statements and then head back to give him a hand."

"Okay." She glanced around the room. "Well, better be off. Don't want to keep the super waiting, do we?"

Chapter Six

The traffic on the motorway thinned as Eva pressed north. As she passed a Sainsbury's supermarket lorry in the nearside lane the road stretched out in front of her. An image of Naomi seated at her computer screen entered her head. Where was she now? How badly was she hurt? Eva felt a sharp pang in her chest.

The surrounding countryside had flattened, offering open views across a patchwork of agricultural fields. But her brain refused to focus. Her stomach clenched as her mind wandered back to that day in France where this nightmare began.

A sea of foreign words swam in the garage air around her. Eva's eyes were glued to the packages in the door panel. Drugs. They had to be drugs. Why else would they be hidden away in the door panelling?

The French mechanic threw his arms up in the air. He spouted words Eva couldn't understand. She glanced across at Naomi whose gaze was fixed on the door. Her mouth hung open, face petrified. At that moment Eva had no idea what to do.

Suddenly, the Frenchman bent down and collected the screws. Gently moving the packets aside, he rewound the window and replaced the panelling.

As soon as he finished he looked up at her with a mixture

of fear and anger in his eyes. He made a shooing motion with his arms. When Eva didn't move, his voice became excited and he pushed her arm towards the car.

Eva reached down for her purse, but he shook his head vehemently and motioned again for them to leave. She grabbed Naomi, pushed her into the passenger seat and climbed into the driver's side. The tyres screeched as she spun off the forecourt and down the road out of town.

Neither spoke. Eva pressed her foot to the floor, cornering the mini around sharp bends, down country lanes, through tiny villages, heading in no particular direction. All the time she churned over the events in her mind. Something about the French mechanic's reaction told her that he wouldn't call the police. Yet it didn't stop her race as far away from the town as possible, leaving the incident behind. But it wasn't left behind. She was taking the packets with her, hidden in the door panelling.

Somebody carefully secreted those packages, knowing the car was being driven back to the UK. Eva didn't do drugs. She hated what they did to people, what they'd done to Naomi. Her eyes were fixed on the road. Naomi referred to herself as a social user, but Eva knew she struggled to stay away from the stuff. One of the reasons for this holiday was to secure a break from it. And cocaine isn't cheap.

Anger began to fester like an ulcer in Eva's chest. She pulled the wheel to the right and braked sharply, bringing the car to an abrupt stop at the side of the road.

"What's going on?" Naomi said.

"You tell me."

"What?"

Eva shot Naomi a penetrating stare and jabbed her thumb at the door beside her. "Well, these didn't pop up out of thin air!"

"I don't know anything about them." Naomi's head shook

violently.

"No?"

"Really! I've no idea."

Silence followed. Eva's stomach reeled. "I don't believe you," she snarled.

"Honestly, Eva. Please."

"I thought you'd given up the drugs?"

Naomi shrunk back. "I have. I promise. I haven't touched a line in weeks."

Eva didn't respond. She turned her attention back to the road, as if it contained a clue that would jump out and grab her.

"Anyway," Naomi said, filling the silence. "It looks more like heroin than cocaine."

"Great!" Eva's voice cracked as she raised a hand to her forehead. "Well, you should know."

"I've never touched heroin. I'm not that stupid. But, I saw a programme on it once. It's naturally light brown. Cocaine is white."

"And expensive. Is this how you fund your habit?"

"No!"

Eva turned to face her friend. When she spoke her voice was barely a whisper. "How could you involve me in this?"

"Eva, don't do this. Please!"

Tears pooled in Naomi's eyes, just as they had when she was seven-years-old and one of the older girls pinched her skipping rope in the playground. Friends since primary school, they'd lived in the same road, walked to school together, had tea at each other's houses, played at the local park. Naomi's parents moved away when she was sixteen but, even though there was a school year between them in age, they stayed in touch. Through college and university, they met up in the holidays. Eva felt like she knew Naomi almost as well as her own family. And Naomi had always been a bad liar. Ever since she was young, when Naomi was lying her right eye twitched slightly, her face coloured. Eva scanned her friend's face now, but there was no trace of the twitch and her face was ghostlike. "Well, somebody knows it's here. What do you think?"

Naomi stared back, but said nothing.

"Ring, Jules!"

Naomi looked at her in astonishment. "You're not suggesting… "

"You got any better ideas? This was his idea, the holiday, the apartment, the car. Why do you think he offered it to us?"

"He said I needed a break. He was trying to help… " Naomi shook her head, as if to dismiss the bad thoughts sneaking their way in.

"What about this?" Eva waved her hand towards the door. "He's used us."

"No. He wouldn't do that."

"Then, how do you explain it?"

Naomi pulled the phone out of her pocket. Eva watched, shifting impatiently in her seat as she pressed the digits and raised it to her ear. After what seemed an age, she shook her head. "Voicemail."

Eva sighed heavily. She faced the road, considering their options. "I think we should call the police."

"The police… in France?"

Eva slapped her hand across the steering wheel. "Why not? We haven't done anything wrong!"

"But they might not believe us, or even understand."

Eva mulled this over. Naomi had a point. The police would ask a million questions: Where did you stay? Where are you travelling to? Who does the vehicle belong to? They might put them in a cell until they could organise an interpreter. They might not believe them.

Eva drew a deep breath. "Maybe we should empty them out?"

"Leave them here?"

"Why not?"

"What if kids come by and find them?"

Eva climbed out of the car and looked around. They were in a country lane. She could hear the autoroute in the background. She couldn't see any houses, church spires, outbuildings; just rolling countryside. It would have been a beautiful aspect in different circumstances.

But that didn't mean that there wasn't a village somewhere nearby. And the French did love to cycle these country lanes.

She turned to Naomi who had climbed out to join her. "What do you suggest?"

"I don't know. I mean they belong to somebody. Or rather somebody is expecting them. Won't we get into trouble if we dump them?"

Eva narrowed her eyes. "You're not suggesting… "

"I'm not suggesting anything. We just need to think this through."

"Let's drive to the nearest town, find an industrial bin and empty them out." But even as Eva spoke the words, a thought crept into her mind. She looked back at the vehicle, shining in the afternoon sunlight. She had seen a programme on smuggling a few years ago where they stripped a car down to show all the little crevices where illegal goods could be stored: tiny gaps between the ceiling panelling and roof held hand guns, the spare tyre had been opened and filled with packages of drugs. The car could be riddled with drugs and goodness knows what other illegal substances. And how would she retrieve them? She didn't even have a screwdriver.

"We need to dump the whole car." Eva spoke slowly as her brain formulated the idea. It seemed the only option. They could leave it for Jules to collect himself. It was his problem. But how would they get home?

The girls sat on the grass verge beside the car and pooled

their cash. They barely made fifteen euros between them. Eva cursed herself for maxing out her two credit cards, living life on an overdraft that exceeded its limit until she got paid the following Monday. She only took the holiday because it was a freebie. Jules covered the budget flights out, the short ferry crossing back, arranged for them to have use of his friend's apartment in Milan. Naomi's situation was no better. Having drained her account of the last few pounds for spending money, she hadn't even left sufficient funds to make her next mortgage payment.

They talked about contacting their parents. The idea made Eva recoil. Her parents wouldn't welcome a telephone call interrupting their holiday in South Africa, even if she could reach them. Especially a call asking for money.

Naomi was convinced her father wouldn't help, particularly since he knew the holiday was arranged by Jules.

Naomi stood and rubbed her hand across her forehead, knocking her sunglasses off her head. They rattled as they hit the floor. As she picked them up, her face slackened. She faced Eva. "Look, I reckon Jules brought this car in for someone. We know he comes out to the continent all the time to bring in cars. Perhaps they picked this particular car and organised this."

"I don't care who organised… "

"Bad people deal in this sort of thing," she interrupted. "And they won't be happy if their goods don't arrive."

"I won't be happy if we get arrested. Christ, Naomi, smuggling illegal drugs into the country? We could go to prison!"

"That's assuming we get caught. Look, we're out of choices. We need the car to get home. I say ignore them. In the unlikely event that anyone stops and searches us, we'll just deny all knowledge. It's not our car, remember?"

Eva stood very still for several minutes, working her

options. There had to be a way out of this. Every sinew in Eva's body screamed that this was a bad idea. But what was the alternative? Wherever they dumped them here, they might get into the wrong hands, a child even. "I don't believe I'm doing this."

Eva swallowed and turned her attention back to the road in front of her. She caught the large blue sign for Glasgow at the last minute and swung a sharp left onto the slip road. A lorry blew its horn, but she ignored it. What mattered now was to get as far away from Hampton as possible. She needed time to think.

Chapter **Seven**

Helen spotted Superintendent Jenkins as soon as she entered the incident room. He was stood at the window in her office, staring out at the car park below. Although not a particularly tall man at five foot, nine inches, his mere presence seemed to shrink the room to a tiny box.

She halted in the main office to fill a plastic cup from the water dispenser. Spencer twisted in his seat to face her. "Morning, ma'am." He followed her eye line. "He's been in there for twenty minutes."

Helen's heart sank. Jenkins was known for his diplomatic approach to policing. There were brief moments when he'd shown great support, lent inspirational knowledge to a case, but only when it fit with current policy targets. He disliked protracted investigations and switched allegiance as quickly as a dirty politician. "Any new developments?" she asked.

He shook his head.

She emptied the cup, chucked it in the bin and moved forward uttering, "Okay, cover me." Spencer's grin warmed her back as she approached her office.

Jenkins turned as soon as the door clicked open. "Morning, sir." She scooted past him, dropping her briefcase and bag behind the desk.

"Helen." He moved around and settled himself into the

chair opposite, crossing one leg over another. His right foot, suspended in the air, twitched slightly. “You’ve had another shooting?”

The word ‘you’ve’ was not lost on Helen. She didn’t answer immediately. Instead she sat behind the desk and leant down to retrieve her notes from her briefcase. She gathered his testiness was due to her being out of the office. Jenkins was certainly no fan of her preference for the hands-on approach to interviewing witnesses. He preferred his DCIs to manage an investigation from a desk where they collated evidence, read witness statements taken by DCs and barked orders at their team. Losing her inspector to sick leave had only bolstered him further. He’d amped up the pressure these past few months, but she’d fought it every inch of the way. The matriarchal approach just wasn’t Helen’s style and it vexed Jenkins intensely.

Striking in appearance, his dark eyebrows and lashes contrasted with a full head of combed back, grey hair. But Helen had noticed a marked difference in him since he’d been passed over for promotion the previous year. His eyebrows hung deeper over his eyes, the frown marks more prominent in his forehead. He’d always been a private man, lacking humour (unless it was of his own making) but he emerged even more driven, focusing heavily on targets and public relations.

“Sir?”

He adjusted his position and she caught a brief whiff of his aftershave. “So, where are we?”

Helen flipped open her notes. In the short time they had worked together she’d grown accustomed to his not reading her situation reports, although he cursed like hell if they weren’t emailed to him at the appropriate time. She sat back in her chair and gave him a brief overview of the case.

“We’re building up a picture of Naomi’s life at the moment,” she said as she finished up and closed her notebook, "particularly her last hours. And we've circulated Jules Paton's details nationally in an effort to locate him."

"Right. What are we doing about the informant?"

"The phone used by the informant isn't traceable on our systems and we can't site it either as it's seemingly off at the moment. The quality of the recording isn't great, but we're playing it to everyone that knew Naomi. Hopefully, somebody will be able to identify the voice."

Jenkins nodded slowly and stared across at the wall for a moment, tapping his chin with his right forefingers, another habit of his.

Helen glanced past him into the incident room. She could see one of her officers calling across the room to somebody, another on the phone, others clicking at keyboards, rustling through filing cabinets. It never ceased to amaze her how a thin plasterboard wall could enable her to cut the sounds and movements from her mind.

Her eyes rested on a soft toy rat that hung over the white board listing the job allocations for that morning - somebody's joke at Pemberton's expense. It was incredible how quickly, when it came to humorous incidents, word got around. The jokes had started at briefing this morning: 'I hear there's a rat in the camp. I think I smell a rat, sergeant… '

"Okay. That all seems in order," Jenkins said and abruptly stood. "Let me know of any developments as soon as they occur."

"Certainly, sir."

He turned as he reached the door. "Don't forget our meeting with MOCT at eleven thirty in the conference room."

Helen stifled a groan. It hadn't slipped her mind that Midlands Organised Crime Team, or MOCT, were coming down to assist in their cold case shooting investigations, or that the introductory meeting had been arranged for that morning. "I was going to send Pemberton on that one, sir. It'll be a good developmental move… ”

“He’s at Memington Hall.”

Her jaw tightened. “I realise that. I’ve got the autopsy at twelve.”

“Delegate.” He turned his head to the office behind him where Spencer was on the phone, waving his arms about vigorously. “Send him.”

“Sir, I strongly… ”

“I need you there,” he said, enunciating every syllable. “You can use the press conference afterwards to appeal for witnesses to the current case. Let’s play this one down as an argument between lovers that went wrong. We won’t mention the murder weapon. With any luck we’ll have it wrapped up in a few days.” He scratched the back of his ear. “We are dealing with public perceptions here, Helen. Let’s not turn this into something it isn’t. We’re there to promote the help we are getting from MOCT to solve our outstanding murders. A united approach against gun crime. Keep it positive.”

Helen fought to keep her reserve. Autopsies were key to a murder investigation. She hated missing it. Just as she inwardly cursed the politics of modern day policing, she recalled the intelligence on Paton. He’d been associated with cocaine supply… How big a player was he? Local intelligence had been quiet for a while. Had he moved further afield? If so, he may have attracted the interest of the area organised crime team. Maybe she could salvage something here - use the meeting with MOCT to glean some background on Paton? It had to be worth a try.

“I’ll sort it,” she said.

“Good, see you there.”

Helen sighed as she watched Jenkins wander back through the main room and disappear from sight. She eased back into her chair and rolled her shoulders, listening to the cartilage in her neck pop and crackle. She was no longer thinking about politics. There was another reason why she hadn't wanted to attend the MOCT meeting: Detective Inspector Dean Fitzpatrick.

They met a year ago, on a week's residential training course in the West Country - 'The Proceeds of Crime Act'. She recalled Dean entering the room that first morning; his very presence lifted the atmosphere of the group of strangers instantly. Dean possessed that special gift of acknowledging everybody in a group, saying just the right thing at the right time, pressing just the right buttons to make everyone feel special. Coupled with dark, athletically handsome looks and a killing smile, he was infectious.

After break they were paired together on a syndicate exercise. Initially wary of his charm, Helen couldn't fail to be pleasantly surprised by his practical, easy nature and impressed with his knowledge of legal application.

As the day progressed, she slowly peeled her shutters back. Over lunch they discussed sailing. Both Helen's boys had taken lessons the summer before at Pitsford Reservoir, just outside Hampton. Dean was a keen dinghy sailor. He laughed at her accounts of the boys learning to tack, leaning over the side of the boat to keep the sail upright. Over dinner they discussed family. He explained how he was separated from his wife and talked about his daughter, Lucy.

By the second day they were studying the role of gambling, money laundering and asset seizures in organised crime by day, and tearing each other's clothes off by night. He was a generous, tender lover and, when exhausted from sex, they lay and talked, him about his various hobbies of golf, swimming and cooking; she about her family, her boys. She was flattered by his genuine interest in her.

When the course ended, they exchanged numbers. With Dean in Nottingham, a two hour drive north of Hampton, Helen had been sceptical about a future relationship. The following week he surprised her, by calling and texting most days. On Saturday evening he drove down, took her out for dinner to Georgios beside the canal. She remembered it well: she ate risotto, him cannelloni. It was the first time she'd worn a dress in years and it felt good. Afterwards they'd spent an exhilarating night together in a hotel nearby.

In spite of the distance between them, the relationship continued on this level for several months. A few hours grabbed here or there between shifts, the odd night together arranged around family commitments. Helen didn't make a point of dating police officers and they agreed to keep the relationship secret for a while.

It hadn't been the first time Helen had been drawn to a man since her late husband, John. She had indulged in a few flings over the last ten years. But there was something about Dean. Something that made her stomach flip, gave her a lust for life. Something that reminded her of how much she'd missed these past years.

After four months, Helen plucked up the courage to introduce him to her boys. It was a Saturday afternoon, they went out for pizza and stopped to take a walk in the park on the way home. Dean won Matthew over almost instantly with his knowledge of gold medals in rowing in the last Olympics. Robert, initially reluctant, soon followed when Dean produced a ball from the boot of his car and they had an impromptu game of football in the park.

A month later they all went away to Cornwall for a weekend together. Helen was walking on air. Nothing could burst her bubble. Until he left her after that holiday and headed home. That's when she received the text message.

Hi Honey, I'll be home around seven. Can't wait to see you. D XX

A simple message in many respects, but a message that said so much. And in that split second her elation hit the floor.

The following day, back at the station, Helen looked up an old friend she'd trained with at Bruche police training centre in Warrington. DS Celia Barren worked for the Nottingham force, just like Dean. She remembered the call as if it was yesterday. They spent a few minutes catching up, talking about Celia's daughter and Helen's boys.

Finally, Helen asked her if she knew Dean.

"Fitzpatrick? Of course I do. Everyone knows Dean. Why do you ask?"

"Just interested."

"Interested?" Celia paused. "Oh, no, Helen, not that kind of interested?" Helen didn't respond. "I can see why, but no chance there. He's still very much married."

Even as she recalled the conversation Helen felt her heart drop all over again. "I heard they were separated?" she had asked.

"Not as far as I know. He keeps it all private, but I do know they're still cosied up in the same house together. They live in the next road to me."

That's why I was never invited to Nottingham, she'd thought. So many times it was promised, and every time it fell through for whatever reason. Even now, she remembered the lump in her throat, the pain in her chest. How could she have been so stupid?

She'd excused herself, ended the call as soon as politely possible and replied to his text message. Eight simple words, *I think this was meant for your wife.*

What hurt Helen more than the lies and the deceit was that he was still with his wife, even now. Helen never wished to break up a marriage. But for the first time in ten years she had really let someone in. And she wasn't interesting, attractive, clever or funny enough to keep them.

When she didn't return his calls, a barrage of text messages followed. Not wishing to be played for a fool twice, she'd forced herself to delete each and every one of them, unread. When he arrived on her doorstep a week later, she refused to see him. But closure hadn't made the pain or humiliation less easy to bear.

"Ma'am?" Spencer's soft tone jolted Helen back to the present. Lost in her memories, she hadn't heard her door open, seen his face appear around the edge. He held up an empty coffee mug.

Helen managed a flat smile, shook her head and quickly told him about the autopsy. As he retreated she collected her bag and made her way out to the ladies room.

Relieved to find it empty, she washed her hands and splashed water over her face. When she looked up into the mirror she hardly recognised herself. Her face was pale and washed out. Dark rings hung below her eyes. Helen searched through her handbag. At the bottom she found an old pot of blusher and applied a light covering, then smoothed her lank hair and tucked the stray strands behind her ears. She snatched another glance, sighed and turned to leave.

Just as she turned down the corridor towards her office she spotted him. Her knees immediately weakened. He was standing there, military style, hands clasped behind his back, talking to another plainclothes officer she didn't recognise. Suddenly, the other officer let out a chuckle. Dean smiled, reached round and tapped him on the arm. They looked like two old friends, sharing a joke. For a second she contemplated turning and walking back in the opposite direction. Then he looked up and she realised she had no choice but to approach. She would be meeting him in less than an hour anyway, no point in putting off the inevitable.

"Well, well, look who it is!" Dean said, a smile spreading from ear to ear.

Helen ignored the flip in her stomach and forced a smile as she approached them. "DI Fitzpatrick."

"Helen! It's good to see you," he cried, ignoring her reserve. He locked his eyes on hers, his gaze intense.

She deliberately turned her flushed face away from him, towards the other officer.

"Oh, this is DS Edwards, my deputy," Dean added hastily, as if he had forgotten he was standing next to them. "I see we're going to be working with you on your gun crime cases."

Cases, Helen thought. They're people. Dead people. "So I understand." An awkward silence followed. "Well, it's good to see you," she said, shuffling to the side. He didn't move to let her by. For a split second, she could feel his eyes on her, the air between them charged. A familiar 'just stepped out of the shower' odour filled her nose. It was intoxicating.

She forced herself to snap out of it. "We have another murder. I'm a bit tied up at the moment."

"Yeah, I just heard about that. Another shooting?" Dean asked.

"Young woman, shot twice in the chest," Edwards added.

"Looks like we arrived at just the right time," Dean grinned.

Helen formed her lips into a thin smile. "You've done your homework. If you'll excuse me?"

"Of course, see you at the meeting." He moved aside and she continued down the corridor.

When she finally returned to her office, she shut the door and closed the blinds. Helen leant up against the wall and rested her head back on the cold plaster. For some reason she had wanted this moment to be so different. For some reason she had wanted to look triumphant, so that he could see what he was missing. But she couldn't fathom out why.

Chapter Eight

Situated an hour north of Glasgow, Aberfoyle was a small town nestled in The Lomond and Trossachs National Park. Eva stopped for a moment to watch the tourists wander up and down the main street that offered eateries, outdoor clothing stores, gift shops and a visitor centre. She marvelled at how, even in low season when the weather was at its harshest, people still travelled here from all over the world to enjoy the breathless beauty of rural Scotland.

Having stopped at the Co-op on the corner, she was now stocked up with bread, milk, tea and eggs. She filled up at the petrol station, grabbing a large bar of Cadburys from the counter before continuing on her journey.

Eva had been coming to Scotland every year for as long as she could remember. The familiar surroundings felt like a baby's comfort blanket and the tension trickled out of her shoulders as she pressed on into the rural heartlands.

Turning off the A821, the winding country lanes drew her further into the Scottish countryside. She slowed to pull into a field entrance, jumped out, leant her elbows on the gate and drank the fresh, clean air. The field was inhabited by three large cows, hair hanging down over their eyes, curved horns protruding from their heads. One of them gazed in her direction for a second, before lowering his head to the grass.

Eva watched them gently grazing. They whiled away their days eating grass, basking in the sunshine, sheltering under trees in bad weather. Always together, always looking out for one another. A mixture of envy and melancholy washed over her. What kind of a friend was she, running off and leaving Naomi like this?

She pushed her head up and closed her eyes as the thick breeze brushed her face. During their last conversation she had been annoyed with Naomi, frustrated at her inability to cope with the situation they found themselves in. Yet Naomi was right to be petrified. Guilt stretched her heart into a tightrope across her chest. She should have stayed, supported her friend, faced up to their problems. But Naomi wouldn't have wanted that.

Eva thought of the black gloved hand. Had they seen her face on Naomi's screen? She swallowed, blinked open her eyes back to the present. The cows had moved away to the other side of the field. She climbed back into the car and, as she revved the engine, made a point of opening the window.

The sharp wind rustled through Eva's hair as she pressed the accelerator. Grief turned to anger and she allowed her rage to flourish in her driving, revelling in the twists and turns that eventually led her to the road that ran alongside the vast Loch Ard, flanked by beautiful conifer covered mountains, past the Macdonald 'timeshare' resort and hotel where she stayed in her early years, and into the small sprawling village of Kinlochard.

When she reached the Wee Blether tearoom adjacent to the old shop, she made a sharp left, past the post box, the tiny primary school, through the scattered houses and up into the mountains. The sun shimmered across the top of the loch as she slowed and turned left into Lochside, the two bed bungalow her parents' bought eight years ago, situated almost half a mile outside the village.

Twenty minutes later she was seated on the veranda at the back of the property, cup of tea in hand, overlooking the loch. She pondered how different her life would be if they'd dumped the drugs. They brought them back out of fear for their lives. The wrong thing for the right reason. Why now, were they being hunted down?

The hot fluid warmed her. She gazed across the loch. The isolation and sheer beauty of the landscape slowly drained her of the troubled memories that haunted her brain. For the first time in twenty-four hours, she finally felt safe. With her parents still away on holiday in South Africa, nobody would find her all the way up here. Would they?

She closed her eyes and relished the warmth of the sunlight soothing her face. It seemed nobody had told Scotland about the snow down south.

The branches of two silver birches at the bottom of the garden batted against each other in the wind. The sound was distant at first, then louder, then louder still. Suddenly, she realised that it wasn't the trees at all. She turned urgently towards the sound of the gentle footsteps, scraping across the decking.

***

"Glocks, Berettas, Baikals - all automatics. These are just some of the weapons we've retrieved from the criminal underworld. We have recovered a few revolvers, but they tend to be on the decline. Usually illegally trafficked in from former war zones such as the Balkans, although a few replicas are made in this country, all are readily available on the black market if you have a few grand to spare."

Jenkins and Helen were seated around the end of the long table in the conference room. Helen looked at the images of reclaimed guns on the screen, then watched as Dean in his slick black suit stood back and pressed another button on his laptop. The image on the screen changed.

"Don't be fooled by the media," Dean continued, turning to face his audience, "knives are still the weapon of choice in gangland Britain. Guns tend to draw too much national attention, as we've seen recently, so are generally used to scaremonger and frighten, or carried as a status symbol. But the numbers are rising." He pointed at a graph that showed a crinkled line turning upwards. "What the press don't know, is that there are a lot more out there than we have figures for, or care to imagine."

Dean raised his hand and brushed it across his dark hair. Helen felt her stomach bounce. "We are working very closely with ballistics on the intelligence side to see if we can establish any links with current outstanding cases of gun crime throughout the UK."

Helen glanced out of the window as she fought to keep her emotions in check. A strapping wind had wiped the clouds from the sky, allowing the sun to melt the remaining snow spots. Heavy rays penetrated the window, warming her left shoulder. Her mind turned to Operation Aspen as her investigation had now been named. How was the autopsy going? Had they retrieved the other bullet? She checked her watch. Did they have an ID on the informant yet? A sharp look from Jenkins turned her attention back to the screen.

"With improvements in forensics over the years, those involved in gun crime have become shrewd," Dean droned on. "Regular users tend to stick to 'clean' guns, meaning those not involved in an incident previously. After a shooting, they break them up and dispose of them, either bury them or chuck the pieces in a river or lake. But in the current climate, we have found that more and more are getting sold on. It is still far cheaper to buy a used gun than a clean one."

Helen stifled a yawn. "The shot of every gun is different,"

Dean continued, "it leaves a unique mark on the cartridge shell. The organised gangs have picked up on this. In the recent shooting of Germaine Long in London we actually have CCTV footage showing two people with hoods pulled down over their faces, collecting the cartridge cases off the pavement before they flee the scene, no doubt in an effort to reduce the evidence available."

This last remark shook Helen's senses. She recalled Pemberton's comments at the crime scene, that they couldn't find the shells. Could this be an organised, calculated killing?

Dean switched off the machine and sat down.

Jenkins took a deep breath and leant his elbows on the table, "So, what can you do to help us with our outstanding cases?"

"The guns used in your shootings in Roxten were Baikal IZH-79s, right?" Dean said. He looked directly at Jenkins who nodded. "We have been working closely with colleagues in neighbouring forces on their outstanding gun crime and similar Baikals are cropping up. We want to locate the source of these weapons. We'll base ourselves here for a couple of weeks as we continue our enquiries."

"How long before we see results?" Jenkins asked.

"Hard to say. We're hoping the pooling of intelligence may throw up some end users."

Helen thought back to the scene of the crime: the rabbit warren in Roxten. A prominent name popped into her mind. "What can you tell us about Chilli Franks?" she asked. Stephen Franks, nicknamed Chilli for his fiery personality, was proprietor of the Black Cats nightclub in Roxten, a suspected front for drugs trafficking and organised crime.

Dean's face turned blank at her interruption. He shook his head.

"Oh, come on!" Helen hissed. "Nothing goes on in the rabbit warren or the whole of Roxten for that matter, without a nod from him. We know that Richard Elsdon, our main suspect in the Harvey case was linked to him. He used to work at Black Cats as a barman."

Dean sat back in his chair. "We've all heard the stories. It's not a crime to keep criminal associations. But whatever Chilli was in his younger years, we've found nothing to suggest he is criminally active now, and no connection with either of the dead boys."

Helen could barely believe her ears. Formidable in his younger years, Chilli was the right hand of Jimmy Percival, regarded as Hampton's very own gang leader during the 1980s.

Chilli was Percival's 'fix it' man in those days, suspected to be responsible for Hampton's most violent crimes. It was alleged he'd chopped two fingers off an associate who'd skimmed off Jimmy, plunged a rival's hand into boiling water for information on their gang and, his signature dish, slashed the faces of Jimmy's adversaries with a Stanley knife. Numerous arrests failed to convert to convictions through lack of evidence, absence of witnesses, or traced witnesses withdrawing statements. With half of Hampton Town Hall on Jimmy's payroll, Chilli appeared almost Teflon coated.

Putting Chilli Franks behind bars placed a severe dent in Jimmy's operations and was one of the biggest investigations of James Lavery's career in Homicide and Organised Crime. Helen remembered the case well from her childhood - Chilli had blinded a man by throwing acid in his face. Her father worked around the clock in close conjunction with witness protection, to secure witnesses and gather enough evidence to make the case solid. He called Chilli Franks 'rotten to the core' and his elation was obvious when 'the most dangerous man he had ever put away' was sentenced to fifteen years imprisonment.

By the time Chilli was released, almost ten years ago,

Helen's dad had passed away and she was a rookie herself. She remembered how beat constables were briefed to keep a close eye on his movements, particularly when Jimmy took Chilli back into his operation as a 'driver'. But, although pulled back into the world he'd left, Chilli appeared a shadow of his former self, a calmer individual who kept a low profile. Months passed and police interest waned, intelligence taking them elsewhere.

A couple of years later, Jimmy died of a heart attack and bequeathed Black Cats to Chilli. Again, Chilli was under the eye of the police, scrutinising his every move. But he took the reins quietly, went out of his way to ward off police attention. She recalled the first time they'd crossed paths. As soon as he heard her surname his eyes darkened, a muscle flexed in his cheek. He said nothing, but he didn't need to, his face spoke a thousand words.

As she rose through the ranks, Helen had watched him expand his operations to include a couple of nail bars and a hairdressing salon. Occasionally he attracted police attention, moments when Black Cats was linked to drugs supply, selling alcohol to minors, prostitution. Each time they were unable to build a case against him. But he always gave her the same wolf-like stare as though something was bubbling beneath the surface.

Helen wasn't fooled. Chilli's record may have been clear since his prison stretch, but that was only because he employed the best lawyers in the business. You needed a gold plated warrant to get near Black Cats these days.

"Look," Dean continued, "it may suit him for people to suspect his involvement in order to gain respect in his line of business. But there's no intelligence to suggest his personal involvement."

"Presumably you'll share your intelligence?" Helen asked. She'd worked with specialist units in the past and they were notoriously cagey with their information. Everyone had their own agenda - they wanted the source, those that smuggled the weapons in. She was more interested in locating the killers of the two boys.

"As much as we can."

"I thought we were working together on this?" She shot a glance at Jenkins who pressed his lips together and frowned. How was she supposed to come up with answers if she wasn't given all the necessary information?

"Helen," Jenkins interjected.

Dean lifted his hand to Jenkins in a conciliatory manner, and nodded. "The spread of too much information at the moment may jeopardise the operation of my guys working in the field and put them in danger."

"Only if it is leaked."

"Exactly."

"Are you suggesting that somebody in here would do that?"

"I'm not suggesting anything. Just that, at the moment, the decision has been made at the highest level to keep the information close, until we have completed our mission. It won't be for too much longer."

"In the meantime, how are we supposed to progress these two murder enquiries?" she asked.

"I hear you had another shooting last night?" Dean said, changing the subject.

"Yes, a twenty-four-year-old local woman named Naomi Spence," Jenkins said. "Perhaps Helen could enlighten us?"

Helen suppressed an angry sigh and gave a laconic update on Operation Aspen. As she finished she asked whether Dean's team were familiar with Jules Paton.

"We do know of him," Dean said. "Jules Paton is a middle class lad who dropped out of university eight years ago. He's originally from Worthington, although I believe his parents don't have much to do with him these days. He started a business, sourcing and supplying specialist cars. Recently, I believe he's moved into the vintage market."

"You seem to know a lot about him. Why the MOCT interest?" Helen asked.

"I believe his name has come up a few times… "

"In relation to what?" Helen interrupted.

"Drugs mainly." Dean shook his head dismissively. "He's a party lad, a suspected cocaine user. We think he might be involved in the supply chain in some way, but we're not really interested in him, more so in those above him."

Helen considered this a moment. If they were investigating organised crime, guns and drugs usually went hand in hand. She narrowed her eyes. "What can you tell us about him?"

"Not much at the moment."

His curt tone vexed her. "If you have any information on his whereabouts you need to share them." Her voice bristled. "We need to speak to him urgently."

"We have no idea where he is," Dean said. "I can assure you that if we get intelligence that is likely to assist with any of your investigations, we'll feed it back. We are here to help."

"What about family, friends, connections? Somebody must know something?"

"I'm not sure we have much there." Dean shrugged a single shoulder. "He doesn't have much to do with his family. His ex-wife lives in Roxten. I could have someone dig her address out for you."

"What about Chilli Franks? Any association there?"

Dean sighed and shook his head. "Nothing."

Helen cursed loudly.

"Helen, there's no room for grudges here," Jenkins said. "We need to focus on the operation."

Helen snorted but they seemed impervious to her anger. Instead Dean focused his attention on Jenkins. "I suggest, for the purposes of the press at least, we treat this current case as an argument between lovers, the chief suspect being a drug addict. We don't want any suggestion that there is a serial gun killer on the loose."

Helen glanced at Jenkins, whose face lit up at these final remarks. Didn't take much to please the super.

***

"Hello, my dear."

Eva stood and darted back. "Oh, it's you." Relief squashed the air out of her lungs. "You startled me."

"Were you expecting someone else?"

Eva stared at Annie Buchanan's fresh face and wavy auburn hair, parted at the side and cut into a short bob. She had worn her hair that way for as long as Eva could remember and she couldn't help thinking how it widened her face, making it look as dumpy as her frame. "I wasn't expecting anyone. I mean… "

"Neither was I." She cast a protective glance back at the property. "Your mother didn't mention you were coming otherwise I'd have freshened up the place, got you some essentials in."

Living a quarter of a mile down the road, Annie was their closest neighbour. When they first purchased the property, her persistent visits and interest had eventually led to Eva's mother jokingly calling her the 'eyes and ears' of the village. She couldn't have realised how right she would be. As soon as a retired Annie became aware that Lochside was to be used as holiday accommodation, she offered her services as a cleaner come housekeeper during their absence. She had to find some way to supplement her pension.

"It was a last minute decision," Eva said and nodded, as if trying to convince herself.

Annie eyed her suspiciously.

Eva was grateful that her parents were only a week into their three week holiday. By the time Annie reached them, Eva would be back in Hampton.

"Well, can I get you anything? Bread, milk, eggs?"

"No, thank you. I stopped in Aberfoyle on the way."

Annie continued to stare for a while, then glanced across at the Loch. "Well, you've picked a good week. Hasn't been so warm in March these past ten years." She turned her attention back to Eva. "How long are you staying?"

Eva pushed her mouth into what she hoped was a convincing smile. "A few days. Holiday at work I needed to use. How is your granddaughter?" she asked, keen to change the subject.

"Shona? Same as usual. On the computer. She tells me she's working, but I'm sure she's just chatting to her mates. I don't know what it is with young people these days. All this beautiful countryside and all she wants to do is tap away at those keys."

Shona's parents had died in a car crash when she was barely out of nappies and Annie raised her single-handedly, bringing her out to Kinlochard when she was only eight-years-old. Eva allowed herself a wry smile. Kinlochard must feel like the loneliest place on Earth to a teenager.

"Well, I'll be going then," Annie said. "Let your mother know you are low on oil. Probably want to get a delivery in case we have a cold snap."

Eva nodded. With no gas supply to the village, they relied on kerosene to fire their central heating. "Will do."

She watched Annie walk out of the side gate and sunk deeper into the chair. It seemed you couldn't disappear, no matter how hard you tried…

Chapter **Nine**

A frustrated Helen made her way back to the office after the press conference that afternoon. The morning felt like a complete waste of time, the meeting with MOCT revealed nothing in terms of new information on the boys' killings and her current investigation was played down during the press conference, limited to her appealing for witnesses to the location and movements of Jules Paton who now, according to Jenkins (even though they had no solid evidence to support this), was their number one suspect.

The event was dominated by Jenkins and Fitzpatrick declaring their alliance in the fight against Hamptonshire gun crime. A public relations exercise designed to show that Hampton force had employed additional resources to investigate the fatal shootings, to reassure the public that no stone would be left unturned until they were solved. Even the Assistant Chief Constable was present, there to earn his own political capital in the media cabaret.

As she reached the canteen, her stomach kicked out reminding her she hadn't eaten since breakfast. When the Local Authority built this modern out-of-town Police Headquarters, they promised a gymnasium with facilities including tennis courts, badminton, a football pitch - all welcome in view of the police's new policy to test the fitness of existing officers at regular intervals throughout their career. They'd also promised a canteen serving hot and cold food to keep them healthy through the long, laborious hours the job demanded.

As usual, ambition exceeded budget allocation, eventually leaving them with a gymnasium restricted to a room with two bikes and a selection of free weights on a stand flanked by two shower rooms; a canteen consisting of a small room of laminated tables and chairs alongside a drinks machine, another selling chocolate and confectionary, and one offering cold snacks.

Helen grabbed a cheese and tomato sandwich out of the machine. It resembled rubber, like the toy food her boys played with when they were young. The frustrations of her morning ate away at her. Even though she'd taken the accelerated promotion scheme, racing through the ranks to make DCI in less than ten years, she wasn't driven by the success and kudos the ranks offered.

All she wanted, all she had ever wanted, was to be like her dad - to catch the really bad guys. She took a bite out of the sandwich. The dry bread clung to the roof of her mouth as she remembered fondly how many an evening he would come home with some tale about a chase, an exciting arrest. They all shared his elation at convictions, despair at unresolved cases. He couldn't relay intimate details but he didn't need to, they simply felt the investigations through his moods. His job was his life and it was infectious.

After successfully leading her first homicide enquiry last November, Helen had felt that same elation all over again. Yet at times like this, when public relations threatened to take over and wear her down, she gripped the real reasons for her existence. Helen was well aware of the need for public reassurance. She couldn't fail to be with Jenkins' constant reminders. But with a dead girl and a killer on the loose, right at this moment that's where her priorities lay. She finished half of the sandwich, binned the rest and made for the door.

On the way back to the incident room, she caught up with DC Spencer on the stairs. "Hi Steve. How was the autopsy?"

His dark, pointy features creased into a frown. "Damaging."

Helen was intrigued. Spencer had worked on the homicide team for the past six years, and before that had been a detective on area. He would have attended endless autopsies during his career. "In what way? Was she raped?"

"No," he interrupted, shaking his head. "No sign of any sexual interference."

"Then what?"

"Tortured," he said quietly, shaking his head. He looked across at her.

A short silence hung in the air. "What do you mean?"

Spencer's face was pallid. He looked visibly shaken. "Cigarette burns on the back of her neck." He held up his fingers, as if he couldn't believe what he was saying, "Four of them." Helen started, but remained silent for him to continue. "Faint marks around her wrist too, suggesting her hands were tied at some stage. Gooding reckons it was probably rope, as there's a burn mark where she fought to break free."

Helen couldn't remember rope at the scene. Perhaps they'd taken it after they killed her.

"There's also a clump of hair missing from the left side of her head," he continued. "Gooding thinks the killer grabbed it to keep her still while he burned her. One burn is smudged, jagged, as if she managed to get away."

Helen recalled Naomi's contorted body. The striking red hair spread across her face. She had fallen on her left side, inadvertently hiding the bald patch on her head. They stood in stunned silence for a moment. "Are you okay?" she asked.

"I will be. Could do with a fag though."

She nodded. "Anything else of any significance?"

"Fibres on her tongue, suggesting she was gagged too.

Helen felt goose bumps appear on her arms and was grateful she was wearing long sleeves.

Spencer stared into space as he continued, "She'd eaten, looks like a meal of pasta, tuna and sweetcorn very soon, maybe even minutes before she died. It still sat in the stomach undigested. From the defensive bruises on her arms and the state of the lounge, Gooding is pretty sure she was caught by surprise. They burnt her a few times, presumably to see if she would tell them where to find whatever it was they looking for. Then a brief tussle followed before they shot her."

"Any skin samples, hair under her fingernails?"

"Nothing. He's pretty convinced that the killer wore gloves."

"What about the missing bullet?"

"Lodged in her spinal column. Gooding retrieved it." He pulled a pack of Lambert & Butler out of his pocket and held it up briefly. "I'll just be a few minutes."

"Of course."

She left Spencer to wander outside to take solace in a cigarette, and made her own way back up the stairs to the incident room. Helen's mind was awash. The torture made sense in a way. The killer was desperate to find something that he assumed was in Naomi's house, something he thought Naomi had hidden. But what?

Her phone buzzed and she looked down at it, curiously clicking the button to open the text message: *Really need to talk. Are you free for dinner later? Dean x.*

The kiss at the end made her blood boil. Did he really think that he could pick up where they left off? Pushing her phone deep into her pocket, she stomped up the stairs, feeling every step.

By the time she reached her office a pain seared the surface of her brain. She reached for her bag, popped two paracetamol and drank them down with the old tea on her desk. The cold fluid made her flinch.

As she sat down in her chair her mobile trilled. The Dad's Army theme tune indicated it was her mother. Thoughts of her boys entered her head as she pressed the answer button, her mother rarely rang her at work.

"Hi, Mum. Is everything okay?"

"Hi, darling. Yes, all fine. I've had a call from Auntie Jo."

Helen couldn't resist a brief smile. Jo was John's sister, the boys' aunt. For as long as she could remember her mother had referred to her as 'Auntie Jo'. "Oh, how is she?"

"Alright, I think. She's coming to stay for a few days."

Helen balked. Although Jo lived in nearby London, busy lives over the years had reduced their contact to cards and phone calls on birthdays and a single visit at Christmas. It wasn't like her to turn up impromptu. "It's not a good time at the moment. I'm up to my eyes with work."

"I did try to put her off. I told her you had a case on and won't be around much, that perhaps she should come another time, but she insisted."

Helen could very well imagine her mother trying to delay a visit. Jane Lavery tolerated Auntie Jo but if she was honest her very presence exhausted her within the first hour.

"Apparently she'd like to spend some time with the boys," her mother added.

That didn't sound likely. Only a couple of years older than Helen, Jo was a career girl in banking and had chosen not to have children. Helen recalled her getting engaged to her long-term partner, Tim, some months earlier on holiday in Antigua. Perhaps they'd had an argument? This was all she needed. Another headache.

Jane Lavery seemed to sense her daughter's frustration. "Sorry, love. Anyway, her train arrives at seven thirty. I just phoned to let you know. I'm making up your spare room."

Helen ended the call. For some reason her mother's voice

made her think back to Chilli Franks. Undoubtedly, the most important case of her father's career, that name would be ingrained into her mother's brain. Chilli's contempt for her father was openly demonstrated on many occasions during the trial. She remembered hiding behind the kitchen door as a child, listening to her father's frustrating stories: The cup of urine he chucked in James Lavery's face when he visited him in his cell, the repeated threats against his wife and family. Her father called them, 'Shallow threats of a condemned man.'

Chilli had been out of prison for ten years and there hadn't been any repercussions to her family. Maybe James was right and the threats were shallow. But there was still a darkness about Chilli, something untoward. She felt it in her bones.

Helen stared back at her phone. She drew the message from Dean back up and her fingers moved over the keys quickly to type: *Busy tonight.* She let out a deep breath as she pressed send. One headache dissolved.

***

Eva woke with a start. She shot forward, glanced about in bewilderment for a moment. The loch sloshed up against the shores, the water grey now that the sun had receded. She shivered. How long had she been asleep? As she moved to sit up, a spasm of pain struck her back. Maybe falling asleep curled up in the chair in the midst of a northern breeze, had not been her brightest move.

Her mind turned to Naomi. She wondered how she was. If she should call her. Was she in hospital?

Maybe she should call the hospitals near Hampton? But she wasn't a close relative and, even if they would talk to her, they might ask awkward questions.

Maybe she should contact Naomi's parents. Although Naomi hadn't got on well with her dad for some time. She'd want to keep this from them. And she certainly wouldn't thank Eva for spilling the beans.

They'd agreed to keep the secret to themselves. Tell no-one. But that was before the attack.

Eva's thoughts collided. She slowly gathered herself to a standing position. As she did so, a pain shot through her head. Coloured lights flashed across her peripheral vision indicating the onset of a migraine.

She moved into the bungalow, carefully locking the door behind her and ambling across to the bedroom. The sight of the bed felt like a roaring open fire on a chilly winter's evening. She kicked off her shoes and climbed in fully clothed, wrapped the duvet around herself and sunk into the soft mattress. Only sleep now, would dull the immediate pain.

Chapter Ten

Pemberton turned the wheel sharply and pulled into Forge Way. The area reserved for parking was situated at the rear of the properties, which were enclosed by tall picket fencing, exposing their back gardens through narrow slits. Most of the gardens were laid to lawn, one had a patio at the top, another a bench outside the back door. A flash of colour in the garden on the end caught Helen's attention. A conifer battled for space in the overgrown near corner of the garden, its branches feathering through the gaps in the fencing, obscuring the view. But through the far corner she glimpsed a blue slide, a couple of footballs and a goal.

This had been DI Fitzpatrick's one concession, the address of Jules Paton's ex-wife and kids. He'd presented it to her at the press conference earlier in the company of Superintendent Jenkins, as if he was doing her a huge favour.

Yesterday she'd been looking at photographs of two dead victims who'd lain in the roads nearby. Now she was back in the rabbit warren again.

They exited the car and made their way up the side alley between the houses, past an overflowing wheelie bin to the front entrance of number forty-two. Heavy beats of music thudded from the house next door.

As Helen raised her fist to the door a loud wail rose from

within. She gave Pemberton a sideways glance and knocked firmly. There was a scurry inside, the patter of young feet across hard flooring. The crying abated. Two small hands slapped the pane of frosted glass that ran down the middle panel of the door.

The hands were rapidly removed. A jingle of keys, a click and the door opened. Dressed in tight jeans and a black, fitted top, Karen Paton stood in front of them in bare feet. Her dark hair was scraped back from her face and tied in a high ponytail. She wore no make-up, yet the beauty in her young face was striking: neat dark brows framed deep brown eyes, edged with thick black lashes. Helen guessed she was in her early twenties. The young boy with the offending hands, around two-years-old, was balanced on her hip, fresh tears still visible on his face.

Helen held up her card. "Good afternoon, Karen. I'm DCI Lavery and this is DS Pemberton."

Karen made no attempt to invite them in. She simply nodded, her eyes switching from one to another. The child wriggled in her arms and she tightened her grip. "I can't tell you anymore than I told you on the phone," she said, exasperation filling her tone as the child continued to wriggle.

"We just want to ask you some questions about Jules, Karen," Helen said. "May we come in?"

The child was squirming hard now, writhing around. Karen reluctantly moved aside to let them in and as soon as the door was closed, she put him down. He immediately scooted behind her.

Helen bent down. "What's your name?"

He stared at her for a moment, before moving further behind his mother's legs.

"Not like you to be shy, Ben," Karen said and rubbed his head tenderly. "Don't you like the police lady?"

He looked up at his mother and grinned, then hid his head

in her leg. "You'd better come through," she said, lifting him back onto her hip.

Helen and Pemberton followed them down a narrow hallway, past a closed door on the right, stairs blocked by a wooden baby gate to the left, and into a square kitchen. The fittings were basic, grey formica cupboards with mock marble work surfaces. An older boy sat at a round pine table in the middle, drawing a picture. He wore a blue jumper with a gold school emblem, although he barely looked old enough to be at school. He stopped and stared at them.

"Hello," Helen smiled.

He said nothing, but continued to stare, wide eyed. A thick aroma of warm milk pervaded the room.

Karen put the toddler down, then turned and placed her hands on her hips. "I'm sorry but I think you've had a wasted journey."

"We just need to ask you a few questions," Helen said, "it shouldn't take long."

The elder boy lowered himself down from the table and ran to the back door, swiftly pushing his feet into a pair of green wellingtons.

Karen Paton turned to face him. "Callum, if you're going outside to play, you need to put your coat on," she said.

He grabbed a navy jacket off the back of a chair and went outside without uttering a word. The door slammed behind him.

Finding herself next to the fridge, Helen studied the photographs encircled by a plethora of fridge magnets, drawings and paintings that decorated it. Pictures of the two boys playing football, one of them holding a fishing rod, another of them posed by a large building that Helen didn't recognise. She paused on one of Karen, dressed up on a night out on the town, then several others of her below that looked as if they'd been taken professionally.

"These are nice," she said. "Where did you have them taken?"

Karen spied her suspiciously. "I used to do some modelling before I had the kids."

"Is that where you met Jules?"

Karen guessed where the line of questioning was going. "Yeah. He was at one of the shoots." Her voice was deadpan, her face a brick wall.

Helen looked back at the photos. Karen Paton was certainly very photogenic.

A loud wail rose from behind them, "Want to go out too!"

Karen turned to look at her younger son. "Okay. Put your boots on first."

"Don't want to!" He rushed across to the door and reached for the handle.

"Ben!" She moved quickly and positioned herself between the door and the toddler. "No," she said firmly, ignoring the others in the room. "If you want to go outside, you wear your boots and coat."

Ben let out a shrill scream and threw himself on the floor.

"Looks like you've got your hands full," Helen said. She pressed her lips together in sympathy.

Karen briefly nodded, although her face held a 'how would you know?' expression. She turned her attention back to the toddler who was banging his hands on the floor.

Helen glanced around the room. Apart from some freshly peeled potatoes standing in an uncovered pan next to the cooker, a kettle, breadbin and single kitchen roll, the surfaces were clear. She recalled their earlier phone conversation when Karen had confirmed that her and Jules were separated, although he has open access to the children and comes and goes as he pleases. She also maintained she hadn't seen him since Saturday and had no idea where he was and no way of contacting him. The problem was Helen didn't really believe her.

She suddenly became aware that the crying had abated.

The toddler was fiddling with a small box, picking out raisins and planting them in his mouth. She watched Karen lift him onto the side and he swung his legs as she helped him into his jacket, fastening each button separately, then slipped red wellington boots over his feet. His eyes were still fixed on the box of raisins as she pecked him on the nose and lifted him down. She handed him another box and opened the door. "Give those to your brother."

As Karen turned to face them, Helen pointed at the empty chairs in front of her. "May we?"

She gave a reluctant shrug as they sat.

"Difficult age," Helen said, tilting her head towards the garden.

"You got kids?" Karen's tone was abrasive. She clearly felt her mothering skills were being questioned.

"Two boys," Helen said. "Teenagers now."

Karen looked genuinely surprised.

"Why don't you sit down?"

Karen sat in the chair nearest the back door and eyed Pemberton suspiciously as he got out his notebook and pen. "I don't know anything," she said.

"It's fine, Karen. You have nothing to worry about. We just want to ask you some questions about Jules. Detective Pemberton here will make a few notes."

"I told you everything I know over the phone. I saw him last Saturday, when he dropped the kids off. He said he was going away for a while."

"When will he be back?"

She shook her head. "No idea."

"What about contact details, a mobile phone number?"

She shook her head again.

"Oh, come on, Karen. Surely you must have something. What would you do if one of the boys got hurt or you needed help?"

"Call my dad."

They sat in silence for a moment.

"Does he go away a lot?"

"Yeah. It's his work."

"What kind of work?"

Karen gave her a sharp look and twisted the silver, celtic ring on her forefinger. "He buys and sells used cars."

Helen let the silence linger for a while. "How long is he usually away for?"

Karen shrugged. "Sometimes a few days, sometimes a week, sometimes longer."

"Where does he go?"

"Wherever the cars are, I guess," she looked away. "You'll need to ask him."

Helen stared at her until she met her gaze. There was something uncomfortable about her. Karen twisted her ring again. The thudding music from next door had stopped. The fridge hummed in the background. Helen recalled Henry Spence's account of Jules' relationship with Naomi. One line stuck in her head. '… he started to control her, knock her about.' She angled her head, "How long have you two been separated?"

"Over two years now. We broke up just before Ben was born."

"That must have been hard."

Karen's fingers worked the ring, twisting faster now. "Not really. Mum and Dad help out a lot. And Jules still comes around, takes the boys out."

"Was he ever violent towards you?"

Karen snorted. "Jules?"

"Yes."

"Never!" She looked from one detective to another. "Jules isn't a bad man. Just couldn't keep it in his pants. Even after we split he still wanted to look after me, kept buying me stuff."

She looked around the kitchen. "He didn't want us to move here. Said it was too rough. He wanted to keep us in Hampton, in a nice house around the corner from him. But my parents live in Roxten. This is where I grew up. I know he helps, but he's away a lot and my folks help with the boys." She turned her gaze towards the garden. "I don't know how I'd manage without them."

More silence. Helen could hear the scratch of Pemberton's pen against the paper.

"It's because of her, isn't it?" Karen said.

"Who?"

A shadow crept across her face. "Naomi. She was killed. I saw it on the news."

"What do you know about Naomi?" Helen asked.

"Not much. Jules was seeing her for a couple of years. Bit stuck up if you ask me, but the boys liked her." She snorted again, "Not difficult to get a toddler to like you when you buy them things and pump them full of sweets."

Helen smiled sympathetically. "You didn't like her?"

"I never said that. Only met her a couple of times." She cast her eyes to the floor.

"What about Jules?"

Karen looked up sharply. "You don't think *he* killed her? Is that why you're looking for him?"

Helen looked down to see a red mark had formed beneath the ring on Karen's finger.

Karen followed her eyes and tucked her hands in her lap.

"What do you think, Karen?"

"I think nothing," she said. "Nothing!" Her voice was filled with anger, but her face looked like she wanted to cry. "They split up a couple of months ago. And he had nothing to do with her murder. He just isn't capable."

***

As they approached the alley that led to the car, Pemberton stopped to light a cigarette and cast her an inquisitive glance. He looked as if he expected to be berated, especially in view of the fact that she had recently given up. But Helen was not about to pass judgement. Instead, she checked her phone. There were two missed calls: one from Dean, which she deleted, the other from Spencer. She dialled him back.

He answered on the second ring, as if he was waiting for her call.

"Hi, Steve. Any news?"

"Yes. A slight breakthrough."

Helen's stomach lurched. She could hear the sound of an engine purring in the background. "What is it?"

"Some of the victim's friends said Naomi went on holiday to Milan with her best friend, Eva Carradine, a week or so ago."

Helen felt a rush of adrenalin. Out of the corner of her eye, she could see Pemberton tilt his head to get her attention. She lifted a hand to silence him. "Where are you now?"

"I'm just heading back to the office. We managed to get her address from the spa at Memington Hall where she was a member. Want me to head out there?"

"Where is it?" Helen retrieved her notebook and scribbled as he spoke. "No, don't worry," she said. "We'll take that one. And Steve?"

"Yes?"

"Well done."

***

The engine hummed as they drove out of the estate. Helen considered Jules, Karen and Naomi: the love triangle. The difference between Karen and Naomi struck Helen. From what she'd learnt of Jules Paton, Naomi's background seemed more similar to his own. But she could see why Karen caught his eye.

They pulled out onto the main road leaving the rabbit warren behind, and passed an industrial estate encased within a six-foot high brown fence that was in dire need of a paint job. From the road, only the tops of the buildings were visible but, having visited there on many occasions, Helen knew these units housed garages, printing firms, engineering factories and even a recruitment office.

As Pemberton slowed to join a line of cars waiting at the traffic lights, Helen's gaze fell on an imposing Victorian building painted entirely in black. The sign read *Black Cats*. Straddling the corner of Henderson Street and Albert Road, on a Saturday night the queues to enter the nightclub ran almost down to the entrance of the rabbit warren estate itself. A pair of chilling, green cat's eyes were painted on the black background above a neon sign, which lit up red when the club was open.

The bald headed, gaunt face of Chilli Franks entered her mind. She recalled Dean's earlier words, 'we've found nothing to suggest he is criminally active now.'

Helen thought back to Chilli's release from prison. He'd taken his nephew, Nate, under his wing. She remembered Nate from her early years in the force. The accident baby of heroin addict, Sheena Franks, Chilli's youngest sister. As Sheena suffered from postnatal depression, a psychosis that deteriorated into manic depression that dogged her life, she rejected Nate at birth. For the majority of his early years, he was passed around family and friends with intermittent periods back with his own mother who clearly lacked interest. Finally, she took an overdose, slashing her wrists in a hot bath when Nate was just nine-years-old.

Helen was one of many cops who'd been called to his school for several violent incidents before he reached the age of eleven. He struggled academically, was a loner and Helen remembered there being something odd about him, an uneasiness she couldn't place. She recalled that Nate moved in with his auntie Petra, Chilli's older sister, after his mother's death. But it was no secret Nate idolised his uncle, having visited and written to him in prison. They stayed close after Chilli's release and rumours were rife in the rabbit warren that Nate unofficially lived with his uncle. For a while, social services kept a close eye. But Nate's school attendance started to improve, he enrolled at the local boxing club and stayed off the streets and slowly their interest dwindled. Whatever influence Chilli had on his nephew appeared beneficial.

Since his release, Chilli had marketed himself as a reformed character, an honest businessman with a strong influence in the parenting of his nephew. But she struggled to believe that she was labouring under a misconception.

The lights changed. Pemberton turned left, leaving the club and Roxten behind them. They passed a burnt-out car on the grass verge displaying a police aware sign, then scores of housing estates tucked behind lines of tall privet hedging as they pressed on towards Hampton centre.

Helen's mind switched back to Karen Paton. She considered the photo she'd seen on her fridge, on a night out with the girls. Maybe it was taken at Black Cats. She certainly looked a lot more glamorous and relaxed than she did today, worrying that ring around her finger until it grazed.

Helen turned to Pemberton, "Did she seem frightened to you?"

He briefly faced her, before switching back to the road. "Karen Paton? Like a rabbit caught in the headlights."

Chapter **Eleven**

Hours later, Helen burst through her front door and heeled it closed. Heavy rainclouds had advanced into the skies over Hampton throughout the afternoon and were now emptying their load with a vengeance. She dropped her briefcase down, suppressing a shiver as she unbuttoned her overcoat.

A high-pitched beep sounded twice and she paused to search through her bag. Another message from Dean: *Really need to talk. Have some information that may assist your current case. Could you squeeze in a quick coffee later?* Helen stared at her phone. What information could he have now that he couldn't share earlier?

Frustration bubbled inside her. For the last few hours the investigation had been thwarted by obstacles: Dark had confirmed with Naomi's parents that Eva Carradine was one of her oldest friends, but they'd reached a dead end when they visited Eva's address as a male student answered the door. The spa address records were out of date and Eva hadn't lived there for the past six months.

In desperation, they approached the DVLA for an updated address, then the electoral role, but they all followed suit. Naomi's other friends didn't seem to mix with Eva, not enough to know her address. Why hadn't Eva updated her records? To add to her frayed patience, the phone company's computers were down and they were still awaiting Naomi's call records.

With Eva and Jules both missing, she was starting to wonder if they weren't both involved in some way. They could check with the Department for Work and Pensions for Eva's new address, but not until the morning as they were closed. This felt like dead time.

Jenkins' decision not to inform the press of the details of the murder weapon felt like a noose around her neck. It was normal to hold back information; they shared only what they felt would assist the investigation. But with the press fixated on gun crime, unless they caught the killer quickly, this decision would come back to bite them. Every tick of the clock taunted her.

Helen reread the text message from Dean. As she wrestled off her wet coat, she wondered whether Dean had discovered the location of Jules Paton. Or had he uncovered more background on Karen Paton? Whatever it was, she realised that she couldn't afford to ignore it. She pocketed her phone and popped her head around the lounge door to find Robert on the sofa, watching television.

"Hi, Mum." He looked up briefly, before fixing his attention back on the screen.

"Hi, darling." She rested her hand on her youngest son's bony shoulder. "How was school?"

"Okay." His voice disappeared into the television.

"What are you watching?"

"Friends re-run. It's one of my favourites."

She nodded and smiled to herself at the depth of his voice, the last remnants of boyhood receding just a few months earlier. "Where's Grandma?"

"In the kitchen," he said, eyes glued to the screen, a smile tickling his lips.

She crossed to the kitchen and pushed the door open. Seated at the breakfast table, Jane Lavery looked up from her magazine and smiled. Blue eyes shone out from a wonderfully clear complexion, only gently wrinkled around the eyes and mouth. Her grey hair was pulled back from her face and tied at the nape of her neck. "Hello there!"

Helen smiled fleetingly and glanced around. Her nose twitched at the gentle aroma of garlic in the air. "Where's Jo?"

"She phoned. Delayed in London, apparently. She'll be here around nine. How was your day?"

Helen glanced up to check the time. Eight o'clock. "Just about to get longer. I've been called out again, I'm afraid." The lie stung the back of her throat as it escaped.

Jane nodded and stared at her knowingly. "Sorry about that. Do you have time for a bite to eat? I've made lasagne."

After John's death, committing to a full-time position in the police force as a single mother had presented a major challenge. Helen found resolution in moving back in with her recently widowed mother and over the years her mother acted as housekeeper come childminder. Jane Lavery occupied her life with her grandchildren and the arrangement enabled Helen to balance the unsociable shifts and demanding hours of the police force, whilst she raised her boys.

Inevitably there were clashes, days when Helen loathed her mother's intrusion in her personal life, days when Jane resented her daughter's very existence; two women from different generations battling for space and supremacy in a shared home. But generally, the arrangement suited them both in its own way. Recently, they'd moved into this detached house with adjoining flat, giving them both a degree of independence, although her mother still spent the majority of her time in their shared kitchen.

"Maybe later, thanks Mum. You okay?"

"Fine, thank you."

"Where's Matthew?"

"In his bedroom."

Helen headed up the stairs. The first few days of a murder investigation left little spare time for sleep, let alone family, and she took every opportunity to check in with her boys, even if it was only for a few precious minutes. She reached Matthew's door, knocked once and strode in.

A rather dishevelled Matthew leapt off the bed, hastily lifting a sweater to cover his bare torso. But it was what was underneath Matthew that made Helen gulp. A hand shot out with verve. It swept a mass of long, dark hair away from the face of a girl who sat up and pulled down a skimpy t-shirt over her bare stomach. Helen just caught sight of the blue stud in her navel before it was covered.

For a second, Helen froze. Then retreated. She shut the door and rested the side of her head on it. When she had agreed to allow Matt to join the Air Cadets last year, she hadn't bargained on him discovering the world of girls.

Suddenly, a damp shiver rippled down her back, reminding her that she needed to change. The rain had soaked through her coat, wet trousers clung to her ankles. She withdrew to her own room, grabbed a black jumper from the closet and sat on the bed unbuttoning her shirt.

This wasn't the first time she'd encountered a girl in Matthew's room, but certainly the only time she'd interrupted something. Helen closed her eyes, desperately trying to recall her own memories at sixteen. Like him she was still at school, studying for her GCSEs. Was she interested in boys, experimenting at this age? She cast her mind back twenty years, but no particular memories came to light. Until John…

As she threw the jumper over her head and stood to fasten her jeans, she thought about the boys' father.

Helen met John at university and they married soon after graduation when they discovered she was pregnant with an unplanned Matthew. He joined the Army and she played mum. They were married for four years before he died suddenly on a routine helicopter flight from Nuneaton to Oxford. Not a day passed when she didn't think of him in some way; miss his laugh, his friendship, his zest for life. At times like this she missed his support too, even though he would probably have burst out laughing and turned the whole event into some kind of joke.

For some reason her mind switched to Dean. Dark and athletically handsome, he couldn't be more different to John. She remembered how he charmed her mother, wheedled friendship out of her boys, and then let them all down. He would be the last person her mother would expect her to meet this evening.

Helen moved back across the landing and hesitated outside Matthew's room. Her fingers lingered on the handle momentarily, before she changed her mind and headed back down the stairs.

As she entered the kitchen, her Mother handed her a parcel. "Lasagne on the run," she smiled. Spending the majority of her life with serving police officers, she was well versed in the unusual habits forced upon them.

Too guilty to refuse, Helen took the foil-covered container and placed it in her bag. "Thanks. Did you know Matthew has a girl in his room?"

"Yes, Leah." Her mother nodded. "They're just listening to some music."

"They were doing a lot more than that when I walked in."

Jane Lavery turned her attention back to the dishwasher. Mugs clicked together as she unpacked.

Helen raised her brows. "He's only just sixteen."

Her mother stopped for a moment and met her gaze, a model of composure. When she finally spoke, her voice exuded a quiet confidence. "I'm sure it's all very innocent." She turned back to the dishwasher.

Helen stared at her mother's back astounded, wondering

when she had suddenly embraced liberalism. But this was a conversation for another day. "Make him come downstairs, please?"

Her mother looked back at her and nodded silently.

Helen glanced at the clock. "I'll speak to him later. I need to go now." She held up her bag. "Thanks for dinner." And with that she sped out of the kitchen, threw a jacket over her shoulders, called a goodbye out to Robert in the lounge and banged the door shut after her. It had taken less than ten minutes.

Using her bag to shield her head from the unrelenting rain, Helen ran to the car and hurried in. Once seated, she rubbed the back of her neck irritably at how her mother's values had mellowed somewhat over the years. She certainly hadn't been this laid-back with Helen in her teens.

She leant forward and turned over the engine as thoughts of work swept back into her mind. She glanced down and flicked the switch to change the radio channel to BBC Hampton, hoping to catch the news. It was always handy to know how far ahead, or indeed behind you, the press were. Instead she was confronted with a Kings of Leon song, "Sex is On Fire". She promptly turned it off. That was all she needed.

Chapter **Twelve**

The moment she was through the door of Hayes Coffee House, Helen spotted Dean. He was seated in the far corner, phone glued to his ear, wearing the blue top she bought him last year. Meeting him here, like this, felt wrong somehow. She hesitated awhile and watched him. He seemed to be having an animated conversation with someone on the phone. Curiosity drove her feet forward.

She'd almost reached him before he noticed her. He immediately stood and pocketed the phone, sending a stray serviette to the floor.

"Everything okay?"

A smile stretched across his face. "Of course."

She paused. "Because you looked like you were in the middle of something."

"No, it's fine. You know what it's like in this job. Everybody wants a piece of you." His face softened. "I'm so glad you came."

She extended a wary hand, but instead of shaking it, he pulled her close to him and kissed the side of her face. As their cheeks brushed, she inhaled that same odour. Combined with the strong smell of coffee and vanilla in the cafe, it was intoxicating.

She nodded abruptly, retrieved her hand and sat, averting

her gaze to look around the cafe as she battled to keep a lid on her composure. A young girl, probably early twenties, sat on one of the large sofas in the window, bent over a laptop, her head softly tipping to music from barely visible headphones. Two women were deep in conversation on tall stools beside the bar. The waitress fiddled with what looked like an old CD player behind the counter.

The peacefulness of the atmosphere calmed her. She turned back to Dean, "There was something you wanted to discuss?"

"Yes, of course. Shall we order first?"

She looked up at the menu behind the counter, an automatic gesture - she knew exactly what was on the board. "Just a latte, thank you."

Helen watched him look towards the counter. The waitress was over in an instant. "Two lattes, please. And two of those double chocolate cookies." He flashed Helen a smile.

"Oh, not for me… "

"Who said they were for you? I might be hungry."

The waitress' giggles dissipated into the air as she retreated. When he looked back at Helen there was a twinkle in his eye. "So, how have you been?" he asked.

"Fine."

"You finally got the Homicide Team then?"

"Yes."

"Pleased?"

The muscles in her thighs tightened. He wasn't going to make this easy. The last thing she wanted was to engage in small talk, but if she left now she had gleaned nothing. And she needed something. "Of course." She forced a fleeting smile. "Hard work though."

He sat back in his chair and sighed heavily. "Know that feeling."

Silence hung in the air. A surge of laughter turned Helen's head to the two women at the counter who appeared to be chuckling together at some private joke, lost in their own world.

"How are the boys?"

Helen turned back and fidgeted uncomfortably. "Good."

"Still playing footie?"

She forced herself to be polite. "Robert is, yes. He's in the youth league finals on Sunday."

"Wow! I'll have to see if I can get over to watch it."

Helen shook her head as she spoke, "I don't think that'd be a good idea." She looked down and found a deep scratch, gouged in the corner of the table. She ran her finger along it.

"Helen, we need to talk."

She raised her eyes to meet his. "Yes, you said you had some information about the case?"

He leaned forward. "I do. But first we need to talk about us."

Helen immediately stood. "I have no… "

"Sit down, please?" The pain behind his eyes irked her. "Just hear me out? That's all I ask."

Helen sat down slowly. This was the conversation she dreaded. The one she wanted to avoid.

"You and I had a huge misunderstanding… "

She widened her eyes as she interrupted, "You lied. You said your marriage was over. You were separated."

He shook his head. "I didn't lie. My wife and I were separated last year. But we hadn't sorted out the financial arrangements, so I was living at the same house in the spare room. That way I could still be around Honey."

"Honey?"

"My daughter. That text message you received, the one you thought was for my wife? It was meant for Honey. You are right next to each other on my phone."

Helen desperately tried to recall the few details of his life that he had told her. He had talked about his daughter. She recalled her being around the same age as Matthew, although they'd never met. "Isn't your daughter's name, Lucy?"

Dean smiled gently. "Honey is her nickname. I've called her that ever since she was a kid."

She knew that Lucy loved to perform. She remembered how proud he was when she was offered the role of Sandy in a local production of Grease last summer… She racked her brains. Not once did she remember Dean calling Lucy that nickname. She eyed him suspiciously. "Why should I believe you?"

"Because it's true. I've moved out now. I wanted to make a clean break, to show you that I'm serious about you."

Helen closed her eyes and shook her head. A lump the size of a golf ball pushed its way into her throat. This was more than she could bear. "It's too late."

"Don't say that." He moved a hand towards her.

His touch prised her eyes open. She dragged her hand back. Right now, she wasn't sure what to think. "Why didn't you say so?"

"You wouldn't take my calls remember? I sent you endless text messages, which I don't suppose you read?"

Helen's mind reeled. She had consumed herself in her own sadness, rolled herself up and protected herself from the calls, the messages. The only way she could deal with the blow was to block it from her mind. Until now.

The waitress arrived with their drinks. They were accompanied by two large cookies on separate plates. She placed them down by his coffee. As soon as the waitress retreated, he pushed one towards Helen. "Everyone knows that chocolate is good for you," he grinned.

Now she saw it. The reason she had fallen for him: the mischievous wit, the boyish charm. This is what had reminded her of John, what made her chuckle. But this, coupled with remarkably handsome looks, was a recipe for disaster.

She ignored the biscuit, looked him straight in the eye. "What was it you wanted to discuss, Dean?"

His mouth was full of cookie and he wiped his lips slowly. She cursed the rush of excitement that hit her. "I want to have a little chat about Jules Paton. Perhaps I can help you with some background."

Helen jerked her head back. "You said you didn't have anything?" Dean didn't answer. He finished the cookie on his plate, scooping up the last of the crumbs with his index finger. "What exactly can you tell me?"

"Well, I guess you know all the obvious – twenty-eight-years-old, five foot eleven, skinny, blond – we call him 'Willo The Wisp'…

"Dean. We've got every officer in the county looking out for him. We know what he looks like."

"Sure. Well, he was studying sociology and politics at university until he crashed out in the second year. We think that's where his coke addiction started."

"We know that too, he was at Nottingham." Helen scratched the back of her neck. "Do you have something new for me?"

She watched as an intense expression spread like a stain across his face. "He came back to Hamptonshire when he left university and looked for jobs to fund the party boy lifestyle."

Helen rose from her seat. The chair squeaked on the tiled flooring. "Dean, if you haven't got anything new to tell me…"

Dean grabbed her arm. "Give me a chance? Please?"

She slowly sat, but her legs still twitched.

"He took jobs in insurance, sales, anything - used his charm to worm his way in."

You should know, thought Helen.

"But the money was never enough. So, we think he started supplying, selling at big events like parties, weddings, that sort of thing."

Helen frowned. "Then why haven't we brought him in?"

"Because he hasn't been caught in the act." His mouth twisted awkwardly. "It's a bit complicated."

"Oh?"

Dean sighed. "Jules' family. They were kind of friends of mine."

"Am I hearing you right?"

His face turned sheepish. "Look, it's no secret. I went to school with his older brother. We were in a band together. Haven't seen him in years, but I bumped into Jules a while back. He knew I was in the job and offered some information."

Helen massaged her temples. "He was an informant?"

Dean's face contorted. "Not, technically…"

She lifted a brow. "An unregistered informant?"

Dean sighed and looked at the table. When he eventually raised his eyes, they were intense. "We met up a few times. He gave me information. Possible deals and criminal associations. Nothing credible as it turned out. There was talk of a shipment of drugs. But it was always on the horizon." He sat back in his chair, scratched the back of his ear. "It all stopped a couple of months ago."

"What happened?"

"He withdrew. Became difficult to get hold of. Said he wanted out, not only with me, but also with the guys he was working with."

"Why?"

"No idea. Then a week ago, he stopped answering my calls and disappeared altogether."

***

Nate flexed his triceps as he hovered in the shadows. His victim should have been back hours ago. He rested his eyes a second, blinked, then froze again, like the street entertainers dressed as statues in the city centre.

Nate had developed a knack for patience, honed through experience. He cast his mind back to an encounter at school with Celia Birtle. Celia had been the most popular girl in senior year with long golden curls that looked as natural as sunshine; large blue eyes, a flawless complexion and legs that went on forever. Every testosterone filled guy in the school wanted to get into her pants.

Most kids gave Nate a wide birth through school. He had no interest in his peers, didn't share their obsession with music, football or comics. Being alone never troubled Nate. Nobody bothered him - he wasn't sure whether that was because he was bigger than the other kids or a result of being Chilli Franks' nephew. But he didn't care. He focused on his boxing and spent hours in the gym every night. By the time he was sixteen he had a six pack and arm definition an Olympic athlete would be proud of.

But the day the teacher chose Celia to be his science partner, he'd felt sick to the pit of his stomach. Partnering was bad enough, but with a girl? Conniving, cold, self-centred beings. Yet, unlike the others, Celia had chatted to Nate. She told him about her pet Spaniel called Sally, her holidays, her parents and older sister. His cool silence didn't seem to bother her. A couple of times she shared jokes behind her hand when the teacher wasn't looking and they laughed together. For the first time Nate experienced a touch of warm friendship and it felt good.

It didn't last. He remembered the moment it all changed. It was the last day of term. They had spent the lesson extracting DNA from a banana. After class, Nate paused in the corridor to search his locker. He heard voices behind him, two lads from his form teasing Celia about her 'new friend'. His back was turned, they didn't realise he was there, lost in the sea of other students. In her musical voice she laughed and responded, "Nate looks like an alien with that wiry hair and acne all over his face and neck."

Nate's jaw had tightened. He couldn't believe his ears, he had to turn, to see her, to be sure. He could still see her now if he closed his eyes; the way she tossed her long, flowing curls behind her neck and grinned, perfect white teeth. A grin that fell flat when she saw him, a face that turned tomato red. He didn't move, just stared back at her until she bustled away into the crowd.

When the new term resumed, Nate ignored Celia, but he didn't forget. For weeks he planned, plotted and watched until he knew her movements inside out. Six weeks later, when she returned from babysitting late one Friday evening, Nate was hidden in her front garden, obscured behind the hawthorn hedge. As she closed the gate behind her, he grabbed her around her mouth, hit the back of her head hard, gagged and blindfolded her.

He remembered the moment like it was yesterday. He could still smell the sweetness of her perfume, the shampoo on her hair, the washing powder on her clothes. He could smell her fear. Whilst Celia's parents watched the ten o'clock news behind their drawn curtains, he cropped her beautiful hair to the bone. He still had a bit of it at home. A sliver of skin remained attached for a while, but that had shrivelled and disappeared over the years.

Celia didn't return to school for a couple of weeks and when she did, hats and scarves covered her head. The fact that he was never caught, simply added to Nate's excitement. She never explicitly said so, but he could tell she suspected him. Whenever they passed in the corridor, her eyes turned fearful. If they brushed past one another in the canteen queue, she stiffened.

Nate blinked and stretched his arms out in front of him, then drew them back and knocked his fists together, *clink, clink, clink,* before he froze again.

He was an animal stalking his prey. And as soon as they made a move he would be ready to pounce.

***

Helen stared at Dean, hardly believing her ears. Jules as an informant certainly muddied the waters somewhat. And an unofficial one could make for a potentially very difficult situation. Dean knew police officers were required to declare any criminal associations. Although Jules had no record to speak of and they had received no intelligence on him for some time. No recorded intelligence anyway.

"What do you know about our victim?"

"Naomi Spence?" He shook his head. "Not much. I think he was quite keen on her in the early days, but for the last year she's been more a trophy girlfriend. I don't think she was involved in any of his deals."

"He separated from her two months ago. Do you think it's connected?"

He shrugged.

"You must have a theory?"

"I think he got himself into something he shouldn't have. Maybe he siphoned off a shipment. Who knows? All I know is that he's disappeared."

Helen sipped the last of her coffee and checked her watch. Quarter to ten. She didn't want to leave her mother to entertain Jo for any longer than necessary. And she needed time. Time to process this new information, away from Dean. "I ought to get going," she said and stood to pull her jacket over her shoulders.

He nodded, lifted his head to the waitress who immediately scuttled over.

Dean paid the bill and they stepped out into a cloudy, dark night. The rain had stopped. Dampness rose from the pavements and pervaded the air around them.

"Would you like to do anything else?" he asked.

Helen wasn't listening. She was looking across the street into a flat above the mobile phone shop. The light was on, the curtains undrawn and a girl sat alone in the corner beside the window, gazing at a screen in front of her. As she watched this perfectly normal activity, an idea crashed into her mind.

"Helen?" The high pitch in his voice brought her back to the moment. "Are you okay?"

There was something she needed to do. She turned back to him just as his phone began to trill. "Fine. Thank you for the coffee," she said quickly. She nodded to his pocket. "You ought to get that. I'll see you tomorrow."

And with that she headed off down the street to her car. Jo could wait another half an hour.

Chapter Thirteen

Helen pressed the brake as she drove past the blue and white tape, plastered around Naomi's home. A fresh faced blond constable, barely out of his teens, stood outside the entrance like a guard at Buckingham Palace. She knew an officer would be posted there until CSI finished working on the property. Barely twenty-four hours had passed since the murder and with the killer ransacking the whole house, as well as accessing the loft space, they had a huge area to meticulously examine.

Her mind followed the killer's movements. Either they knew Naomi, her routine, her home with its front and rear access, the fact that the house three doors down was empty, that the loft space was open; or, they had been watching her for some time. Hours, days, maybe weeks.

Helen cast her mind back to Tuesday evening. She tried to put herself in Naomi's shoes. She left work just after seven, arriving home about seven fifteen. Naomi's red Fiesta was parked up the street, almost thirty metres from her home. They'd had heavy sleet on Tuesday, eventually turning to snow. It must have been a bind not to find a space closer to her front door. Helen imagined her grabbing her bag, her heels clattering the wet pavement as she ran down to her warm, dry home.

Helen slid across her seat, opened the door and climbed out of the car. The Fiesta had been removed for examination. This was about the spot where it was parked. She looked at her watch. Almost ten minutes past ten. She glanced up and down the street. All was quiet. She pulled her torch out of her pocket and shone it across the ground. The officer guarding number eight didn't move, didn't even spare a fleeting glimpse in her direction.

She wasn't really sure what she was looking for. Any clues or evidence would have been removed by now, but she continued for several moments, before moving down the street to number eight.

"Evening." Helen waved her ID at the plastic guard.

He peered at it, curled his mouth into a smile that didn't reach his eyes, nodded and stood aside. He didn't speak a word.

"I'll just be a few minutes," she said. He snapped another nod as she climbed through the tape.

Helen paused inside the entrance and switched back to the previous night. There was no evidence to suggest Naomi rushed about when she arrived home. Her damp jacket was hung on the wooden hat stand in the hall, her bag placed on a hook in the cupboard beneath the stairs. Helen wandered down the hallway. Her shoes squeaked on the black and white tiles as she missed the CSI paper and she edged back onto it.

She entered the kitchen. What would Naomi do? Go through her post? There wasn't any left on the side, but Naomi didn't seem the type to leave it out, almost obsessive in her tidiness. Helen remembered seeing some bills carefully fastened together with a paper clip - gas, electric, council tax, hanging out of an open drawer the night before.

What would she have done next? Checked her answer phone for messages? Helen crossed to the lounge. She stood very still for a moment, trying to piece together Naomi's last movements. She recalled Naomi's landline phone, a black hands free. They'd checked and there were no outstanding messages.

Naomi must have gone upstairs to change. Again, Helen retraced her steps. In the bedroom, she stole another gaze into Naomi's ordered closet. Naomi had changed into a loose green vest and black jeans, but she hadn't slung her suit over a chair like Helen would have done. She must have hung it up in the wardrobe, placed her shirt in the washing bin. Helen fingered the numerous suits in Naomi's wardrobe. They felt oddly sticky through her latex gloves.

She gave up, hesitated briefly to glance at the loft hatch, and moved back downstairs. She recalled the autopsy results: the gastric examination of Naomi's last meal. Helen stood at the bottom of the stairs and closed her eyes. She could almost see Naomi filling the pan, putting it on the hob to warm up, opening the small tins of sweetcorn and tuna, salting the boiling water, immersing the dried pasta, lowering the heat.

Where would she have eaten the meal? The kitchen was tiny. Helen thought back to her student days, before she had children to provide an example to. They had almost always eaten in the lounge, plates balanced on their laps. But what then? Turn the television on?

She recalled the window she'd peered through earlier tonight - the girl sat in the corner of the room, working on a computer. Her computer had been situated in the alcove between the fireplace and the window, just like Naomi's. What if Naomi had been on her computer when she was surprised by her killer? Maybe she was completing a late report for work, answering a few emails.

The killer climbed through the loft, quietly navigated the stairs and carefully opened the door. If she had worked on her computer in the corner, she'd have faced the wall. Perhaps there was music in the background, masking any slight sound.

He could easily have crossed the few metres to the corner, jerked her back, gagged her.

The torture explained the requirement for surprise. He wanted something, she wouldn't tell him where it was. He grabbed her hair to hold her in position. Tied her wrists. Burnt her. Pulled the cloth out of her mouth. She still wouldn't say. Wouldn't or couldn't?

Maybe she pulled away and broke free. He chased her, knocking over furniture, a mirror from the wall. She freed her hands. The bruising to the backs of her arms and across her legs showed they fought.

Perhaps she had fallen to the floor, sobbing, clutching the pains at the back of her neck. He had walked away. She thought he was leaving. Maybe she made to stand. Then he turned back and she saw the gun. Perhaps she tried to reason with him. But it was too late. He shot her twice in cold blood, before turning the house upside down in his search.

Helen turned to face the corner of the room. The desk was bare, the PC already seized as evidence, due to be examined. Tomorrow she would get every technical expert in the station to make it a priority to check Naomi's last movements online.

***

Eva opened the sugar bowl and shook the few grains visible at the bottom. She hated tea without sugar. Although the migraine had abated, she'd woken with a parched throat, the darkness seeping through her window, the only clue to the time. She hastily drew the curtains with a shiver.

She pulled open the cupboard beside the kettle and moved aside the fresh box of tea bags, the jar of coffee. Her heart sank. No more sugar. There was usually a good store of basics in the house to welcome them for every visit. Annie Buchanan made sure of this. Except, as she had made so clear earlier, she hadn't been expecting this visit.

Eva was half tempted to wander down the road to the Buchanan's house to borrow some, then thought better of it. She couldn't face more conversation. There was always the shop. Tomorrow was Thursday. It opened around ten o'clock. Eva's face contorted. Although she had met the shopkeeper, Ken Saunders, and his wife, Valerie, on many occasions in the past, they still viewed her as an outsider, and her visit would, no doubt, prompt questions. And, right at the moment, questions were just what she wanted to avoid.

She crossed the room and slung the hot tea down the sink. There was nothing for it. Tomorrow she'd have to head back into town.

***

By the time Helen reached home, Jo had arrived, unpacked and already shared half a bottle of wine with Helen's mother who looked distinctively relieved (and slightly wobbly) as she excused herself to bed. Helen warmed through the lasagne she'd carried around with her all evening, poured herself a glass of Shiraz, kicked off her shoes and relaxed on the sofa, feet curled beneath her.

She watched her sister-in-law fill her mouth with more wine. Whilst John was tall and lanky, Jo was slim and demure. John's wide eyes had looked oversized for his face giving him a comical quirk yet, coated in mascara, Jo's were striking. John's dark hair stuck up untidily across the top of his head, Jo's hung down in a sleek, short bob. But he shone out through her face, from the expressions she pulled, right down to the dimple in her left cheek and Helen found the resemblance strangely comforting.

Every part of Helen's weary body ached. In the midst of a murder enquiry, the last thing she needed was to gossip with a relative she only saw twice a year. "So, what brings you here in the middle of March?" she said as she dug into her dinner.

Jo laughed out loud. "God, Helen. Trust you to be direct! Not interrupting anything, am I?"

Helen smiled. "I didn't mean that," she added, rolling her eyes. "It's just so unusual for you to visit like this."

"And there's me thinking you had a man hidden somewhere." She made a play of looking behind her, down the side of the sofa, bending her head towards the door.

Helen couldn't resist a chuckle. "Not that exciting, I'm afraid. So, what's up?"

"Can't I come visit my nephews?"

"Any time you like. It's just not like you, that's all. Nothing wrong, is there?"

"Course not. How are things with you?" she gushed, taking another gulp from her glass.

Helen glanced at her plate and pushed the food around with her fork. "Fine."

"Fine!" Jo's voice pitched up a level. "Come on, I haven't heard from you in ages. What have you been up to?"

"Busy, work, you know."

"I'm not interested in your work! What about your love life?"

It never ceased to amaze Helen how much interest John's only sister paid to her relationships. "Non-existent," she replied.

"Oh, you're so boring. My brother's been dead for over ten years now. Don't tell me you've taken a vow of celibacy? Come on. You need a bit of excitement in your life," Jo continued. "What happened to that Dan fellow last year?"

"Dean," Helen corrected as she forked another mouthful of lasagne into her mouth.

"Dean, that's the chap. I remember meeting him at Robert's birthday bash. Seemed like a great guy. The boys loved him."

Helen felt herself cringe. This conversation had rapidly moved out of her comfort zone. "Been over for ages." She shook her head, looked at the floor.

"Oh, what happened?"

Helen recalled Dean's explanation earlier. If he was right then she was a hot-headed, stubborn woman who'd wrecked the only true relationship of any value since John. But did she believe him? "It's a long story."

"When did you last see him?"

Helen wriggled uncomfortably. "Actually… about an hour ago."

Thoughts of Dean unsettled her. Was he telling the truth about the text message? Or was he a consummate liar? She desperately wanted to believe him, but every time her mind entertained the notion, DS Barren's pithy words hung in the air around her: 'still very much married'. And who was he arguing with when she arrived at the cafe this evening? Was it really work? Helen met Jo's gaze. "Not like that. We're working on a case together."

"Really." Jo nodded, knowingly. "Well, see if you can fit some sex in. You look like you could do with some. All work and no play makes you dull."

Helen couldn't resist a smile. Brash was Jo's middle name. That was one trait she didn't share with her brother. "What about you?" Helen asked, keen to shift the conversation.

Jo dropped the smile and lowered her eyes to her glass. "Just needed a bit of space."

"Problems with Tim?"

She looked up. "No… Well, not exactly, not at the moment anyway." She stretched out the word 'moment' and Helen wasn't sure if this was intentional, or a result of too much wine.

"What do you mean?"

"I'm pregnant."

Helen opened her mouth and closed it like a fish in water. Jo was closing in on forty with a senior position in banking, a three figure salary and, by her own volition, never wanted kids of her own. She'd lived with Tim for as long as Helen could remember. "Oh," Helen said finally.

"I don't know what to do." Jo shook her head as she spoke.

Helen stared at her glass for a while. "Does Tim know?"

Jo's eyes widened. "Absolutely not."

"What do you want to do?"

"I'm not sure really. When I look at your boys I think, maybe I could do it. They're so good."

"I caught Matthew in his room with a girl earlier this evening, in a very compromising position," Helen said. She had searched for Matthew on her return home, only to find him in bed (on his own this time, much to her relief), uncharacteristically having an early night. She made a mental note to get back early tomorrow evening to catch up with him.

"Oh, come on Helen. He's sixteen. My cherry had been well popped by that age."

Helen winced. "Too much information."

Jo ignored her. "What about my job? I'd have to go back to work."

Helen cast her mind back fifteen years. When Matthew arrived she had been barely out of university, with no job to speak of. She remembered waiting for maternal instinct to overwhelm her, ready to turn her into a blackberry picking, jam making, Earth mother. She was still waiting two years later, when Robert came along. In spite of the deep love she felt for her children, Helen had never been a natural stay at home mum. Shortly after John's death she joined the police force and the boy's grandmother adopted the everyday roles: doing the school run, organising their clubs, baking with them. And Helen rushed home from work to tuck them up in bed when shifts allowed, and took them to the park on her days off.

"They do have nurseries these days. Or maybe you could have a Nanny?"

"Mmmm," Jo replied, thoughtfully. "Or maybe you could lend me Mrs L?"

They both laughed. Jo had referred to Helen's mother as 'Mrs L' for the whole of their acquaintance, a habit which annoyed Jane Lavery intensely. Jo leant down for the bottle, tilted it to one side to check for any remaining drops.

"How much of that have you had?" Helen asked.

Jo gave a watery smile. "Don't worry. I've only had a couple. Gave most of it to your mother. Thought she could do with letting her hair down a bit."

Again they laughed. Jo's mouth followed into a full-blown yawn, which she made no attempt to cover. She reached to the floor and clicked some buttons on a laptop that sat open beside her. Helen watched her, perplexed.

"Facebook," Jo snorted. "It's a curse."

Helen watched Jo shut down her laptop, stretch to the ceiling and give a wry smile. "Well, that's me, I'm going to turn in." She leant down and collected her shoes from the floor. "Don't want to be accused of keeping you from your work now, do I?"

Helen smiled, pushed the half-eaten food aside, stood and gave her a brief hug before watching the door close behind her.

She retrieved Robert's laptop from the corner of the sofa and switched it on. Helen had opened a general Facebook page under a false name with high privacy levels to enable her to research for work. She found social networking an amazing phenomenon. People were consumed with identity fraud these days, yet they spread their life across Facebook and Twitter like butter on toast. Photos, birthdays, names of pets, hobbies, anniversaries were all on display. Technology made it so easy to trace people and with this kind of personal information on tap, it wouldn't be too difficult to guess their passwords. The possibilities for the criminal fraternity were endless.

Helen logged on and searched for Naomi Spence. She recognised Naomi's ginger tresses in her profile picture immediately. Her wall was full of condolence messages from friends, family, even an old college tutor. She had obviously been very popular.

Helen looked across at the list of her friends. Jules Paton was listed. She clicked to view his page. The last entry he made had been over a week previous. She briefly flicked through his photos. There were many of him and Naomi. Their break up can't have been acrimonious, at least not on his part. Not enough to remove them. Many of the other pictures featured cars of various types and colours.

She pressed the key to return to Naomi's page. Again she looked through her friends until she came to Eva Carradine. A blank profile faced her. Helen frowned and clicked on the image to move to Eva's page. The screen changed. Eva's account came up, but required she message her or send a friend request and be approved, in order to view her page. Whereas Naomi and Jules' accounts were open for all to access, Eva had fixed higher privacy settings. As she returned to Naomi's page, she thought of the holiday the girls had taken. March wasn't the warmest time of year to go to Milan.

Chapter **Fourteen**

Helen stretched her arms back. The heat in the incident room made her throat dry. Having finally obtained Eva's address from DWP first thing, Helen had gone out there to find it empty. She'd spoken to her neighbour, a student named Eleanor, who said she hadn't seen her for a couple of days, but was able to supply her work details: an insurance firm called Warmton & Co., in Hampton. Enquiries later revealed that Eva had phoned into work sick on Wednesday morning. So, where was she now?

"The informant called the victim several times over the days running up to the murder, sometimes two or three times a day." Pemberton looked up from the phone records and rubbed his chin.

Helen crossed to his desk and perched on the edge. "Is there any pattern to it?"

He lowered his eyes. "Doesn't look like it."

"What is strange is that they also called her one, two, three, four - hell, at least half a dozen times after eight o'clock on Tuesday evening." Pemberton picked up his pen and tapped it against his lower lip several times. "According to our reports, Naomi was dead by then."

"That doesn't make sense," Helen raised a brow and cast her eyes over the sheets.

"And, this is interesting… " Pemberton leant back in his chair. "Another call was made from Naomi's missing mobile to the informant on the day after the murder!"

"Somebody's using her phone," Helen said. "Get on to the phone company. See if you can find out where that call was made."

She scanned the listings. There were several calls, some of which were long in duration. A stalker would normally make numerous short calls. Did whoever was using Naomi's phone know the informant? She thought back to the crime scene. Whoever killed Naomi knew the layout of her house including the open loft space. The level of violence indicated they were looking for a male killer, but the informant was female. Could it be Jules, or Eva, or both? She turned to face the rest of her team. "Still no ID on the informant's voice?" Heads shook around her. "What else do we know?"

"Got it!" Dark exclaimed. "The camera picked up Eva Carradinc's car on the M6 near St Anne's services at two o'clock on Wednesday morning." The room fell silent. She flicked back through her notebook. "Naomi's parents mentioned last night that Eva's family have a second home in Scotland," Dark continued. "Naomi joined them there for a holiday last year. Somewhere near Loch Lomond, but they don't know the full address."

"And we still can't locate Eva's parents?"

Dark shook her head.

Helen had taken the boys to Scotland on holiday last year. They stopped at services just south of Glasgow, private services offering organic, home cooked food. She remembered it well, the boys, hoping for a fix of fast food, hated it. Even her Mother had grumbled about the choices of couscous and salads. "If I'm right, they are private services. Give them a ring and see if she spoke to anybody. And see if they have any CCTV footage."

"Right guys, we've got technical examining the computer this morning so we'll see where that leads us. We've appealed for anyone with information on Eva and Jules to come forward on the victim's Facebook page. The feed will appear on their personal pages as well. We've also circulated their details to other forces. Let's concentrate on finding them."

Just as Helen turned to go to her room, she heard Pemberton's voice again, "Oh, my."

She spun round. "What?"

"The address. We asked the phone company to site the call made by the informant's mobile on Tuesday evening." He shuffled the papers around on his desk until he found what he was looking for. The room hushed as everyone turned to Pemberton.

"What is it?" Helen asked.

He marched over to the map on the wall. "Thought so."

Helen sighed loudly, "What?"

"The call to the ambulance service was made from within two hundred metres of Eva Carradine's address."

Helen narrowed her eyes and approached the map.

"Look," Pemberton said.

She followed his finger from Eva's home across to the victim's house which was clearly marked, along with other key points: Memington Hall, Jules Paton's house. She cast her eye down at the scale of the map. "If Naomi returned home from Memington around seven fifteen, cooked dinner, got changed, we estimate she was killed between seven thirty and eight o'clock..." Helen pointed at the two addresses on the map. "That journey would take at least forty minutes. How the hell would anyone have been able to get from Naomi's house, to here, in less than half an hour?"

Pemberton shook his head. "Couldn't have done it."

"Then how did they know Naomi had been attacked?"

***

Eva turned right at the bottom of Kinlochard Hill and onto the winding road that led into town. It was another bright spring day. Slivers of sunshine peeked between broken tufts of cloud. On many a holiday up here, when rain pummelled the mountains and lochs, she'd wished for weather like this. It was ironic it should arrive now, when she would have welcomed rain, or even snow, to flood the narrow roads and cut them all off for a few days.

She gazed across the loch. With the sun's sparkling rays rebounding off the water, the firs in the background stretching up the mountainside, patchy blue sky beyond… It struck Eva that she had never taken the time to paint the scenery up here. She loved art, especially watercolours, indulging the calming effect on her mood. Maybe if she immersed herself in it now, it would wipe the haunting images from her mind, the feeling of dread that weighted her down.

Eva collected her thoughts. Was that only Tuesday evening? It didn't seem possible. Naomi – where are you? The desperate need to speak to her friend ate away at her like maggots.

Anger infused her blood, the rage inside her building as it travelled around her body. How could Jules let this happen? She thought back to Friday evening. When they arrived in Granary Avenue to deliver the car to Jules, he'd greeted them at the door with a wide smile, his arms flung out, like they were old friends who'd been away for months.

When they'd ignored his gesture and pushed past him into the hallway, his face had immediately fallen. "Is everything okay?"

The air in the small hallway rapidly became charged as the girls recounted their story. They interrupted each other, voices rose, anger sliced through their words. Naomi started with the window problems, the garage; Eva followed with their panic at the discovery, their terror at being left with no funds, forced to negotiate customs and bring the 'packages' back into the UK.

Jules looked genuinely alarmed. But all attempts to intercept with apologies were shouted down. He wasn't going to wriggle out of this one. As the screams and allegations were joined by Naomi's tears, red blotches appeared on his neck.

When they finished, he shook his head. "I'm so sorry. It must have been awful for you."

This is the moment when he tries to empathise, to pretend he's on our side, Eva thought. Jules was ever the diplomat. He possessed that rare ability of twisting what people said, worming his way into their conscience, much like a politician. But she couldn't afford to let him kill the moment with phoney explanations and false promises. Not this time.

She turned to Naomi, her eyes peeled back in anger, beseeching her to respond.

Naomi dried her eyes. "Bad people do this sort of thing, Jules," she said. "Really bad people."

He buried his eyes in the floor. Swallowed. "I don't know what to say."

"Why don't you start by telling us who the car is for?" Eva asked.

Desperation crept across his face. "I-I can't."

"Can't or won't? What was in those packets?"

He shook his head.

"Christ, Jules, how could you get mixed up with these sorts of people?" Eva gritted her teeth. "How could you put us in danger, put our future in jeopardy?" She turned to her friend. "How could you do this to Naomi?"

He stepped back, turned to Naomi. "You have to believe me. I didn't know this was going to happen."

Eva had no time for explanations. Naomi always felt like the sister she'd never had. All their life they'd shared secrets and confidences: laughing and partying through the wild teenage years, hugging and crying when Eva argued with her stepfather, flunked university; when Naomi's cat was run over, her first boyfriend cheated on her, her grandma died. But it was a much changed Naomi that Eva hooked up with after university. All the fun and frivolity of a party girl played beneath the surface, yet there was a lack of confidence in her that Eva had never seen before. She witnessed a torrid relationship with the enigmatic Jules. They seemed drawn to each other, yet there was something unnatural about their relationship. Naomi had developed a social use of cocaine that she couldn't seem to stop. Two months ago, when Naomi was spending out on more cocaine, unable to keep up her mortgage payments, Jules and Naomi had a huge argument and separated. Not a drug user herself, Eva was secretly pleased. But it didn't last long, the bond between them drawing them back to each other like moths to a flame.

Up until this moment, Eva had supported her friend in her moments of crisis and battled to keep her opinions to herself. But she'd grown to detest Jules' presence, his stake in her friend's life, the way he tarnished her world. And now this? This was unforgiveable. She drew a deep breath and when she spoke her voice was steely, "Who else knows we brought that car in?"

He looked puzzled. Shook his head. "Nobody."

"Then there won't be any repercussions?"

She watched realisation dawn on his face. "Of course. N-no. I'll make sure of that. You guys are safe."

A deer at the side of the road made Eva blink and brake suddenly, jolting her back to the present. Safe. How wrong could he have been? The deer turned to look at her with soft brown eyes, before disappearing into a nearby copse. Eva ran a hand through her hair. Jules, where are you?

He would be with Naomi, at the hospital. Yes. Despite their toxic relationship, Jules still loved Naomi. He just couldn't wean himself off the coke. But he would look after her. Wouldn't he?

Eva pressed on as the sun played peek-a-boo through picture book clouds. On the approach to the town she saw a sign for workmen in the road. A traffic light ahead switched to amber, then red and she halted. For a few moments she watched three workman standing over a large pothole on the side of the road. They appeared to be discussing it, one pointed to the edge of the hole, the other shook his head.

Instinctively, she reached for her mobile. Having lost her BlackBerry on holiday, she bought this Nokia when she got paid last Monday, a cheap 'pay as you go' until the insurance paid out. Thank goodness she'd taken the time to fill out the contact lists already. She switched it on. The screen stayed blank. Frustration clawed at her as she remembered… She had stopped at the services on Wednesday morning to phone work and when she tried to turn her mobile on, it was dead. She'd had to use a phone at the services. And in her haste to pack she'd left the charger behind. Her stomach dropped.

There was no landline at the bungalow either. Eva remembered her disappointment, as a teenager, her stepfather annoyingly saying that modern appliances spoilt the peace and tranquillity of the place. She glanced across at the neighbouring field. It seemed to go on and on, meeting the horizon in the distance. She would have to wait until she reached Aberfoyle and find a payphone.

Time stood still up here. Everything slowed down. Apart from Eva's mind which, right now, raced faster than ever.

Chapter **Fifteen**

Helen glanced around Eva's lounge. After the discoveries in the incident room that morning, Pemberton contacted St Anne's services. He traced a security guard who confirmed he had seen someone that matched Eva's description asleep in a Ford KA early Wednesday morning.

With Jules and Eva missing, Helen couldn't rule out the possibility that they had worked together on Naomi's murder. Both had disappeared and failed to answer the press and Facebook appeals and both were unreachable. She applied for warrants to search their houses in the hope of finding something that either linked them to the murder, or presented a clue as to their whereabouts, and arranged for two separate teams to search each property - she led Eva's, and Pemberton Jules'.

A faint sweet smell tickled her nose, like crushed up rose petals. Helen looked at the brown, leather sofa, the hessian rug, the desk at the far end, the DVDs stacked untidily beneath the flat-screen television. The old fireplace had been boarded up, covered with a modern chrome electric fire, although the original wood mantle still hung over the top. Helen wandered over. A mirror hung on the wall, wooden models of the 'three wise monkeys' adorned the shelf. Something stuck behind the far monkey caught her eye and she squinted, drawing her face closer to look. An unframed photograph sat there, a large white border around the edge, as if it had been printed out from somebody's computer before they had a chance to size it correctly.

The photo was of the heads of two women, both smiling, posing for the shot; one was definitely Naomi, the blazing hair a giveaway. Helen looked at the other girl. Although she wore sunglasses, she matched the description of Eva given by Naomi's work colleagues. She also bore a resemblance to the girl that appeared in the photograph at Naomi's house. She turned it over in her hands, hoping for some inscription on the back, but it was bare.

Helen looked up as Dark entered the room. "Not much in the bathroom. Toothbrush and paste are missing and I can't see any make-up lying around. I'll check the bedroom."

Helen nodded and moved into the kitchen. As she passed through the door she instinctively touched the side of the kettle. Stone cold. It hadn't been used in a while. She glanced around at the ring of dried coffee on the side, the used mug in the sink, a pile of clean plates on the side. Something niggled at her. She crossed back to the lounge.

The arrangement of furniture wasn't quite right: the rug was wonky, the sofa and the coffee table sat at a strange angle. It was as if they had been knocked about and then thrown together in a hurry.

She crossed back to the kitchen. She pulled open a couple of drawers and rummaged through a mass of receipts in one, another full of different kinds of bills in no particular order. The drawer next to the sink contained Eva's passport sitting on a pile of papers, some of them curled and torn at the corners. They looked as though they'd been pushed in haphazardly and caught on the gap at the back of the drawer.

She opened the passport, leafed through the blank pages and sighed. Since the opening up of Europe, British passports revealed little these days.

She worked through the other papers: a water bill, a scrunched up receipt for a local store dated Monday, an Indian takeaway menu. Her hands halted at an airport boarding pass from East Midlands Airport to Milan Bergamo dated Saturday third of March. One way. Where was the return? She lifted a leaflet on Reiki massage from a salon called Serenity. Below was a car deck location card for P&O Ferries from Calais to Dover on Friday ninth of March. Helen glanced from the ferry card to the flight pass. Why fly out and drive back? And where did they pick the car up from?

***

Jenny Wilson noticed the time and jumped up. Almost ten thirty. She opened the back door and gazed around her back garden. It wasn't like Boots to be late. Jenny had grown accustomed to her arriving at the door, usually around eight thirty in the morning, crying for her food. Never having fed the cat before, she marvelled at how it adapted to a new routine so quickly. In fact, Jenny quite enjoyed it. She would love a furry friend, something to keep her company on these long days at home since the children had left. A cat would be nice, but Stuart refused point-blank whenever she raised the subject. He always maintained that he was allergic, although she'd never heard him sneeze or wheeze once in Boots' presence.

She grabbed her coat, slipped her feet into her rubber gardening shoes and trotted out into the garden. "Boots!" she called at the top of her voice. All she heard was the sound of a pigeon cooing nearby. She stood and looked around the garden for a while, then heaved herself down the steps and through the break in the hedge that led into Jules Paton's garden. "Boots!" she called out again. For a brief moment she thought she heard a softened cry but, whatever it was, it was soon muted by the sound of the wind rustling through the magnolia beside her.

Jenny slid the key into the lock. The back door clicked open. She stepped forward, peered into the kitchen. The cat was nowhere to be seen. Feeling slightly uncomfortable, as if she were intruding, Jenny walked up Jules Paton's hallway. "Boots!" she called. "Where are you, honey?"

She stole a sideways glance into the lounge through the open door to her left. Nothing. Jenny made a few more steps. She reached the front door. All was quiet. She resisted the temptation to lean down and collect the pile of post and was just about to climb the stairs when she heard a definite meow. It was coming from the garden. She turned on her feet. When she got to the back door she called out again and waited, straining her ears.

Yes, there was the reply. It was Boots' high-pitched meow, she was sure of that. She followed it down to the far end of the garden and halted at the edge of the lawn in front of the garage.

"Boots?" The meow came again. It was coming from inside. She glanced down at the battered old door. There was a gap at the bottom, where the wooden panels had rotted away, barely big enough for a fist. Silly cat, she thought.

She looked up and down the door. Half way down there was a doorknob next to a keyhole. More in hope than expectation, she lifted her hand and turned the knob. To her surprise, the door opened.

Before she had time to focus in the darkness, a white cat with four black legs meowed loudly, skipped over and rubbed itself around her ankles. She looked down. "Aren't you a silly girl, getting stuck in here?" She bent down and stroked her head affectionately.

A strange smell filled her nostrils. A damp patch of fur on Boots' back caught her fingertips. She lifted it to her nose and sniffed. It smelt like… ammonia. She moved back to it, running the pads of her fingers over the warm clump. "What have you done here?" she asked, gently.

An arthritic pain shot through her knees. Jenny winced as she stood. Then she raised her eyes and saw the legs dangling in the air in front of her.

Chapter **Sixteen**

Smatterings of shiny sunlight bounced off the blue water as Eva cornered the loch on her way back to Kinlochard. After much searching, she managed to locate a payphone in The Forth Inn on Aberfoyle's main street. She'd phoned Naomi, then Jules, listening as both phones rang out before they switched to voicemail. Where were they?

Freddie Mercury's voice filled the car with 'Who wants to live forever… ' Eva leant forward and hiked up the volume. Queen was her mother's favourite band. She remembered watching a Queen concert with her mum as a kid, allowed to stay up late on one of the odd occasions her stepfather worked nights. She wondered if her mum was touring South Africa now listening to them on the iPod Eva bought her last Christmas. She thought Eva was back in Hampton at work right now. Not driving past Loch Ard, listening to the same music.

As she swung the car into Kinlochard and rose up the hill through the village, an idea pushed into her mind. Perhaps the Macdonald hotel up the road had Wi-Fi. Most hotels did these days. She could call by the bungalow, pick up her laptop, head back to the hotel and check Facebook. Rarely a day passed when Naomi didn't make some entry. Buoyed up by her new plan, Eva pressed on.

She sang along with the radio, the decibels in her voice releasing their own endorphins. Maybe she could persuade Naomi to come up and join her for a few days. Take a short break to recover.

She crossed the undulation in the road before she saw the police car, flaunting its presence outside her parents' bungalow.

The shock hit her like a bucket of ice water. She slowed, gazed across as she crawled past, ready to accelerate at any moment. The car was empty.

The sound of the radio was drowned out by the sound of her own blood rushing in her ears. She sped up, slamming her Ford KA around the bends.

Finally, she pulled over. She was in the heart of the mountains now, surrounded by a forest of fir trees. She rubbed her forehead. If the police car was empty, where was the officer? She imagined him knocking at the door, peering through windows, going around the back to take a look. The curtains were all undrawn, the bed unmade, her clothes strewn over the chair…

Eva struggled to swallow the sickly bile that rose in her throat.

At that moment the clouds merged, swallowing the last of the sunshine. What should she do? Go back to meet the police? But why were they there?

She opened the window and drank the fresh air. A strong smell of pine trees flushed her airways. Gradually the mist in her head started to clear. Right now she needed to get as far away from here as possible. Once again, she was on the run.

***

Helen stood on the pavement outside Eva's house and peeled the latex gloves from her hands before she answered the call.

Pemberton didn't introduce himself, "Ma'am, I've good news and bad news."

She looked up. The clouds had thickened in the sky, plugging any hope of sun in Hampton for the rest of the day. "I'll take the good news first."

"We've located the friend."

Helen felt a frisson of excitement. "Where is she?"

"At her parents' bungalow in Scotland. A small village called Kinlochard, an hour north of Glasgow. Local police are there now."

"Is she with them?"

"Not yet, looks like she's gone out. But they've looked through the windows and can see clothes and personal items, so they're just waiting for her to return."

"Brilliant! How did you find her?"

Pemberton described how a local Kinlochard girl named Millie Buchanan was a friend of Eva's on Facebook. Millie had seen the appeal that morning and alerted her grandmother who contacted Strathclyde police.

"Okay, what's the bad news?"

"The news delayed us slightly," Pemberton said. "We've only just arrived at Jules Paton's house for the search."

"What's up, Sean?"

"Jules Paton has committed suicide. His body was found by his neighbour this morning."

Helen started. "Where's the body?"

"In the garage, hanging from the rafters. And you'll never guess who's here."

***

Back in her office, Helen stared at the photos of Jules Paton's body hanging from the central rafter in his garage. He was tall, about six foot two she guessed, and thin. A white shirt covered his torso over pale denims coated in faeces. The colour had drained out of his face leaving a pale grey tinge. His eyes hung open, dry and desperate.

She clicked to another photo, taken from a different angle. In the corner of the still she could see a kitchen chair on its side beneath the body. Hanging was one of the most common forms of suicide. A feeling of sadness washed over her. Suicides always left her feeling hollow.

Having just come from Eva's house, Helen couldn't attend Jules Paton's house in person. Everything about the scene, complete with note of admission, smacked of suicide. But Eva was still missing. If she was involved, or worked with Jules on Naomi's murder, CSI may find forensic evidence at the scene, in the garage, nearby, indicating her presence. The last thing she needed was a defence barrister arguing that hairs and fibres belonging to Eva had been transferred by Helen or her team that morning.

At times like this, Helen was grateful for the expertise of Pemberton. They thought the same way, adopted the same hands-on approach to policing. As soon as she'd processed his call earlier, she'd set him into action; tasked him to go through the scene with a fine-toothed comb, note everything, however insignificant it may initially appear. He took photos of the garage, then recorded the scene on his mobile phone and emailed her the footage. The CSI photographs would eventually be available, but Helen wanted to see the scene through Pemberton's eyes. It was the next best thing to being there herself.

Helen looked past the body in the photo. Cardboard boxes were stacked in the corner, a wooden workbench down the side, cluttered with various tools and garden accessories; a lawn mower and edge cutters leant against the far wall alongside a metal stepladder. There was a hole at the bottom of the door where the wood had rotted. This is where it was suspected that the cat crawled in. The cat that drew the neighbour's attention to Jules' dead body.

The footage continued into the house. A single piece of paper rested on the kitchen table. The suicide note.

SO SORRY FOR WHAT I'VE DONE.
NAOMI DIDN'T DESERVE THAT.
IT WAS THE DRUGS TALKING.
I CAN'T LIVE WITH MYSELF.

She stared at it awhile then pressed play and moved on. The front room looked as if it had been preserved in a museum, completely untouched. A stash of post still sat by the front door. She scanned through until she got to Jules' bedroom. A black leather jacket rested across a pine rocking chair. The camera zoomed in on the label, *Toujours*, and on the area that should have housed the second button up from the bottom, which was missing. He'd photographed a Baikal handgun, encased in a clear evidence bag, recovered from beneath the bed.

Earlier, Pemberton explained that when he arrived at Jules Paton's house that morning, he'd been surprised to find CSI crawling over the property. He immediately phoned the control room inspector who told him they'd taken a call at ten thirty that morning from Jenny Wilson, reporting the discovery of Jules' body. When he asked them why his team wasn't informed, the inspector was sheepish. The controller had missed the markers on Jules Paton and Operation Aspen, and referred it to local CID.

Pemberton later discovered that Inspector Fitzpatrick's team had seen the log and offered to deal, as Paton was linked to their enquiry. The duty detective sergeant was only too happy to oblige. With a major affray in Hampton centre last night, local CID were tied up dealing with multiple offenders.

Anger clouded Helen's vision. It seemed Inspector

Fitzpatrick hadn't informed her team. She had the distinct feeling he was muscling in on her enquiry. She grabbed the phone and dialled.

Dean answered on the fifth ring, just before the voicemail kicked in. He sounded distracted.

"What's going on, Dean?"

"What? We're at Paton's house. He committed suicide this morning…"

"I know that! You didn't think to call me?"

The line crackled. "What?"

"Jules Paton is a potential suspect in my murder investigation. We had a warrant to search his property this morning."

Dean hesitated a moment. "Yeah, I saw Pemberton here. God, Helen, I thought you knew. I just… well saw this as an opportunity to get into his house, search for intelligence." He sounded rattled. "I'm so sorry."

She swept his apology under the carpet. "What do we know?"

He shared how Jenny Wilson had followed the cat's cries and discovered the body. Helen listened intently, but said nothing. When he finished he cleared his throat, "I had no idea he was in this state, Helen… "

She chewed the side of her mouth. Dean had shared that he knew Jules. That he was an unregistered informant. "How long had you two been in contact?"

"A few months, maybe longer." His tone softened as he continued, "He wasn't a bad lad. Not really. Just needed to grow up, and kick the cocaine."

She let the words soak in. "Anyone spoken to the neighbour?"

"We took a statement from her this morning. She's pretty shaken."

Helen recalled Jenny Wilson's moon-shaped face, Jeremy Kyle on the TV, her interest in the investigation. She remembered how she had felt after seeing her first suicide. For days, weeks, maybe months afterwards, she would see the face in her mind. She felt a pang of empathy.

"Are we sure it's suicide?"

"No doubt, he even left a note… "

Chapter **Seventeen**

Helen replaced the receiver and turned over the mornings developments in her mind.

The outward airport and inward ferry tickets found in Eva's flat sat uncomfortably. Why would Naomi and Eva fly out to Milan for a week in March? She recalled a travel programme she'd watched on Italy a couple of weeks back with her mother. They'd only covered Milan briefly. She tried to remember the draws: shopping, culture... The kaleidoscope of colourful clothing in Naomi's wardrobe flashed into her mind. But they'd scrutinized Naomi's bank accounts and the state of her overdraft indicated she certainly wasn't a candidate for shopping. And with average temperatures chasing fourteen degrees, they weren't sun seeking either. Culture maybe? But why fly out and drive back? Where did they stay and where did they get the return journey car from?

Records showed that the informant's call was made within two hundred metres of Eva's address, although this was too far away to actually witness the incident. Why had she disappeared on the night of Naomi's murder?

She switched to Jules Paton. The evidence found at the scene in Granary Avenue all pointed towards Jules murdering his ex-girlfriend. Gooding estimated Jules had been dead for at least twelve hours. Eva had been sighted in Kinlochard yesterday afternoon before vanishing again. But where was she now?

Too many questions, too many holes. She clicked another button, brought up the image of the suicide note again and stared at it.

A knock at her door broke her concentration. Dark's impish face appeared. "Fancy a coffee, ma'am?"

Helen nodded. "Thanks. Any news on Eva Carradine?"

Dark shook her head. "Not yet. They've got uniform waiting at the property in Scotland."

"What about forensics?"

"We've had preliminaries, but they don't really tell us anything."

As Helen rubbed the side of her face she spotted Jenkins approaching through the incident room. From the buoyancy in his step, she guessed he was already aware of the morning's developments. Dark followed her eyes. "Think I'd better make that two," she said and hastily retreated.

"Helen!" he cried as he entered her office. "I hear you've had a bit of a result."

"There have been some developments."

Jenkins snatched back his sleeve, glanced at his watch. "I've a meeting with the assistant chief constable in half an hour. Be good to pass on some positive news."

Helen sighed inwardly at his drive for brownie points and gave him an overview of the morning's events. He remained silent and calm throughout, although she got the distinct impression he already had a heads up on the details and evidence regarding Jules Paton. She finished up, "Whilst we are tying things up, I would like to continue the search for Eva Carradine. I can't help feeling… "

Jenkins sat back in his chair and exhaled loudly. "That won't be necessary, Helen."

"What do you mean?"

"It seems pretty straightforward that Jules Paton killed Miss Spence and then himself."

"We still don't know that for sure."

His face tightened. "We have the jacket matching the button found in the victim's hair, a suicide note of admission and a gun that fits the criteria. It's only a matter of time before ballistics confirm it was the gun used in the attack."

"What about the unidentified female informant?" Helen said, feeling every inch of the frown stretch across her forehead.

Jenkins scratched the side of his nose. "There are always anomalies in a case like this. Killers don't generally offer explanations. You should know that, Helen."

"The call was made within two hundred metres of Eva's address," she said vehemently.

"Anybody could have seen or heard something peculiar, driven home, then pricked their conscience and called an ambulance. More likely it was an acquaintance from the drugs scene. Someone Jules paid to make the call. We may never know. No-one identified her voice and since the actual call can't be traced to Miss Carradine, there's no reason to pursue her."

"I still think we need to find her, to rule that out."

"Helen." Jenkins' eyes hardened. "People take time out, for whatever reason. I'm not wasting Hampton's budget or the resources of any other force looking for a grown adult who decided to take a break in Scotland. I believe she even called her work. She'll turn up when she's ready. In the meantime, I want this one wrapped up."

"But the timing… "

Jenkins shook his head. He stood abruptly, just as Dark entered the room with two coffees. "Inspector Fitzpatrick has offered his team to build the file on this one, which is very decent of him given our tight resources. Get your team to liaise with his, and pass over anything that is relevant. The order has come from above. I want you back on those cold case review shootings. We're under a lot of pressure there." With that, he swung out of the office, past Dark who was still clasping two cups of coffee, and was gone, leaving Helen to seethe.

***

Eva pressed her foot on the brake as the lights turned red. The drive to Glasgow had taken an hour, but felt like it passed in an instant. Her head was spinning. Why were the police at Lochside? Were they looking for her? The only person who could help her now, was Naomi.

The lights changed and she pulled off again. She'd almost reached the city centre, in the midst of Friday lunchtime traffic. The roads were heavily congested. She followed the car in front of her at a snails' pace past boutiques, a lighting shop, a Chinese takeaway, a sandwich bar. She braked again as a driver tried to squeeze into the tiniest of parking spaces in front. Eva glanced across at the pavement as she waited: a couple walked hand in hand, hoods pulled over their heads to protect them from the gripping wind, a young woman battled with a pushchair and a toddler who was screaming at the top of his voice; a man in a black suit strode out of a newsagent with a file clutched to his chest. Then she saw it, on the corner of the road, a blue iridescent sign in the window - an internet cafe. She could try to contact Naomi from there, via Facebook.

Her eyes darted about in desperation. A grey concrete multi-storey car park sat barely a hundred yards up. The driver in front of her gave up trying to shoehorn his vehicle into the tiny space and they crawled forward again. She turned at the earliest opportunity into the car park, took a ticket, parked on the second floor, and made her way back up the road.

Her breaths ran short and sharp as she reached the cafe. A bell tinkled above her head as she entered. The desk was empty and she glanced around, her eyes resting on an aquarium filled with tropical fish, positioned near the door. They moved around the tank serenely, as if they didn't have a care in the world. She paused to watch them. They looked so relaxed.

Out of the corner of her eye she saw a movement. A teenage girl had moved away from a computer. She turned and watched her scoop up her jacket from the back of the chair and exit the shop. Eva flipped back to the fish in the aquarium. It suddenly occurred to her that they were a paradox: their whole world existed on a strict balance, a slight change in water temperature, conditions or plant life would initiate stress and they could die. A slight change. Their world could change in an instant. Just like hers…

She shuddered.

"Can I help you?" The voice behind her came from nowhere.

She jumped and turned round to see a teenage boy facing her. A student, she guessed by the grungy clothing, with a scrawny body, screwed up features, a face littered with spots and hair that didn't look as if it had been brushed in a month. She quickly recovered herself. "I'd like a computer for half an hour."

"£8 an hour, or £5 a half."

She rummaged in her bag, pulled out a five pound note and handed it over.

"Thanks, any coffee?"

She shook her head.

"Okay, take that one." He pointed towards the computer at the end, the one just vacated.

"Thanks."

It took less than ten seconds to log into Facebook. Her

fingers worked the keys urgently. The anticipation made her tap her feet as the computer changed screens.

The message that faced her at the top of the screen hit her like a bolt of lightning:

POLICE ARE APPEALING FOR WITNESSES TO THE MURDER OF NAOMI SPENCE ON TUESDAY 19TH MARCH. IN PARTICULAR THEY WOULD LIKE TO SPEAK TO HER CLOSE FRIENDS, JULES PATON AND EVA CARRADINE. ANYONE KNOWING THEIR WHEREABOUTS SHOULD CONTACT HAMPTON POLICE IMMEDIATELY…

Eva didn't get any further. Her breath halted. A pain seared in her chest. Murder?

She thought back to the scene on Tuesday evening. She had seen a tussle, Naomi had been attacked. But not for one moment had she allowed her brain to entertain the thought that Naomi might have been killed.

Eva stood. The room swayed around her. She was suffocating, as if a layer of cling film covered her head, blocking her airways. She heard a voice in the background, but failed to focus. The room was swimming.

She could hear strange noises, notes in the background. Her feet left the ground and she was floating, as if in a dream when the unimaginable becomes reality. She could see Naomi in the distance, her beautiful red hair tumbling over her shoulders. She was laughing, her head thrown back. Then, as she raised it, her face was frozen in alarm as the hand covered her mouth.

A tugging sensation. Her feet scraped the floor.

Suddenly, a blast of cold air hit Eva directly in the face. She blinked hard, twice. Took very deep breaths. Slowly, in and out. Her vision started to clear.

Eva could see people in the window of a cafe opposite, a man on a mobile phone on the pavement nearby. A couple walked past hand in hand. A car horn beeped in the distance.

"Are you alright, Miss?"

She followed the voice, looked up into the eyes of the grungy lad who had taken her money.

"Miss?"

Her thoughts spiralled. She blinked, then turned and ran.

Chapter **Eighteen**

Nate grabbed two bottles of Cobra beer from the fridge, popped the tops and offered one to his uncle who sat in an armchair, arms placed on each rest, head relaxed back. His bald head glistened in the light of the bare bulb overhead. Dark eyes stared at the ceiling.

When his uncle didn't acknowledge his presence, Nate placed the beer on a small table, decorated with coffee mug and beer bottle rings. Loose ash from the overflowing ashtray in the centre skipped into the air as the bottle hit the hard surface.

Nate heard raised voices in the street outside: a high-pitched woman screeched words he couldn't decipher, a low husky tone shouted over her. A door slammed shut. All was quiet.

"You did good, Nate," his uncle eventually said. He gave a slight nod, but his eyes were still fixed on the ceiling.

Although Nate swelled inwardly, he had learnt not to show his feelings. It might look arrogant. And his uncle hated arrogance. Instead he stared at the only human being who had ever shown him any kindness, awestruck.

Nate barely remembered his mother. He recalled occasional moments with a woman he later identified from photographs as his mother: a tiny, mouse-like face, crowned with short dirty blond hair, pallid skin, vacant eyes. As a young boy he remembered being in a room with her and stubbing his toe on a door. He'd cried out, rushed to hug her. As they collided she'd frozen. Her hard eyes and closed frame formed an image so vivid it lodged in his memory. And from that moment on, he avoided contact. But whenever she was present, the air felt tight, the tension palpable.

Uncle Chilli lowered his chin to make eye contact. He let the stare linger slightly before he spoke, "Make yourself scarce now, son. I'm expecting company."

Nate showed no reaction, just stood, exited the lounge and climbed the staircase.

He reached his bedroom and sat on the edge of the bed. A grubby, unkempt duvet spilt out of its case next to him. Nate glanced at his watch. Six thirty. He folded his arms behind his head and lay back. Time to open the club soon. He knew his uncle had done a stretch, but he never discussed his crime or his prison life with Nate. Since his release, he'd built a business running Black Cats nightclub and bar, extending his empire to include a couple of nail bars more recently, yet Nate knew it was his secret operations, the drugs supply and prostitution, that were the real earners. Officially, Nate was on the payroll as a bouncer and driver, although his favourite jobs were the undercover 'special assignments' and, in recent years, Chilli had entrusted many more of these to him.

He rolled his eyes as he recognised a pair of knickers with a black lace trim on the floor. Bloody hookers. On his sixteenth birthday his uncle had thrown a party in the club's private room. He was introduced to the girls and asked to pick. They all looked the same to him, all ass and tits.

One approached him, sat on his lap and thrust her tongue into his mouth. He remembered that moment like it was yesterday. He could taste a mixture of garlic, and cheese and onion crisps. He'd pushed her off roughly, too roughly and she fell to the ground. His uncle had taken him to one side, 'We don't hurt the girls, son,' he'd said. 'They can't earn if they're sick.' Enough said.

Since that evening there were always girls available when Nate needed them. He was mechanical, dismissing them when his needs were satisfied. He didn't raise his hand to any of them again, and he didn't kiss them on the lips either. You never knew where those dirty lips had been.

A noise downstairs caught his attention. It sounded like a chair had been knocked over, a glass crashed to the floor. Raised voices followed. He heard his uncle's cutting words above them, "It's not good enough!" Nate sat perfectly still. His hand raked across the acne pits on his face. Chilli shouted a lot these days.

Nate grabbed his Xbox remote control and selected 'Call of Duty'. While the game loaded he thought about his uncle's associates. One day, he would be involved in these meetings. One day, he would be at the centre of the operation, take over from his uncle. He fisted his hands, knocked his knuckles together. *Clink, clink, clink.* Then he really would be THE MAN.

***

Helen's shoes beat the linoleum flooring on her way to Dean's office, late that afternoon. She still smarted from her conversation with Jenkins, convinced that the disappearance of Eva Carradine was connected to the investigation. If she could get Dean on side, perhaps they could join forces to persuade the powers that be to keep tabs on Eva?

Dean's team were located on the floor below Helen in one of the spare suites kept for review teams, incident rooms and special projects. Faces turned as she entered the suite. She recognised a few members of his team she'd seen around the station and tipped her head at them. The layout of the room was the same as the Homicide and Major Incident suite and she made for Dean's office in the corner. The blinds were drawn.

Just as she raised her fist to knock on his door, she heard a voice behind her, "Can I help you?"

She turned on her heels to face a young detective in a tailored, black suit. Her dark hair was cropped severely short. "I'm here to see Inspector Fitzpatrick."

"He's a bit busy at the moment."

Helen widened her eyes. "I'm sure he'll spare me five minutes."

The detective stared back at her protectively. Just then a voice piped up from the back of the room, "It's alright Maggie, you can let the DCI through." Helen followed the voice to DS Edwards who had just walked through the door.

The young DC flushed immediately. "Sorry, I didn't realise… "

Helen managed a kind smile. Rank in senior detectives wasn't always obvious when they were in plain clothes. "It's fine, really." The young DC moved away hastily to hide her embarrassment. Helen nodded to Edwards, knocked once and entered, without waiting for invitation.

Like Helen's, Dean's desk faced the door. He sat behind it. He was bent forward, head buried in arms that were folded in front of him, his phone scattered haphazardly to his side. He looked up, startled at her intrusion.

She paused fleetingly, then pulled the door closed behind her and approached his desk. "Are you okay?"

He nodded and smiled weakly, but his face was flat.

She inclined her head to the door. "Had a job to get through security!"

When he didn't respond, Helen suddenly became aware of something. She'd never seen cracks appear in his calm façade before. He'd always been confident and in control. She couldn't help but wonder – in the short time they were together – did he ever really let her in? She thought she knew him so well. There was a time when she would have claimed to know him better than anyone.

"What's up?" she asked.

He lifted his head and gestured for her to sit on the chair opposite. His mouth opened, then closed again, as if he didn't trust his own voice.

The anxiety in Dean's face flicked a light switch in her mind. She had seen this deadpan expression in colleagues before. The average police officer views multiple dead bodies throughout their career. And every one leaves a mark. But there was something about suicide, something desperate that clung like a barnacle to a rock. Especially if you knew the victim.

His phone buzzed next to him. Helen glanced at it, then at Dean. "Are you going to get that?"

He picked up the phone, pressed a digit and cast it aside.

Dean rubbed his right hand up and down his face. "I keep seeing his eyes." He swallowed loudly. "Desperate, dead eyes… " Helen's instincts told her to comfort him, wrap her arms around him, pull him close. But she didn't want to do anything that may convey the wrong impression. "I should have known," he continued. "I could have done something."

She was desperate to ask about Eva, seek his support in her continued search. Only now just wasn't the right time.

"Right, that's it," she said and stood. "We're getting you out of here."

He shook his head. "No… "

"We'll go for a coffee," she interrupted.

He ran his hands through his hair. "There's no need."

Helen wasn't listening. She'd moved around the desk and was wrestling his jacket onto his shoulders. "I insist."

Chapter **Nineteen**

As soon as they walked through the door of The Angel Tavern, Helen felt eyes burning into her. It was one of those old-fashioned pubs with a jazzy carpet that stank of stale beer and a bunch of regulars at the bar who gaped at every stranger that entered. The gazes lingered as she followed Dean to the bar and she knew why. Even in plain clothes, cops stood out in a place like this. She might as well have worn a name badge.

After parking nearby, Helen had tried to steer Dean into Hayes cafe, but the look on his face at the mere suggestion silenced her. There was only one kind of solace he sought this evening. She watched as he ordered a pint of Guinness for himself, a vodka and coke for her.

The gentle music in the background was drowned out by the hoard of teenagers that surrounded the pool table at the end of the bar. A couple of young heads looked up momentarily, their attention quickly taken by the next shot.

Helen took her drink and followed Dean to a table tucked away in the far corner, away from the intrusive glares. The music seemed louder in the private space and she could make out Sting's dulcet tones, although couldn't place the song.

Dean took a huge gulp of his pint and placed it on one of the many beer mats scattered on their table.

"Are you okay?" Helen asked as she sat next to him on the

lumpy cushion that covered the wooden bench.

He didn't speak for a moment. When he turned towards her, a shadow of despair crept across his face. "He was so young."

Helen swallowed. The job exposed you to the most horrific situations on occasions, those that most folk wouldn't experience in a lifetime. For the most part, you become numb, training sets in and you adopt an empathetic but detached approach. But every now and then, some events catch you, drive a needle below the surface and leave a residue behind that's hard to erase.

She had seen the same anguish in her father's eyes on many occasions. That kind of deep despair that hit home when all hope was dashed. She looked away, gave him time to regain his composure.

The walls were plastered in painted woodchip, yellowed from years of smokers before the ban. It was curled in the corners, peeling back from the wall. The photo of Naomi seated at the piano at the Spences' house entered her head. She was young too, young, talented and beautiful…

The song changed to 'Every Breath You Take'. She listened awhile. When she looked back at Dean, his eyes were fixed on his glass.

"There was nothing you could do," she said gently.

He lifted his head to face her. "How do you know?"

The question took her aback and she thought for a moment before she answered, "He was… " She hesitated, not wanting to say the word 'informant'. Because Jules wasn't an informant. Not officially. "… helping you with enquiries," she said. "There was no way of your knowing what a mess he was in."

"Mess?" Dean hissed the word out.

"People don't commit suicide unless they're desperate," Helen said, battling to keep the conversation calm. "If he killed his girlfriend… ”

“If?”

“Well, we still have to establish… ”

“*We* don’t have to establish anything. We have his jacket, the note. He killed her, then himself.”

The anger in his voice jarred her. “You couldn’t have known.”

He rose. “Another drink?”

She stared at her glass, still two thirds full and shook her head. This was going to be more of a challenge than she thought.

As he disappeared around the corner to the bar, Helen thought about Jules Paton. Jules had admitted to murdering Naomi before killing himself. It was clean. But something didn’t feel right.

Dean returned with another Guinness, accompanied by a chaser this time. The thick scent of whisky filled the air as he planted himself next to her. He threw his head back and downed the chaser.

“You’re not responsible,” she said, in almost a whisper.

“Responsible for what? The murder of Naomi or the suicide of Jules?”

His words startled her. She said nothing, ran her eyes up and down his face.

“You have no idea,” he snarled.

“About what?” Helen was starting to feel uncomfortable. “I have no idea about what, Dean?”

His face folded like an admonished child. “Don’t listen to me. I’m just feeling sorry for myself. Just wish I’d seen the signs, could have done something.”

Helen pushed her lips together. The first rule of being a handler of informants was not to get personally involved, but there was a very fine line between befriending them and keeping them at arm’s length. Sometimes the only way to get the information needed was to draw them in. And this had implications. This was one of the main reasons why registered informants were dealt with by specialist officers. To avoid situations like this.

"How long have you known him?" she asked gently.

He didn't answer. Instead, he reached up, undid the top button of his shirt and pulled his navy tie loose.

They sat in silence, listened to the music and sipped their drinks. 'Fields of Gold' played out, followed by 'Roxanne'. It seemed the landlord was a keen Sting fan. Helen was aware that Dean got up, approached the bar at intervals and returned with more drinks. He seemed content to ignore the bleeps coming from his mobile.

Eventually the room started to feel warm. Helen became aware of her movements. She suppressed a yawn. Dean's actions slowed, his speech started to slur. If she didn't get him out of here soon, she'd have to call for backup. She could only begin to imagine the amusement at the station, let alone the landlord at two drunken police officers.

Helen stood gingerly. The room swayed slightly. "I'm just heading to… " She didn't need to finish the sentence. Dean nodded, eyes fixed upon his glass.

When she later emerged from the ladies room, having splashed cold water over her face, Helen heard 'Every Breath You Take' playing again. The same CD. How many times had it played over while they'd been sitting there?

Dean was just finishing the last drop of Guinness when she reached him. The glass clattered as he missed the drip matt on the table. She blinked, the noise jolting her insides. She could no longer watch him wallow here.

"We're going," Helen announced.

Dean was picking at a chip on the side of the table. "Going where?"

"I'm taking you home," she said firmly and before he had

time to argue she grabbed his arm and wrenched him into a standing position. He looked at her, eyes glazed.

"Come on," she said and pushed him around the table towards the exit, ignoring the chuckles at the bar.

A fresh night breeze slapped her in the face as she stepped outside. Her senses awakened. She hadn't eaten since lunchtime and the alcohol had taken a firm grip. She concentrated her mind on the job in hand: to get Dean home safely, without any more altercations to draw attention to them. Neither of them was fit to drive. Her car would have to stay at the station overnight. She'd hail a taxi home.

"Where is your hotel?" she asked.

He pointed right, and she grabbed his arm and edged in that direction, focusing on putting one foot in front of the other.

They walked about a quarter of a mile up the road. A man passed them on a bicycle, followed by a red Toyota, but apart from that they had the road to themselves. Just before they reached the lights, Dean veered off into a side road and stopped three doors down at a white pebble dashed house in desperate need of a good paint job. A small plaque above the door read 'Hotel Merion' in peeling black paint.

In spite of the veil of alcohol, the surroundings made Helen start. "Don't you get expenses?"

"Yeah… Well, I need to keep a bit back to cover bills back home. The ex is bleeding me dry." He didn't look up, his attention drawn to his trouser pocket where he was struggling to retrieve his keys.

Helen didn't reply, just followed him inside to a tiny hallway, a lone table with a bell indicating that it also doubled up as a reception area.

"You're welcome to come up if you wish?" he said, flat intonation implying it would be preferable to standing down here in the empty hallway.

Helen winced. She hesitated for the shortest of minutes.

She'd just make sure he reached his room safely. It didn't mean anything.

His room was on the first floor. The number four hung loosely off the dirty white door. As he fiddled with his keys, they slipped through his fingers and dropped to the floor. They both bent down together. Helen rose quickly. Dean smiled awkwardly. He unlocked the door.

Even later, when she looked back, Helen couldn't explain how or why it happened. One moment she was stood beside the door, the next she was encased in Dean's arms, kissing him with voracious hunger, pressing herself against him with an urgency that suggested the world was about to end. They stumbled into the room. The door slammed behind them.

This was the total opposite of what Helen intended. All evening she had fought to keep her emotions in check. But the urge was too strong to fight anymore. Her whole body tingled with innate animal pleasure as she gave into it, into him, unconditionally.

***

Eva lay on the bed, her body curled into a ball, arms wrapped around her knees. The more she tried to make sense of her situation, the more the demons crowded, blurring her weakened mind.

She fixed her eyes on the black hole of night through the uncovered window. It looked cavernous and dark, emulating her mood. A sparkle in the sky caught her attention. She cast her mind back to when her grandmother died. She was barely eleven-years-old at the time and had been confused by the grief, the tears; uncomfortable with the sadness that descended on the household.

Weeks later, walking back from the bus stop with her mother on a clear, dark night, she felt afraid. She remembered she'd clasped her mother's hand, expressed her fear of the dark, an embarrassing admission at eleven. Her mother had stopped, pointed up at the brightest star in the sky and said, 'Never be afraid of the dark. That's your grandmother, looking down on us, keeping us safe.' Ever since, when Eva glimpsed a bright star, she felt safe, that she wasn't alone.

Eva raised her head hopefully. The sparkle disappeared for a moment, then flashed again. And again. Her heart sank as she watched the intermittent flash of the aeroplane moving across the sky. Even the stars wouldn't offer consolation tonight.

Her iPod sat on the table beside her bed, the only part of her former life that she had with her, apart from a dead mobile phone.

After the internet cafe, Eva had driven around Glasgow, negotiating the throng of shoppers on Sauchiehall Street before heading past the Cathedral and out of the city centre. With no particular direction she drove out into the suburbs - through backstreets, up main roads, across housing estates. Hours passed. She remembered stopping at a park, sitting on a bench, watching blackbirds huddle together on a telegraph pole above, two of them vying for the same perch, before she took to the road again. Eventually, she headed back into the city and stumbled across The Hollies, a two star guest house secluded down a side street, with a car park at the rear.

The proprietor, a middle aged wiry man named John with a wisp of grey hair scraped across his bald head, had regarded her warily when he answered the door - a woman on her own arriving unannounced with no booking or luggage. If she had been capable of rational thought, Eva would have considered it an odd proposition herself. She wasn't sure if it was the empty car park or the dark rings beneath her eyes that persuaded him to relent.

Eva had barely noticed the peach hallway and the hall table displaying informative leaflets on Glasgow highlights.

Her hand trembled as she completed the form with a fake name, dug her hand in her pocket and paid in cash.

Tears brimmed in Eva's eyes. Suddenly, she wished for something she had never wanted before. She felt a yearning to be fourteen again, back in her parents' kitchen, full of hormonally charged attitude, her mother fixing her fruit juice and cereal even though she was perfectly capable of doing it herself.

She brushed a hand across her face as she recalled the rustic, pine kitchen table where she sat to eat her breakfast; her younger brother, Callum, picking at his cornflakes whilst reading the back of the box, her stepfather already left for work. Life had seemed so hard in those days, everything so irritatingly trivial. All she had to worry about was how her hair looked, whether she'd picked the right jacket for school and whether she would achieve her GCSE grades. Now she longed for triviality, to turn back the clock, to live under her parents' support and protection. Only now did she feel like a child in an adults' world.

Chapter **Twenty**

Helen trudged down to the organised crime suite early the next morning. All night, Jules Paton's part in her case had scratched away at the lining of her brain. Was this because she hadn't participated in the search, because she felt a fellow officer had intruded on her investigation, or was there something else niggling at her? She decided the only way to get closure was to take a look at the exhibits. Perhaps if she examined them herself her mind would rest.

Helen slowed as she approached. The last person she wanted to see was Inspector Dean Fitzpatrick. She had awoken in the early hours, slipped out of bed, dressed and scurried out of the room. It wasn't that she regretted sleeping with him; Jo had been right in her observations, it had been a wonderful release. But it didn't restore the purity their relationship once held. She still wasn't sure whether or not to believe his story regarding the text message, whether she could really trust him again, or whether she really wanted to.

Her ears pricked at the sound of DS Edwards' voice. He was talking about an Audi A3 he was due to collect at the end of the week, congratulating himself for buying second hand and saving a few grand. Helen hesitated. A phone rang in the distance - a welcome interruption. She deliberately turned her eyes away as she scooted past the open door. Fitzpatrick's team were bound to discover her visit sooner or later but, for now, she wanted to take a look at the evidence in her own time, without them breathing down her neck.

She made for a door that sat ajar, about ten metres down the corridor on the opposite side, and slipped inside. A startled face looked up at her from beneath a curly mop of dyed, blond hair. The eyes held prettiness, but the face had long since bloated with age. A sleep crease stood out underneath her left cheekbone.

"DC Taylor?"

The woman stood up from behind the desk and eyed her warily. "Yes."

The small space was barely four metres square and furnished with a desk facing the door, a single chair behind. The air smelt musty. Helen wondered how she managed to squeeze her ample frame into the tight space.

"DCI Lavery. Good to meet you."

Taylor seemed to relax as she shook her proffered hand. "Is there something I can do for you?" she asked.

"Yes, I'd like to see the evidence collected from yesterday's search of Mr Paton's property."

"Of course." Taylor cast her eye across the desk and reached for a buff folder. She fished through the enclosed documents and pulled out a few sheets of paper, stapled together neatly in the corner, and handed them to Helen. "This is the full inventory."

"Thank you." Helen swept her eyes down the page: photographs, gun, address books, laptop charger, answer-phone... She turned the page, looked at the next and the next, taking her time. The list seemed endless, all items packaged, numbered and catalogued. Her eyes hovered over the suicide note recorded on the third page, which had been recovered from the kitchen table.

"Right, I'd like to take a look now." Helen flashed a fleeting smile, before she turned towards the door in the corner of the room that led into the exhibits store.

Taylor shifted uncomfortably. "Oh... I'll just need to check with the inspector."

"That won't be necessary," she said. "In any case, I don't think he's in yet."

Taylor crossed to the door, glanced down the corridor, then back at Helen. "I am under strict orders not to disturb the detained property unless he's consulted first."

Helen was accustomed to exhibits officer's being wary of their catch. It wasn't uncommon for pieces to be removed and put back in the wrong place or lost altogether, jeopardising a whole investigation. She also felt sorry for the detective, compromising an order. But she needed to see that evidence.

"Oh, is that so? Well, I understand the need to be careful, but I'm not asking you to give the whole station access. Just me. I assure you I won't remove anything." She formed her mouth into a cool smile.

They stood in silence for a few moments. Helen was just about to pull rank, when Taylor finally reached down for her keys and worked her fingers through them until she found the right one. "You'd better come through," she said and moved to the door beside the desk.

The door clicked open into a large storeroom. Shelves upon shelves were stacked with bagged items, carefully arranged in numerical order. These pieces formed the basis of the case. They would be included in the file that Detective Inspector Fitzpatrick's team would now build for the coroner, who was responsible for examining the evidence and deciding whether Paton was responsible for the murder of Naomi Spence and his own suicide.

The case would not be closed before the coroner's decision had been made and recorded, although after her conversation with Jenkins yesterday afternoon, Helen was pretty convinced that he considered this a formality.

She glanced down at the inventory list clutched in her hand, then back up at the numbers of bagged items and moved down the racks slowly. Helen tried to ignore DC Taylor's footfalls behind her. Her diligence was impressive, although right now Helen wished she was completely alone.

Everything was in order; Taylor had done her job well. She passed the black leather jacket, stopped and pulled it off the shelf. Sure enough the label read *Toujours*. She looked down and could see that the button last up from the bottom was missing, consistent with the one found on the victim.

Helen replaced the jacket, and moved further along the aisle. Just as she reached the last rack but one, she saw it - the suicide note. Helen pulled it down to take a closer look. There were fragments of dust in the bag where forensics had checked it over for prints. She read it through again: *So sorry for what I've done. Naomi didn't deserve that. It was the drugs talking. I can't live with myself.* There was no signature. She stood and stared at it for a moment.

Helen thought back to the other suicides she had attended during the course of her career. Two of them had left notes. In both cases the notes rambled, were incoherent in places, as if the victims sought to mention everyone close to them, deal with all their misdemeanours, before finally ending their life. Paton's was four lines of type: short, perfunctory, almost emotionless…

"Ma'am, are you done?"

Helen turned to face DC Taylor, suddenly aware that they must have stood there for a good few minutes. "Yes, thank you." She replaced the bag.

"Good. Are you all finished?"

The detective had already started for the door. Helen watched her a moment as a thought jabbed her. "Just one minute." She retraced her steps down the aisle back to the jacket, picked it up and read the size. Forty-eight inch chest. She looked at it again, more closely to make sure she hadn't been mistaken. No, it definitely read forty-eight inches. She cast her mind back to Jules Paton's svelte hanging body, and Dean's description of him, 'We call him Willo the Wisp'.

A knock at the door shook the thoughts from her brain. She swung round just as DC Taylor pulled it open to display a very familiar face.

"And what's going on here?"

***

Leaving her car at the guest house, Eva trudged into the city. It was a damp, grey Glasgow morning. The low clouds obscured her surroundings, mirroring the blurred images in her mind. Breakfast offerings had left a lot to be desired at The Hollies. After coffee that tasted like wood smoke, she declined the offer of a cooked breakfast. What she really needed was a proper caffeine fix.

As Eva turned onto the main road, cars whizzed past, a couple walked out of a music shop pulling their jackets around their shoulders deep in excited conversation; a woman passed carrying a bouquet of flowers, a cyclist in fluorescents wove in and out of the traffic. A thick stench of damp fumes mixed with last nights' fish and chips sat in the air.

Further up the road, the sound of a high-pitched yelp caught her attention. She turned to see a Jack Russell, tied up outside the newsagent. That's when she saw the newspapers fastened to the stand, beneath the awning. … She approached the stand and bent to look at the headlines. *Prime Minister in crisis, Fuel Prices Reach All Time High, Duchess Set to Return to Canada.*

Eva stepped back and relaxed her shoulders. Paranoia was eating away at her, gnawing off tiny chunks at a time. What did she expect? A nationwide search, her face covering the front of every newspaper with accompanying headline:

Do you know this woman?

She moved on until she reached a cafe and took a table in the far corner, out of sight from the road. The waitress approached to take her order. They made eye contact. Did she linger a little longer than normal? Eva fidgeted uncomfortably.

As she drank the fresh coffee, Eva felt a familiar rush of adrenalin. She ordered another along with a poached egg. The coffee sharpened her senses. She stabbed at the egg and watched the yoke ooze out onto the plate. From her corner she could see a man in a suit on a high stool at the bar, reading a newspaper; an elderly man carefully tearing open a sugar sachet to add to his tea, a woman sitting alone, working her iPad. It felt warm and inviting, like hot chocolate on a winters eve.

Eva considered her parents' bungalow. She couldn't go back there. She raised her hand and ran her fingers through her hair, twisting it around her thumb and forefinger as she had done as a child, deep in thought. Absently she pulled a clump around and looked at it. Her hair had always been her hallmark - naturally blond, long and silky. People commented on it from her early teens and she'd rarely cut it. It was also how people recognised her. People who saw the Facebook appeal, people who searched for her, people who wanted to hurt her. Her life had changed irrevocably in the past three days. Perhaps now it was time for her to change with it.

Chapter Twenty-One

Helen took another sip of coffee. After their surprise meeting in the detained property store, Dean had guided her back to his office in silence. She felt a bit like a teenager caught playing truant, although she wasn't sure why.

"So, how are you this morning?" he said.

"Fine." She managed a fleeting glance, a flat smile, before turning her attention back to the styrofoam cup in her hand. The gentle aroma of his sporty shower gel filled the room.

"I didn't hear you leave last night."

She looked up in time to catch the softness in his eyes. Her reserve instantly weakened. "I had to get back," she said uncomfortably, averting her eyes.

The marked contrast in his mood was not lost on her. His old sparkle had returned, bolstered by the evening's events no doubt. "I understand. I just wanted to say… "

She missed the rest of his speech, consumed in her own guilt. Was that guilt over sleeping with him, betraying her family that he had upset last year? Or guilt over mixing her private and professional life? But that wasn't a mortal sin. She could be forgiven a moment of pleasure. It was later, after they'd collapsed into a sex-induced sleep, that he had awoken her - gently at first, kissing each of her eyelids, her forehead. Brushing his nose softly against her cheek, moving his lips down, running his tongue over her neck before inserting it firmly into her ear. Spasms of delight ran through her body and she longed for him, pulling him towards her again. But he had resisted, turned her over, brushed her hair away from the back of her neck, caressed it with swift movements of his tongue until she was practically crying out for him. Then, eventually he moved her round and entered her, cradling her body in his strong arms, before leaning down to whisper into her ear, "I've missed you so much." That's where she committed the mortal sin: the tender, slow love making that she couldn't put down to primal need or alcohol. Love making that she could have stopped at any moment if she hadn't enjoyed herself so much. Love making where her feelings for Dean became entangled like a spider's web.

Even now, her head screeched warning signs while her heart told her to rip his clothes off and take him over the desk. In this mood, he was addictive.

"Helen, are you okay?"

She looked up to see his face creased in concern and shook herself tall. "Yes."

He grinned. "Thought I'd lost you there for a minute."

Helen cleared her mind. They had to work together, for now.

"So, we'll take things slowly?"

She raised a flat hand. "Let's just get the investigation out of the way first. Then, we'll see."

"If that's what you want." His face transformed into a cheeky, boyish grin. "Shouldn't take too long to wrap this one up."

Thoughts of the case pushed Helen back into her comfort zone. "I'm not so sure."

"Oh? Is that why I found you in *my* property store this morning?" he said with a wink.

"Something doesn't feel right."

"Helen, we have evidence that places Jules Paton at the

scene, an admission of guilt and a murder weapon. What else do we need?"

"Doesn't the suicide note seem a bit strange to you?"

"Strange? He was mentally unstable. We can't dissect the words of a deranged man."

"And the jacket… "

"What about the jacket?"

"It's about four sizes too big. You said yourself, you nicknamed him 'Willo the Wisp'."

Dean snorted. "He wouldn't be the first person to buy an oversized jacket."

She could feel his eyes glued to her as she stared past him out of the window. A robin landed on the sill, hopped up and down, before fluttering its wings back in flight. "It doesn't make sense."

He sighed heavily. "Why?"

"We still haven't spoken to Eva Carradine."

"Eva who?"

"Naomi's best friend. Don't you think it's odd that she disappeared on the night of the murder?"

He shrugged a single shoulder. "I understand she's taken a holiday in Scotland."

"She was seen at her parents' holiday home, north of Glasgow, yesterday, but hasn't been back. We can't locate her."

He let out another huge sigh, fidgeted in his seat. "We have no reason to suggest she's involved in any way. It's not a crime to take a holiday."

Helen chewed her lip. Hopes of getting Dean on side were slipping through her fingers. "How do you explain the female informant?"

"Perhaps Jules paid someone to make the call, to take the heat off himself? We may never know. But that doesn't… "

"The call to the control room was made from within two

hundred metres of Eva's home."

Dean lifted his coffee to his lips and rolled his eyes in dismissal.

Helen decided to change tack. "What size foot is Jules?"

"Look, I see where you are going with this. He was size eleven. We haven't traced the actual shoes that match the tread of those found in the victim's neighbour's garden yet, but it's only a matter of time."

"It still doesn't make sense. You said yourself you hadn't seen this coming. That Jules was so young, with his life in front of him. That it was such a waste."

"That was shock talking. You know what it's like, Helen. We've since discovered that he'd exceeded the limits on his credit cards, was behind with his rent and hadn't made any cash from cars, his legitimate source of income, for months. He was in too deep with drugs."

His words shook her. Yet more information that she wasn't party to.

Dean sat forward. "Helen you're picking holes in a case where the evidence is compelling. You've done a good job. Let's not make work for ourselves."

He lingered on the word 'you've'. Was she really picking holes? And, if so, why? Was it because the evidence was flawed or she was sore about losing the case? Or, was an affair with the DI clouding her judgement? She cringed inwardly. The word 'affair' sounded serious. It was a while before either of them spoke.

"Maybe you are getting a bit too close?" Dean eventually said. His tone was gentle, soft.

She looked across at him.

"Don't worry, we'll make sure that everything ties up before we close the case properly."

Helen formed her lips into a thin smile.

"Hey. Enjoy the moment," he added, "It's a good result."

Helen blinked and stared into space, feeling defeated. 'A good result… '

***

Back out on the street, Eva turned in the direction of the guest house, glancing at the shop fronts she past, hunting vigorously. A hundred metres down the road she stopped and looked around. A convenience store, a Chinese takeaway and children's clothing store faced her; the Victorian stone fronted buildings with sash windows above them long since converted into flats and offices. A group of school children approached, herded by an anxious teacher. She stopped to let them pass, then pressed on further down the road. She was just wondering whether she'd imagined the salon when she saw it - on the corner of the road leading to The Hollies.

'Movers and Shapers' was a modern hairdressers decorated with black and white striped wallpaper across the back wall in contrast to white side walls, black appliances, and a shiny, black tiled floor. A bell trilled above her as she opened the door and approached the counter. Just as she reached it a face capped with a pink fringe popped up and smiled.

An elderly lady, the only other client, sat at the far end with hair curled into rollers, leafing through a magazine as a girl with a sharp blond bob fussed around her. Eva stroked her own hair protectively. She felt the urge to turn back.

"Can I help you?"

Eva hesitated, biting her bottom lip. "I want a complete change."

The girl's eyes widened. She glanced down at the book in front of her. "Do you have an appointment?"

"No, I'm sorry." Eva's voice faltered. As the girl leant over the book, Eva could see there was a long band of pink wound into a bun at the back of her head.

Pink hair looked up, a smile spreading from ear to ear. "No matter. We're pretty slow this morning. Let's take a look, shall we?"

***

Back home, Helen's foot clipped a pair of trainers as she passed through the hallway. She kicked them aside. A grey fleece spilt out the top of a rucksack leant against the wall. The dense beat of Matthew's music thudded the ceiling.

"Hello?" Her voice dispersed into the air around her.

She wandered through the hallway, surprised to find the downstairs so empty. It was the day before the Easter holidays, a teacher training day, which meant the kids broke up from school the day before. Usually her house was a hub during the holidays.

She made her way into the kitchen and flicked the kettle switch. Feeling a presence behind her, she turned to see Matthew's beaming face.

"I thought I heard someone come in. Alright, Mum?"

"Hi! I'm surprised you can hear anything past that noise."

"Hey! Don't diss the Train, man. They're huge!"

"Yeah, right." Helen chuckled. "All packed?"

"Think so. Can't wait!"

When Matthew shared his ambition to join the Air Force last year, Helen had felt sick to the stomach. If that wasn't bad enough, he followed it up with his longing to fly aeroplanes. Losing John in a freak helicopter accident ten years earlier had made Helen fiercely anti-forces. To this day, any mention of the Army on the radio, of war on the news, of new Navy battleships, made her curse.

But Matthew had done his homework and investigated university courses before he raised the issue. She'd felt compelled to support him, even though the thought of him in the air still made her lightheaded, and encouraged him to join the Air Cadets, secretly hoping a taste of military life might put him off. He'd embraced the idea wholeheartedly. This was his first field trip. Canoeing and rock climbing. At least this time he would be keeping his feet on the ground, although the flying would come soon. She just knew it.

"That's good," Helen said. She glanced at the clock. Just after twelve thirty. "What time are you leaving?"

"Around four. Gran's dropping me at the centre. Are you coming?"

"I can't I'm afraid, I'm sorry. I have a meeting with the super." Her heart dropped. "Thought I'd come back now and wish you all the best."

"Never mind."

Helen smiled warmly. "Where's Gran, and Robert?"

"Robert's gone to Jack's and Gran's gone shopping with Auntie Jo."

Helen stretched her neck back. "Really?" She couldn't imagine Jo and her mother browsing M&S, picking out clothes in Next and Wallis. Jane Lavery hated trawling the shops.

Matt laughed. "Well, Gran dropped her off in town while she went to the supermarket."

"Oh right, listen Matt… We need to have a quick chat before you go on your trip."

"We do?"

"The other night… " Helen cleared her throat.

"What?"

She hesitated. "The other night in your room, with Leah."

He shrugged. "What about it?"

"Look Matt, I know you are getting older, exploring… "

He stepped back and dug his hands in his pockets. "Look, Mum, if this is what I think it is, you're about six years too late. They started teaching us this stuff in year five."

"I realise you know. I'm trying to be practical." Helen

paused searching for the right words. "I don't like the idea of your exploring right now, you're still underage. But if you must… "

Matthew's face folded. "I can't listen to this." He turned to go.

"Just make sure you're careful," she said.

"What?"

"I mean… if you need me to get anything… or your gran…"

"Mum! If I need anything, which I don't, then I'll get it myself. Jesus… I'm going to finish packing."

Helen listened to his feet hit every step of the staircase and his door slam. The music throbbed louder. She pressed her fingers to her temples and leant back against the kitchen side. Once again she longed for John's easy temperament and jovial manner. He would have definitely handled that conversation better. Matthew was so like his father, they plucked the same strings.

She sighed, reached for her bag and retrieved the rechargeable torch she'd picked up for him, along with a tiny expanding camping towel, and headed up the stairs. It wouldn't do to part on a bad note.

Chapter **Twenty-Two**

Helen looked across the desk at Superintendent Jenkins. Telephone clutched to his left ear, he smoothed his right eyebrow between the thumb and forefinger of his free hand. He had been on the phone since she arrived, pausing only briefly to signal for her to sit in the chair opposite, before continuing his conversation. He said very little, yet his mood darkened the room.

Several minutes passed. She gave up trying to decipher his one-sided conversation and glanced around his office, wondering how many of her little cubicles would fit comfortably inside. The conference table at the far end was surrounded by chairs all pushed underneath, the books on the bookcase were aligned in height order, the papers on his desk stacked in neat piles. A laptop sat open in front of him.

The abstract painting on the wall caught her attention: just a few splodges of yellow and orange. There didn't seem to be a pattern and it certainly didn't resemble any recognisable shape. Helen could appreciate the talent of artists, but preferred something she could relate to like landscapes or portraits. It suddenly occurred to her that this was the only personal artefact in Jenkins' office. There were no photos on his desk of family, nothing to indicate a life outside work. It reminded her how little she knew of the man behind the suit.

She'd heard rumours that he was divorced and lived alone but Jenkins never discussed his private life, and she often wondered if that was simply because he didn't have one.

He replaced the receiver, leant back in his chair and steepled his long fingers before he spoke, "Thank you for coming, Helen."

His sour tone caught her off balance slightly. When his secretary had called earlier to arrange the appointment, she assumed that it was to discuss the cold cases. Now she wasn't so sure. "You asked to see me?"

"Yes."

"Helen, would you mind telling me why you still have Scottish police watching Miss Carradine's parents' bungalow?"

"Of course, sir." She was startled he'd discovered this, since she'd requested that all communication came through her. But Jenkins was a skilled detective and, whilst he tended to toe the political line adopted by many senior ranking officers, he did have the ability to consider the wider aspects of an investigation.

She presented a concise update of the case so far - the sizing of the jacket, the suicide note and reiterated the phone call by the female informant made so close to Carradine's address, closely followed by the disappearance of Eva herself.

Jenkins didn't interrupt. He sat, one leg crossed over another, which made his body appear at an angle, hands now folded in his lap.

When she finished he unfolded himself and leant forward. "Helen, I'm going to give you a piece of advice. Don't let enthusiasm spoil your career."

"But, sir… "

"You disobeyed an order yesterday. I specifically asked you to leave Eva Carradine out of it."

"But, considering the facts… "

"There are no facts." His terse calmness cut through her like a knife. "People go away all the time." Jenkins leant back, pinched the bridge of his nose between his thumb and forefinger and closed his eyes momentarily. "Hell, where is the money supposed to be coming from?"

"I'm sure I can… "

"That's enough. There isn't cash for hunches and whims. We have a tight case and the offer of central resources to tie up the loose ends, which is worth its weight in gold. Problem is, any saving we might have realised, you have now blown on a whimsy notion with Strathclyde police force. I'm not going to repeat the evidence that points to a case solved, Helen, but I will say that this investigation is no longer yours. DI Fitzpatrick's team will close this one. Lend him one of your officers to aid the smooth transition. We move on."

His voice softened, "Let's put this behind us. You got a good result on the Bracken Way case last year. You've got another one here. These jobs take it out of you - the hours, the headaches, the decisions. Take the weekend off, maybe spend it with your family. Come back on Monday and let's show the chief what we can do with these cold case shootings."

She stared back at him, but held her tongue.

His face slackened. "Look Helen, you're a good cop. Senior investigating officer on homicide is a difficult job. You have to balance leading an investigation with being a team player. Sometimes that's not easy."

"I don't have a problem leading my team, sir. Actually, many of them share my view… "

"Then it's your job to change their mind," he interrupted. Once again, his tone adopted a harsh inflection. "*You* give the orders. Believe me, you have to kick a few butts from time to time to gain respect in this place. You say, they do. That'll lick them back into shape."

Helen was infuriated. How dare he question her ability

to manage. His empty words and lack of respect for his colleagues made her embarrassed for his rank.

Not for the first time, Helen left Jenkins' office, raging like a bull. He was so wrong, yet he couldn't see it. Couldn't or wouldn't? Where was Eva Carradine? At the bottom of a ravine? Floating in a lake? Since officers reached her parents' bungalow in Scotland, she hadn't returned. Helen pursed her lips. The surveillance on Eva Carradine may have been cancelled, but she'd make sure she lent one of her best detectives to Dean's team. It always paid to keep your eyes and ears open.

***

A stream of vehicles stretched out in front of Eva as she pulled off the M80 towards Callander and slowed to a halt. She sat there for several minutes, tapping the steering wheel. When nothing moved, she cut the engine and climbed out. The view from the side of the road showed a line of traffic stretching to the horizon.

She sighed, climbed back into her KA and turned on the radio, fiddling with the channels until she found what sounded like a local station, hoping for some travel news. When Abba's 'Dancing Queen' filled the car, she turned the volume down to low. She glanced at the car behind her in her rear-view mirror, then turned it to view her own reflection.

She stared at the stranger in the mirror. The severe black fringe accentuated her eyes - they looked bluer, larger; dark lashes curled out of pale eyelids. She couldn't deny that the hairdresser had done a wonderful job, skilfully layering the inverted bob at the back so that it fell softly forward into her face. In other circumstances she might even have liked the change.

An image of her mother skipped into her head. She had

always been so proud of her daughter's natural, blond locks. She'd be so disappointed. Eva raked her hands through what was left of her mane. It felt false, like nylon. Once again she had messed everything up.

***

Helen sighed and shut down her laptop. She was supposed to be rereading the ballistic reports on the Roxten boys' shootings, but her brain refused to focus. She made her way downstairs to join her family. The blare of the television drew her to the living room where she found Jo and Robert on the sofa watching a movie.

"Hi guys," she said. "Anyone want tea?"

"No thanks," Jo said, without looking up. Robert shook his head.

"Where's Gran?"

"Gone to watch her own TV," Robert said, eyes glued to the screen.

Helen looked up to see squirts of blood spray across the television screen. The image changed to a girl's terrified bloodied face, then back to a car windscreen as two lines of blood dribbled down to the wipers. Helen turned to Robert and Jo. "What is this?" Her question elicited no response. She switched back to the television to see the bloodied girl stumble around the car and discover the body of an old man with one eye shot out.

"Ewww." Robert said, still absorbed in the screen.

Jo grimaced. "That's gross."

"What is this?" Helen repeated.

"*Wolf Creek*," Jo answered.

"What?" The alarm in Helen's voice pulled both pairs of eyes to her. "You're not watching this!" She bent down, grabbed the remote and changed channels.

"Hey!" Robert said.

"Robert, it's an eighteen rated film, and a damaged one at that. You're not watching it!"

"Oh, come on," he pleaded. "All my mates have seen it."

"No, way." Helen shook her head and retreated to the kitchen, teeth clenched.

She sat at the table and pressed her palm to her forehead to soothe the ache that was gaining momentum. A tiny thought niggled her. Earlier, the phone company confirmed that the call made from Naomi's phone on Wednesday, the day after she was killed, was made from somewhere in the Roxton vicinity. Did Jules visit his boys and use Naomi's phone before he died? Or did Karen Paton make that call? One thing was for sure. It wasn't Eva. She was in Scotland…

"Are you okay?"

Helen looked up to see Jo standing at the doorway. "Fine. That film was far too old for Robert."

"Sorry. I didn't realise it was going to be that gruesome."

"Christ, Jo! It's an eighteen certificate. He's only just thirteen."

"I've said I'm sorry."

"Well, sorry isn't enough when it comes to kids." The barbed words escaped before Helen could soften them.

Jo stiffened. "Perhaps that's telling me something, eh?"

Helen sighed loudly, trying to calm her acerbic tone. "I wasn't implying that your… "

"Save it!" Jo interrupted. "I need time to think." And with that she stomped out of the kitchen.

Helen placed her head in her hands. The day was turning into a disaster. Her conversation with Matthew hadn't gone well, she'd upset Robert, argued with Jo. As she massaged her forehead, Jenkins' face popped into her mind. Was that why she was so tetchy? Because she'd been taken off the case? Because no-one could see the holes in the investigation? Or was it because, deep down, she was starting to think they might be right.

***

Sleep didn't come easily to Helen that evening. She tossed and turned like a paddle boat in the midst of a mighty storm.

When she finally did drift off, her slumber was haunted by dreams.

She was in Naomi's house, trudging down the stairs. Shrill screams filled the air around her. They were coming from the lounge. The metallic smell of blood seeped out of every crevice. The faster she moved, the more steps appeared beneath her.

The scenery changed. She was standing on the pavement outside Jules Paton's house, an innocent bystander. Karen Paton and Naomi were shouting. She couldn't make out the words. They seemed oblivious to her existence. Naomi became increasingly agitated. Karen's boys tugged at her sleeve, crying.

Another change. Helen was following Naomi down a dusty bridleway. Fields stretched out across rolling country on either side. She had to quicken her pace to keep up. Naomi's red hair hung loose. Wisps reached out and danced in the wind. Helen sped up to reach her. Just as she caught up she felt something brush her shoulder. She glanced behind to see Jules Paton's face. As she turned back, someone had moved in front of her, blocking her path. They collided. Helen stumbled and almost fell. When she recovered herself, she looked up into the eyes of Karen Paton.

Helen woke with a start, blinking her eyes open. She glanced at the clock and nestled back into the pillow. It was only five thirty.

Sleep continued to evade her. Too many disjointed images,

too many thoughts merged together in her mind. But one theme continued - Jules, Naomi and Karen. Had Karen played a role in the murder? She couldn't have been the female informant, her voice was too high pitched, almost mouse-like. But what about the call made from Naomi's missing phone on the day after the murder, traced back to Roxten?

She turned onto her side restlessly and switched back to the interview with Karen. The fiddling of the ring, cutting into her finger. Was she hiding something? Karen's record was clean. Was it dealing with the police that made her so agitated? Or was she frightened for her children? During her service, Helen had faced many cases where concerned parents laboured under the misapprehension that any slight brush with the law meant that custody of their own children would be called into question. In reality, removing children from their families only occurred in extreme circumstances and was a difficult and convoluted process involving social services experts. And from what Helen witnessed, Karen Paton was a good mother.

No, there was something else bothering her, something niggling beneath the surface. She decided to pay Karen Paton another visit. Just to set her mind at rest. It wouldn't be out of place for the police to provide a welfare visit to Jules' next of kin now, would it?

Chapter Twenty-Three

The alarm bleeped at seven, waking Helen with a start. She leapt forward, slammed the snooze button and rested back on the pillow to calm her shallow breaths.

Her head thumped like the beats in Matthew's music and she rubbed her hands up and down her face to ease the tension. After a night of shallow, evasive rest she could feel the warmth and comfort of deep sleep luring her.

Her mind flashed back to recent events: the searching of Eva's house, the discovery of Jules' body, the investigation wrapped up in a tidy pink ribbon by Dean's team. She recalled his words, 'Perhaps you are getting too close to this one?' Then Jenkins, 'It's a good result, we need to move on.'

Daylight crept through the crack at the top of the curtains. Perhaps they were right. Maybe she had allowed herself to become too close. Certainly, the intervention of MOCT into the Spence case frustrated her. It reminded her of year eleven in secondary school: she'd spent months organising a charity fundraising concert and was taken sick with suspected meningitis days before the event, leaving a fellow pupil to take over. She'd hated sitting on the sideline, while someone else took the reins of her baby.

Helen stared at the ceiling, toying with following Jenkins' advice and taking the day off. She could spend time with the boys. But Matthew was away, Robert had arranged to meet friends in town, and her mother had a lunch date with an old friend. Even Jo had said she was going to take advantage of a quiet house to catch up with work this morning. Left to her own devices she would brood around the house. No. She pushed Operation Aspen firmly out of her head. Today she'd go to the station and immerse herself in the review files.

***

Eva stared across the countryside. Soft mist danced on the edge of the field. The view was beautiful, the air clean. She inhaled deeply and held onto the breath, wanting to keep it forever.

She continued further down the road, past a field of sheep, another of cattle. A Land Rover rattled passed, then nothing. She paused beside a gateway and looked out into the distance. Just past the edge of the field there was a loch. She stared at it as Amy MacDonald's 'Mr Rock and Roll' bounced into her ears from her iPod. Only last week they'd listened to it as they drove through France. Naomi and Eva. Together. Last week. A brief recollection of a former life filled her brain, warped by recent events.

She focused on the water. It looked inviting, reaching out for her. Naomi. Icy darkness cocooned her. A lump expanded in her throat. The water reached out again, calling to her.

Her life was a tangled mess. She stared at the loch. It would be so easy. In death the pain would be released. Easy. She suddenly remembered a documentary she'd watched on near death experiences a couple of years ago. The drowning victim's voice spoke in her head, 'Drowning isn't easy, your body fights the water and chokes to death. It isn't a pleasant feeling, not until the water engulfs you and, by then, you are practically unconscious.' She shuddered, wondering if she was really brave enough to try.

An image of her mother pushed into her mind. She would be devastated, not least because Eva hadn't come to her for help in her hour of need. Eva would be losing her pain, but passing on a new desperation and anxiety, one that would glue itself to a parent's heart for the rest of their life.

She threw her head back, stared at the hazy blue sky. The truth was she was too cowardly to try. The weight of her mother's anxiety weighed too heavily on her shoulders. She ached to contact her. But Eva's mother hadn't taken her own mobile on holiday and her stepfather never switched his on. It was only for emergencies…

As she glanced down, something on her finger glinted in the sunlight. Her engagement ring. She recalled how the proprietor of the guest house from the evening before had glanced at it when she enquired about a room. The knowing look she gave when Eva said she needed to take a few days away, to use up holiday at work. A young woman travelling around on her own - must be a relationship break-up.

The importance people placed on that ring finger interested Eva. She had been engaged to Nick for six months before he'd finished it. She kept wearing the ring, but mostly because it offered her safety. On a night out, men would notice and give her a wide berth. And if she saw someone interesting, well, she could always remove it.

She glanced back across the water. She thought of Nick. The bad boy that caught her eye, the one she'd flunked university for on the promise of an engagement ring and a life of excitement. Nick that left her soon after. Although ludicrous, part of her still harboured feelings for him. When she dropped out of university she'd overheard her parents talking in the kitchen. Her stepfather had said, 'The only way Eva will learn to make the right decisions is to experience the consequences.' Trouble was, she never seemed to make the right decision.

After university, she secured a sales job in insurance. It seemed fun at first, but very soon the boredom set in. She rented a house with a loser of a boyfriend who dumped her, forcing her to move to a smaller flat and take in a lodger to cover the rent. Even the lodger, a student from Hampton University called Nicole, didn't hang around. She shuddered. This was never how she saw her life evolving.

A low flying plane droned overhead. She held a hand up to shield her eyes and watched it, listening to the sounds of the purring engine as it disappeared into the tufts of cloud. The emptiness it left behind flushed her brain injecting clarity of thought. She needed to rejoin the land of the living.

Instinctively, Eva placed her hand in her jacket pocket and foraged around. Her heart sank. Her mobile was back at the guest house. She'd bought a new charger in Glasgow and charged it overnight. But having been switched off for so long, she had taken to leaving it behind - in stark contrast to her previous life where she carried it everywhere with her, accessed her emails, Facebook, the internet, sent endless texts. It was time to pick up the threads of her previous life and mend them. She turned on her heels and hurried back in the direction of the guest house.

***

Helen arrived at the station just after eight and felt her heart drop at the sight that greeted her. Parked diagonally opposite was George Sawford lifting his briefcase and coat out of the boot.

Last November, on her first murder investigation with the homicide squad, Jenkins had suggested that Sawford be brought in to assist and share the wealth of knowledge he'd gained through managing serious criminal cases over the past nine years. Helen didn't doubt his competence. What concerned her intensely was his agenda. Nicknamed 'Celebrity Cop', Sawford played golf with most of the chiefs he worked with, entertained local councillors and MPs. His political persona was more important to him than the jobs he worked on, or the colleagues he worked alongside. Getting a result was all that mattered.

Fortunately, his visit was brief. Helen had located the killer within a day of his arrival. Although he appeared outwardly pleased, his tight mannerisms had betrayed his true feelings. He didn't like to be beaten to the finishing line.

Her mind raced. The last she heard, Sawford was on secondment with Police Professional Standards Unit. What was he doing here?

He shut the boot and turned to face her. "Helen!" He closed the short gap between them in seconds. A whiff of musky aftershave brushed the air around her.

"George." She lifted her head in acknowledgement and shook his proffered hand. His fox-like face creased into a smile. He was probably the only male officer in the station smaller than her. "So, what brings you to Hampton?"

"Just checking in on my team," he said. He juggled his overcoat, as it fought to slip down his arm.

Helen creased her forehead. "I thought you were with PPSU?"

"Oh, short term," he said, waving his arm dismissively. "Just on secondment to examine a particular case whilst Bellows was on paternity leave."

Helen pondered inwardly how the PPSU would have suited him. Even though they shared the same rank, he would love to think that he was working on cases that were far too important to share with the likes of her.

"Anyway, now I'm with MOCT."

She managed to quash her surprise before it showed. He

didn't seem a likely boss for Dean. "Oh, I hadn't realised."

"Yes, been with them since the middle of January. Acting Superintendent. Come down to congratulate them on their result. Wonderful news."

Their result. "Mmm."

"Quite surprising. All happened rather quickly from what I've heard?" He extended his free arm towards the door, gesturing she walk with him. Right now, she wanted to move in the opposite direction, yet approaching the station anyway, she was out of options. "I understand you played a part."

Helen fought to keep her composure and said nothing.

They reached the door and he paused, holding it open for her. "Perhaps you'd fill me in?"

She glanced across at him as she passed through the entrance, wondering what he was up to. Previous experience in working with Sawford combined with anecdotes from colleagues had taught her a valuable lesson: he played games and pulled peoples' strings as if they were a puppet, always with his own agenda. Well, she wasn't going to be played. "I think your inspector is better versed to do that since he's taken over the case file."

Sawford didn't react although Helen was convinced she saw the glimmer of a smile tickle his lips. They climbed the stairs together. "Interesting, though," Sawford said thoughtfully as they reached the corridor. The warmth of the building had produced a ruddiness in his cheeks. "And with the ballistics news linking the gun with the Stratton case, it all seems very tight."

Helen stopped in her tracks. "Pardon?"

George turned back to face her. "I didn't realise you hadn't heard. The results just came through. The gun used in the Stratton shooting shared the same characteristics as that in the Naomi Spence murder."

Her jaw tightened. "No, I hadn't heard."

"I'm sure your team will fill you in."

They reached the second floor. George stopped. "Good to see you, Helen." He twisted on his heels and pulled open the door that led to the MOCT suite.

Helen stared into the empty air behind him, feet fixed to the spot. Leon Stratton's shooting was one of her unsolved murders. How could this discovery not have reached her?

Just as the door was about to close, a hand wrapped around the edge. Sawford's face appeared above it. "Helen, just one question, how do you find DI Fitzpatrick?"

The question, out of the blue as it was, knocked her sideways. Was this something to do with her previous affair with Dean? Was he aware of it? If so, how many others were? Or, was he questioning Dean's detective skills, his judgement?

She decided to play it safe. "Well, it's only been a couple of days, George. You'll need to judge that one for yourself."

He nodded and disappeared. Helen stared at the door. It seemed like an odd question. But, as she trudged up the stairs to the incident room, the investigation and the cold cases swamped her mind, pushing any questions about their relationship to a far corner.

The incident room was quiet on her approach. Most of her team had taken advantage of a Saturday off, the urgency of a homicide investigation now passed. Only Pemberton and Dark were present. He hovered over a map of Roxten on the far wall. She tapped away at her keyboard. Having delivered the news to Naomi's parents yesterday, no doubt she was putting the finishing touches to her family liaison officer's report for Dean's team.

Dark looked up briefly as she entered. Pleasantries exchanged, Pemberton turned to face her.

"I understand we've had some more news?" Helen said.

"You've heard about the ballistics results then."

"Sawford told me on the stairs. When did we find out?"

"Them, or us?"

Helen felt frustration clawing its way back in. "What are you talking about?"

"Dean's team knew yesterday," he said. "I found out on the grapevine this morning."

Helen looked at him, incredulous. She wasn't only being pushed aside on the Spence murder, but on the cold cases too. What was Dean up to? Seeking brownie points? She knew that MOCT funding would be reviewed shortly. Maybe he thought if he could gather results like this, there was a better chance of securing it. But on her patch? How could he?

Once again, she had let down her wall and let him in. And once again she had regretted it.

Chapter **Twenty-Four**

Molly, the guest house landlady, was kneeling in the hallway, tidying the information leaflets when Eva opened the front door.

"Hello dear. Oh, don't you look better!" She pushed wisps of grey hair out of her face as she hauled herself up. "The fresh air has brought the colour back to your cheeks." She ushered Eva in, squeezed past her to close the front door. "I've just made drinks. Would you like one?"

Eva immediately felt the warmth of the house wrapping around her. The air was loaded with the smell of freshly filtered coffee. "No, thank you."

"There's been a man here looking for you."

Eva jolted. "What?"

"A policeman actually, although he wasn't in uniform. Stayed and chatted awhile. He was just checking to see if you are okay." She tilted her head to one side and narrowed her eyes. "It sounds like somebody's worried about you."

Eva stared back at her, feeling the air squeezed out of her lungs.

Molly seemed to sense her anxiety. "Don't worry, dear! He was such a nice young man. Just concerned. Left a note. Now, where did I put it?" She rummaged in her pocket, retrieved a creased piece of paper and unfolded it. "No, that's not it. Wait there."

Eva watched her amble into the kitchen. As soon as she was out of sight, she took to the stairs, two at a time. How did they find her?

As soon as she reached her room, she crossed to the bedside table and retrieved her mobile phone, still plugged into the charger. She switched it on, willing it to life.

The door knocked. She jumped, like a child caught peeling wallpaper from behind the settee. "Who's there?"

"It's me, dear," Molly cried out.

Eva opened the door and Molly handed her an A5 piece of paper, folded neatly in half.

Eva stared at it.

Molly smiled at her gently, touched her arm. "Are you okay, dear?"

She fought to get the words out. "Yes."

"Are we staying another night?"

"No… Thank you. I think I need to get back."

Molly gave her a knowing nod.

She closed the door, rushed to her bedside and reached out for her phone, her final bastion of hope. The screen lit. It was searching. She prayed there would be a signal. Yes, two bars! A plethora of messages sprung up from a past life. A life without fear.

As she scrolled through the messages she saw it, a message from Naomi, her best friend. Nothing unusual in that. Except the message was sent the day after she died.

The room turned hazy. She cast the phone aside, sat back onto the bed, a hand clasped to her temple. Slowly her vision cleared. The phone rested on her bedside table and she stared at it, as if it was a grenade ready to explode.

The note sat on the bed next to her. She snatched it, unfolding it slowly. It bore a crested emblem with Strathclyde Police printed below, alongside a telephone number:

PLEASE CONTACT DC GILMORE AT STRATHCLYDE CID ON THE NUMBER BELOW AT YOUR EARLIEST CONVENIENCE.

THIS IS A ROUTINE ENQUIRY. NOT AN EMERGENCY.

Eva turned the paper over in her hands. It certainly looked legitimate. But anybody could produce something like that on a home PC. Anyone could copy and paste the logo.

She reached out for her phone. Tentatively, she stroked the screen. It lit up. She viewed her messages again, and gasped. Naomi's number was top of the list. Another message, sent a minute earlier. Goosebumps pricked her arms. She blinked back tears and clicked to open the message:

You can't run forever.

Eva's body began to shake. A sudden thought struck her. It was possible to trace somebody through the GPS on their mobile phone. With trembling hands she leapt forward and switched it off.

***

Nate surfaced at around nine o'clock the following morning. He pulled on his joggers, made his way downstairs into the kitchen, opened the fridge and glugged juice out of the carton. As he shut the fridge door, he felt a presence. He turned. The kitchen was empty.

He wandered through to the living room. Dressed in a black t-shirt and boxer shorts, Chilli sat on his chair at the far end, staring into space. He looked as though he'd been there all night. He didn't acknowledge Nate, his gaze fastened to a black bin liner sitting beside the table. A red stained Manchester City football shirt, just like the one Richard Elsdon, one of their runners wore, spilled out of the top. Spatters of blood marked the surrounding carpet.

"They think I'm too old for all this," Chilli said, without looking up.

Nate scanned the sofa, curtains and coffee table for more blood. There was none.

"That's the problem when you get to the top," Chilli continued. "Everyone wants your crown."

Nate stared at Chilli as his uncle finally made eye contact. He stood, approached his nephew and slapped him on the back, affectionately gripping his neck. "You're the only one I can trust now, Nate. That's why we're special." He turned to leave the room. "I need you to make that disappear. We've got a busy day ahead."

***

Helen was still seething as she exited her car in the road behind Karen Paton's garden. How could Dean do this to her? How dare he? The sound of her mobile interrupted her thoughts, and she stopped to answer it, surprised to hear Spencer's voice at the other end of the line. At Jenkins' bequest, she'd reluctantly leant Spencer to MOCT as they wrapped up the Paton case.

"What's up, Steve?"

"Ma'am, you asked me to contact you personally if we received anything on Eva Carradine?"

A shot of adrenalin whipped through her. Finally. "What do you have?"

Spencer cleared his throat. "Strathclyde Police located the guest house where she is staying in Scotland and left a message for her to contact them. Although we cancelled their assistance the message didn't get through to the field. Anyway, Miss Carradine responded and they referred her to us."

"She called the incident room?" Helen balanced the phone precariously between her chin and shoulders as she rummaged through her bag for her notebook and pen.

"I've just put the phone down to her. She asked to speak to someone in charge."

With the case now under Dean's jurisdiction, Spencer would normally pass this to him. Helen was grateful for his loyalty. "Thanks, Steve. Who else have you informed?"

"Nobody yet, ma'am. She isn't a suspect here. I thought I'd let you make that decision."

As far as Hampton management were concerned, the murder was solved, the enquiry being closed. Both Dean and Jenkins had made it perfectly clear that Eva wasn't a suspect. There was no evidence linking her to Naomi's murder and, even though the informant's call was made so close to her home address, there was nothing to indicate Eva made that call. But Helen couldn't rest until she'd spoken to her. "Right. Thank you." Helen hesitated. She didn't want to get Spencer into trouble. "Allocate the action to me, would you? I'll speak to her and report back if anything further is required."

"Certainly, ma'am."

Eva had called from a guest house near the Scottish town of Callander. Helen jotted down the details quickly before she rang off and dialled the number.

The call was answered on the second ring, as if somebody was standing beside the phone.

"Hello."

The voice sounded fragile, timid.

"May I speak to Eva Carradine please?" Helen replied.

"Who is this?"

"Is that Eva?"

"Yes."

"I'm Detective Chief Inspector Helen Lavery from Hampton force. You asked to speak to someone in charge?" The line fell quiet, a few short shallow breaths, the only indication of a presence. "What can I do for you?" she said gently.

"I need your help."

"And why is that?"

"Can we meet? Alone?"

Helen turned this over quickly in her mind. Jenkins himself said there was no evidence to suggest that Eva was linked to the murder enquiry and he didn't want resources wasted on finding her. But he couldn't object to her meeting Eva alone. She grabbed her pen and leant her notebook against the fence. "Okay, where are you?"

Another pause. "I'm in Scotland, but I'm driving back to Hampton today."

They agreed to meet at a motorway services just outside Hampton. Helen didn't want Eva to cross the county border, drive through the town, approach her home, until she'd spoken to her.

Her spirits bolstered by the phone call, Helen marched up the alleyway beside Karen Paton's house and knocked on the door. No music blasted from her neighbour today, no sound of children playing.

It was several moments before she heard footsteps up the hall. The door opened. A slim elderly lady with bushy, white hair and striking eyes stared back at her. "May I help you?" A thick Northern Irish accent weighed in her voice.

Helen flashed her card. "I wondered if I could have a word with Karen Paton?"

The woman leant into the card, examined it carefully. She looked up at Helen, suspiciously. "She's sleeping at the moment."

"And you are?"

"Marian. Her mother."

"May I wait?"

"I don't think that would be a good idea."

"How is she?"

"As well as can be expected. Look, I think I know what

this is about and I don't think she is ready for more questions about her late husband at this stage."

Helen nodded. She hadn't told anyone back at the station about her visit which meant she couldn't afford to press the point. "I'll come back at a more convenient time. How are the boys?"

Marian looked taken aback for a moment at the personal nature of the question. "I don't think they really know what's going on. Certainly the youngest doesn't. Keeps asking when his daddy's coming back from heaven."

Helen pressed her lips together. "I'm sorry." She turned to go.

"So am I," Marian shouted after her. "Just hope you catch them."

Helen turned back. "Pardon?"

"The beggers who did this. They might not have been living together, but my son-in-law idolised those boys. The last thing he would do is take his own life, whatever mess he'd got himself mixed up in."

Helen heard the squeak of footsteps on floorboards above. Marian gazed up. "I have to go," she said and closed the door.

Helen hovered on the doorstep a moment. A chink of light peeped through the dark clouds overhead. The suicide note. She knew something was strange about it - Jules hadn't mentioned his boys. A loving father would be sure to mention his boys. Wouldn't he?

***

The white Mercedes crawled past Helen as she pulled out of the estate. She didn't need to view the personalised plate to see who it belonged to. Chilli Franks had been a teenager when his family moved to the rabbit warren. He immediately saw opportunity in Jimmy Percival's interests and ingratiated himself with Jimmy's crowd. Later, when he took over the reins to Black Cats, the club flourished and he expanded his empire and moved to the new estate nearby, just a stone's throw away. Situated on the corner, one of his bedroom windows overlooked the rabbit warren, another reached across to the trading estate opposite. With his obvious wealth, Chilli could easily have afforded to leave the area, take a home on one of Hampton's more affluent estates. But that would take him away from his insidious operations. These days, it was not only home to the city's red light district, but intelligence officers estimated that more drugs came out of the rabbit warren in a single month than the rest of Hampton city in an entire year.

The difficulty was catching him in the act. Many police operations were planned and executed. Some led to prosecutions. But nobody talked and none led them to Chilli himself. He may parade around with his posh car and five bedroomed house, dodging the tax man and evading the police. He may market himself as a reformed character. But Helen knew what he really was: Rotten to the core. Some things never change.

***

The clock on the dashboard read five o'clock as Helen turned into Leicester Forest East Services. The parking area was thick with vehicles, pushing her far from the entrance, near the lorry park, in search of a space.

Helen crossed the car park quickly. The sweet smell of nicotine curled her nostrils as she reached the entrance. She stepped over a used Burger King box, reached in her bag and placed a mint in her mouth. Anything to keep the buried nicotine cravings at bay.

Bodies swarmed the doors. She stood aside to let an army

of teenagers out and held the door for a mother wrestling with a double buggy, the twin toddlers fast asleep inside, ignorant of their mother's difficulties.

Helen located the sprawling restaurant and glanced around. It teamed with bodies, the sports car event at nearby Donington Park drawing more travellers to the road than usual on a March Saturday afternoon. She strained her eyes to see a girl with long blond hair and blue eyes. It was a hopeless task amongst the mass of occupied tables.

She decided to wander around. On the phone earlier, Eva had said she was unable to use her mobile. They agreed that Eva would sit alone and place a closed copy of *Red* magazine next to a can of Coca-Cola on the table to indicate her presence.

Helen passed tables of families eating meals, elderly couples drinking coffee, young lovers holding hands, a table of teenagers clicking on their mobile phones. Time passed slowly. Her arms itched in agitation. Had Eva changed her mind?

Helen tripped on the outstretched foot before she saw it. In her haste to retain balance, she flew sideways against the broad bicep of a middle aged man.

"I'm so sorry," she said, straightening her jacket around her. He waved her away and she turned to scowl at the owner of the outstretched leg: a tall, stringy man who had curled himself into the chair, but simply couldn't fit his legs beneath the table. He looked up, mouthed an apology. But Helen didn't hear it. Her attention was taken elsewhere as a flash of red caught her eye.

She raised her head to meet the gaze of the single lady seated at the table for two.

Chapter Twenty-Five

Eva Carradine sat in the front seat of Helen's Honda and stared out at the sea of cars clogging the car park.

The black hair and severe fringe had initially thrown Helen. She'd glimpsed the magazine, the can, then instinctively glanced over her shoulder. But as she turned back to Eva, the mixture of apprehension and fear behind her large blue eyes was enough to convince Helen that this was her girl.

Once introductions were over, Helen suggested they leave the restaurant and seek the relative privacy of her car. She didn't want their conversation overheard. Eva had followed her silently, looking about suspiciously as they crossed the car park.

Helen crossed her ankles and clasped her hands together as she spoke, "How can I help you, Eva?"

Eva turned her head. "You wanted to see me?"

Helen paused for a moment, maintaining eye contact. "We have been seeking to talk to you in connection with Naomi Spence's murder. Is that the only reason you contacted us earlier? Only, on the phone you said you needed help?"

Eva averted her eyes, as if she wasn't sure what to say next or perhaps how much to say.

"Eva, I can't help you if you won't let me."

Silence hung in the car for several seconds. Eventually,

Eva raised her hand to her head. "It's all such a mess. I don't know where to start."

"Well, why do you think you need help?"

Helen watched Eva remove her hand, then shake her head. "No, I need to start way beyond that."

For the next twenty minutes, Eva told her story, starting with the holiday that she had taken with Naomi at Jules' friend's apartment in Milan, how they had flown out there and driven back through Italy, Switzerland and France to deliver a Paul Smith Mini, a special order for a client of Jules - the favour securing them a free holiday. Eva's account was surprisingly detailed, as if she had turned these events over in her mind many times over the last few days.

"We delivered the car and thought it was all over," she said. She cast her eyes to the floor. "Then Naomi received a call on her mobile on Saturday evening."

Helen sat forward, but said nothing.

"I remember the look of surprise on her face, she didn't recognise the voice. Then it changed to fear." Eva shuddered. "All he said was that he wanted what was missing from the car. We had forty-eight hours to return it, or there'd be trouble. And if we contacted the police, we'd regret it."

"And what was missing?"

"No idea. The call scared us. We panicked. Naomi phoned Jules and relayed the message. She screamed down the phone at him. He just kept saying it was a misunderstanding and we had nothing to worry about. That he was going away to sort it and he'd be back in a few days. But he wouldn't tell us who they were."

"Where was he going?"

"I don't know. Naomi was in pieces."

"What about you?"

"I was terrified. We both were. But I almost felt numbed. The anger kind of took over. I just kept thinking how could

Jules do this to us."

"Why didn't you go to the police?"

"I don't know." She closed her eyes for a second. "We were scared. We just wanted it all to go away."

"And you had no idea who was on the end of that call?"

"No. Naomi said it was a husky, male voice. Anyway, a couple of days passed and nothing happened. I thought it was sorted. Then… " Her voice faltered.

Helen needed to keep her talking. Right now she needed to get as much information as possible. She couldn't afford to let emotions get in the way. "What do you know about Jules?"

Eva shrugged. "Jules is everybodys' friend. He's one of those people that worm their way into your life and you can't get rid of them."

"You don't like him?"

"I don't like what he did to Naomi. She was always a nice girl. But he changed that."

"Was he ever violent towards Naomi?"

"No! But to be honest, you're not the first to ask. Other people noticed bruises on her. Naomi was clumsy. Always falling over, knocking herself. When we were kids she'd have bruises all up her legs. She even fell at work last year and gave herself a black eye." The car turned quiet. People moved about in the car park beyond, but it was almost like a television going on in the background with the sound turned down. Eva's face clouded. "How did she die?"

Helen recalled the details of the autopsy report and decided to hold some information back. "She was shot."

Eva drew a sharp intake of breath. "Jules said we were safe. He promised. I didn't know she was dead." Her head dipped as she choked on her words.

Helen reached into her bag for a tissue and passed it across as the tears that flowed developed into soft sobs. She reached out, placed an arm around Eva's shoulder and pulled her close. It was an unorthodox gesture, something that wouldn't have been approved of, or adopted by her colleagues back at the station. But then they wouldn't have approved of such surreptitious meetings either.

As Eva's breathing started to regain some normality, Helen asked the question that had been tormenting her. "How did you know Naomi had been attacked?"

Eva sat up straight in her seat, wiped her nose and turned towards her. "I saw it."

This was what Helen had been waiting for. But the fact that the phone company sited the call near Eva's house, forty minutes drive from Naomi's, still puzzled her.

"You were there?"

Eva bit the side of her lip. "Not exactly."

"What do you mean?"

"We were talking to each other online over Skype. I saw the hand swipe around her mouth and the struggle in the background through my webcam."

Helen almost screamed out - of course! She thought back to Naomi's house: the desk in the corner, the lopsided chair on the floor next to it. But she'd asked the station technology experts to examine Naomi's computer on Thursday morning. Surely they must have been able to verify that Naomi was logged onto her Skype account and who she was talking to. Perhaps they sent their results to Dean's team, now he'd officially taken over the investigation. If so, why hadn't he shared this information?

Helen looked at Eva. "This is really important." She paused briefly. "What exactly did you see?"

"It was all a bit of a whirlwind. The images kept breaking up, and it was only a minute or so before someone turned Naomi's webcam off."

"Anything will help. Take your time."

"Okay." Eva bit her lip and chewed it a moment. "Well,

we'd only just connected. Naomi was sad. I knew she was struggling - she couldn't push the phone call, the threats out of her mind. Then she heard a noise and said there was somebody in the house."

"Did you see the attacker?"

Eva shook her head. "Just a black, gloved hand and an arm. It looked like maybe he had a black leather jacket on."

"Are you sure it was a man?"

"Pardon?"

"You said 'he'."

"The images were blurred, but he looked hefty, much bigger than Naomi." Eva nodded her head. "Yes, it looked like a man."

"When you say hefty, do you mean heavy built or tall?"

"The images were blurry. I-I can't be sure."

Helen glanced across. "What about facial features, clothes, hair?"

Another head shake. "Too difficult to tell."

"Eva, this is important. Did you recognise him?"

"No. I had no idea she was dead. Really." Her voice was barely audible. "I thought they might have hurt her, but not…"

"You phoned the ambulance?"

Eva nodded.

"Why did you run?"

"I could hardly go to the police, could I? I thought Naomi might be in hospital. I tried ringing her several times."

Helen blinked. That explained the calls on Naomi's phone log, made after she died. "How did you find out?"

"When I saw the police car outside my parents' bungalow, I panicked. I drove down to Glasgow. My phone was dead, so I went to an internet cafe and saw the notice on Facebook. I couldn't believe it. Still can't." Her voice splintered. She stared into space.

"So, why contact us today?"

Eva explained about the note from Strathclyde police and the text messages she received from Naomi's missing phone, after the murder.

Helen narrowed her eyes. "And you're sure the second message was today?"

"Yes, why?"

Helen thought about the first call made from a location in Roxten. It was possible it could have been Jules. But the second came after he died. And she didn't recall a mobile phone on the inventory of evidence recovered from Jules' house. "I just want to make sure we have our facts right, that's all," she said.

"They're coming for me, aren't they?" Eva said softly.

"We don't know that for sure. It might just be scaremongering."

"There's something else." Eva pushed her fringe to one side. "Jules promised to deal with the problem, but I haven't been able to contact him since Tuesday evening. We need to get to him urgently. He could be in danger too."

Helen paused for a second before she answered. "I'm sorry to have to be the one to tell you this, but Jules Paton is dead. His body was found on Thursday morning."

***

Helen peeled the lids of two milk cartons and tipped the contents into the mug of tea. When they did little to lighten the colour, she opened another two, and added several sachets of sugars before passing the mug to Eva.

A couple of calls verified the guest house visitor to be a legitimate member of Strathclyde CID. Spencer was right. Although their assistance had been cancelled, word hadn't got through to the field. But it was the caller using Naomi's missing mobile that really bothered Helen.

Following Eva's revelations, Helen knew she had to act fast. Her priority was to keep Eva safe. She remembered a hotel she'd been to for a cross-border police conference, a couple of years earlier. She pulled off at junction twenty of the motorway and found it easily on the Leicestershire border, just off the main road.

After a brief call to Pemberton, Helen checked Eva in under a false name, paid on her own credit card and moved her into the room. A cloud of silence had descended over Eva since she had heard the news of Jules' death.

"How are you feeling?" Helen asked, dragging a throw off the bed and draping it around Eva's shoulders to alleviate any possible shock affects.

Eva raised a pallid face and nodded her head slightly. "Okay."

"Can I get you anything to eat?"

She shook her head.

Helen smiled gently. "You're safe here, Eva. Nobody knows where you are."

"I still can't believe it."

Helen glanced around the room, giving her a moment to compose herself. It was one of those modern boutique hotels. The wall behind the fuchsia pink bed was papered in a subtle, black and white floral print, and it faced a plain white wall with a flat-screen TV. Eva sat on a black chair in the corner beside the long window, obscured by pink curtains with black tie backs. In the other corner was a round glass table with two metal chairs. The en suite bathroom was located in a short hallway leading to the entrance, and faced a built-in selection of wardrobes and cupboards, obscured by two long mirror doors. The room was bright and clean, but felt superficial.

She briefly turned over Eva's account in her mind. Something was wrong, a missing link. "How long have you known Naomi and Jules?"

Eva took a sip of her tea before she answered, "I grew up with Naomi. We lived in the same road until she was sixteen."

"You kept in contact after she moved?"

Eva nodded. "Even when she went off to university in London and I followed on to Southampton we spoke through email, saw each other in the holidays."

"You came back to Hampton after you finished university?"

"Kind of. Well, I didn't actually finish my degree. Flunked out, just after the start of final year. Met a guy… "

Helen nodded. "How did you meet Jules?"

"When I came back to Hampton, we hooked up and had a night out. Naomi was already seeing Jules, so she brought him and I brought Nick, the boyfriend I gave up my course for."

The line was definite. Helen knew the answer before she asked the question. "You're not with Nick anymore?"

"Nope. Finished soon after."

"You've known Jules a while, then?"

Eva sighed. "I guess so. He seemed to know all the right people to get us into the best clubs and parties. Naomi had contacts through her job too. We had a great time." She hesitated, glanced out of the window. "In some ways I looked up to him. He'd left uni midway through a course too, but he'd managed to make a success of his life, with his own business. In spite of everything, even his parents disowning him, he still did alright." She swallowed. "I just can't believe this… "

"How was his relationship with Naomi?" Helen continued.

"They had a love-hate relationship." Eva squirmed uncomfortably. "Always arguing. They kept splitting up and getting back together. It was like they couldn't live without each other."

"Because of the drugs?" Helen stared at Eva. As expected, the question knocked her sideways.

"Pardon?"

"Oh, come now. We both know Naomi was using. Jules too."

Eva wriggled uncomfortably, but said nothing.

"There's no room for secrets, Eva," Helen continued. "Were you using too?"

"No!" The change in Eva's inflection left Helen in little doubt she was telling the truth. "I don't touch the stuff. A friend of mine, Sadie, took ecstasy during Freshers' Week at uni. One minute she was all over the dance floor, the next she crashed to the floor." Eva's eyes glazed over as she recalled the memory. "An ambulance took her to hospital." She shook her head, almost disbelieving her own story. "It was heat exhaustion. Apparently ecstasy numbs your senses and she hadn't had enough fluids. She almost died." Eva paused and looked up at Helen. "I used to worry about Naomi. I told her about Sadie, but she wouldn't listen. She said cocaine was different."

"Is that why Jules arranged the holiday?"

Eva gave her a suspicious look. "What?"

"Were they arranging to bring something back? Drugs maybe?"

"No! Naomi wouldn't do that." Eva's voice cracked and she cleared her throat as she continued. "They had a big bust up, a couple of months ago. Only Jules wouldn't accept it. He kept turning up on her doorstep. Naomi couldn't decide what she wanted. She was tired. He needed to bring the car back, so arranged our flights out and ferry crossing back. He said the holiday would give her a break to sort her head out."

"You see, I'm struggling a bit with this, Eva. It must have cost a packet to fly you both out there, put you up in an apartment, ferry you back - all for a vintage Mini? My knowledge of cars isn't great, but I'm sure the vehicle can't have been worth that much. He must have been expecting to make a fair bit on the deal?"

Eva didn't reply.

Helen ploughed on, "Did he go out to the continent often?

To collect cars?"

"Now and then."

Thick silence sat between them. "You indicated that someone expected something more than a car. Something that made them torture Naomi and ransack her house for." She halted momentarily, watching Eva's eyes snap up to face her.

"Tortured?" Eva whispered.

Helen shouldn't reveal details of a case to a witness and she knew it. She was pushing herself out on a limb. But, clutching at straws, she hoped the shock tactic would work. "Yes," she said flatly. Eva's mouth hung open. "Are you sure you don't know what was in that car?"

Eva lowered her head. Her shoulders shook as thick tears streamed down her face. Helen wasn't sure how long they sat there. She reached into her bag for more tissues, passed them to Eva and patiently waited for the sobs to abate. And, as they did, Eva explained the problems with the window sticking, the small Frenchman who discovered the packages in the door panelling, describing their terror at driving through the border carrying the strange packets home. She explained how they delivered the car to Jules, the argument that ensued.

When she had relayed the story she sat quietly for several moments. Eventually she looked up at Helen. "What's going to happen to me?" she said weakly.

Helen considered this for a moment. Even if they traced the vehicle and stripped it down, it was unlikely that there would be any trace of the packets. The description convinced Helen that they contained an illegal substance - probably heroin, although there were no photos or evidence to secure a conviction. And the two links to the smuggling, Naomi and Jules, were both dead. Even if they were able to trace the Frenchman, according to Eva's account his behaviour with the girls suggested he didn't wish to be involved, so there was little chance he would be forthcoming. But she had to be careful. She couldn't be seen to advise Eva, or affect the investigation in any way.

"My immediate priority is to keep you safe. When this is over, we'll need to interview you formally. I would advise you to get yourself a solicitor and follow their advice."

A knock at the door made Eva jump. She shot Helen an anxious glance.

Helen stood and approached the door. "Who is it?"

"Me, ma'am." Helen smiled to herself and opened the door to a rather disgruntled looking Pemberton.

"It's like a maze in this place," he said. She moved aside for him to enter, then leant out and glanced up and down the corridor before retreating and locking the door behind her.

"Eva? I'd like you to meet Detective Sergeant Sean Pemberton."

Pemberton nodded at Eva and turned to Helen. "Ready to go, ma'am?"

"Sure."

"You're not going to leave me?" Alarm chipped at Eva's voice.

"The sergeant and I are going to move your car to a safe location. We can't leave it in the services tonight. Their security will be all over it. Now, remember what I said to you. Nobody knows you are here. You are quite safe as long as you keep your mobile phone switched off and don't answer the door to anyone. She reached into her pocket for her card and handed it over. If you need me, call me on that number. Anytime, day or night. Use the hotel phone only." She pointed across to the handset resting on the bedside table. "I will call you myself in the morning."

With a pained expression, Eva took the card and placed it on the table.

Pemberton handed over a Tesco carrier bag. "Some

provisions," he said with a kind smile. "Just in case you get peckish."

Eva followed them to the door. Helen placed a hand on her shoulder and squeezed gently, before exiting. As the door closed, she paused in the corridor for a moment, until she heard the sound of the locks being applied and then strode after Pemberton.

Chapter Twenty-Six

Helen leant her elbow on the car windowsill. Eva's account gave the case a new impetus. Was Jules working with someone to smuggle drugs into the country? Were they an accomplice to Naomi's murder? It certainly explained the problems with the jacket size. The formal suicide note and Karen Paton's mother's words flashed into her mind, '… hope you catch the beggers who did this.' Did Jules really commit suicide? Or was he murdered by a third party in order to conceal their involvement in Naomi's murder?

She considered Eva Carradine. Eva refused to be parted from her mobile phone. With no legal powers to take it, Helen had reluctantly left it with her under strict instructions not to switch it on, but its continued presence with Eva sat uncomfortably with her.

Helen's work had exposed her to many devious criminals over the years. From the little she knew of her, Eva didn't display any attributes that marked her as a murder suspect. Her account of Naomi's attack seemed credible, and the phone call explained why Eva ran away and changed her appearance. They also provided a motive. But a motive for who?

She was sure of one thing: Eva's life was in grave danger. But it was Dean's case now. As tempting as it was to step up and show everyone how right she was, she had to pass the new information over to him.

She pulled her phone to her ear and glanced across at McDonalds where Pemberton had gone to get them coffees. Helen tapped her feet with each ring until the phone switched to voicemail. She pushed out an irritated sigh and left an urgent message, then switched to text, snapping out another quick message. Where the hell was the inspector?

***

Pemberton lifted the cup to his lips and stared out of the window. "This sounds like a case of 'threat to life', ma'am," he said, flinching as the hot liquid burnt his tongue.

After retrieving Eva's car they sat in Helen's Honda in McDonalds car park on the northern Hampton border. Whilst her drink cooled, Helen had given Pemberton a summary of Eva's revelations. She sniffed her coffee. "God, that stinks," she said, wrinkling her nose.

He allowed himself a wry smile. "What did you expect?" His face turned pensive as he continued, "Her nearest relatives are away on holiday, you say?" He stared into space not expecting an answer. "She can't go home, since they undoubtedly know where she lives. You've secured her in a secret location. Job done, until tomorrow."

"At least it gives us tonight to figure what to do next." She glanced at her phone. "Damn the inspector… Where is he?"

Pemberton shrugged and scratched his temple uncomfortably. "Sawford was looking for you earlier."

Helen felt her hackles rise. Sawford was like a joint of rotting meat; he became more pungent the longer he lingered. "What did he want?"

"He came up looking for you. And when you weren't there, he asked me about your relationship with Dean, whether it was personal."

"Pardon?"

"I told him that you'd met on a course last year and hadn't seen each other for months."

"Thank you, Sean."

He gave her a knowing stare. "You're welcome. Anyway, he started asking questions about the case."

"Like what?"

"Who found the gun, the jacket… "

"Why didn't he ask his inspector?"

"He couldn't find him."

"He's on the duty stats for today."

"So Sawford told me. Apparently, they had a meeting this morning and he shot off at lunchtime. Some sort of family crisis."

Helen felt a crack expanding in her chest. That explained why she couldn't reach him. Family crisis. Still lives with his wife…

"Fitzpatrick's been gone all afternoon," Pemberton continued.

Helen's annoyance at Sawford pushed thoughts of Dean's family aside. She snorted dismissively. "He only needs to read the policy log."

Pemberton rubbed his chin. "That's the thing. The policy log disappeared with him."

Helen grunted. The policy log was like a diary to senior investigating officers, where they kept a note of every aspect of their investigation, justifying the reasons why they made a decision at any given time. Dean had probably taken it with him on purpose to save Sawford breathing down his neck. Part of her didn't blame him. "He's probably just pissed off at Sawford nosing in."

Pemberton took a gulp of his coffee. "No, it's more than that."

"What do you mean?"

"He asked me who allocated Dean to the case."

"Dean requested it!"

"Exactly. Sawford didn't seem happy."

Helen shrugged. "Maybe Sawford doesn't want his resources used to build coroner's files on solved cases." She sighed. "Not my problem."

The sound of her mobile interrupted their conversation. She answered on the second ring.

"Helen, it's me. I'm tied up with family stuff. I just got your message."

Cursing the ripple his soft intonation stirred in her stomach, Helen gave Pemberton a hard stare as she spoke, "Hello, Dean. Nothing serious, I hope?"

"Don't ask. You know teenagers. What's up?"

"There's been a development in your case."

The line crackled. "What kind of development?"

"We've located Eva Carradine."

The phone went silent. She could sense him thinking, working his options. "Where is she?"

"She's safe now," Helen said. "But she has raised new issues that turn Operation Aspen upside down."

"In what way?"

"There's a lot more to it."

Another hesitation. "It sounds like we need to question her."

"I've already done that."

"Come on, Helen. Don't be difficult. I don't need to remind you the assistant chief constable passed the case to me." He paused. "Just give me the address."

His persistence irritated her. She refused to be pushed aside again. "No need, Dean," she said firmly. "She's safe for tonight. As you said, you're busy. The urgency has gone for now. Get your family sorted. It sounds like they need you. We'll hook up in the office tomorrow and decide what to do next." And with a feeling of discomfort, Helen clicked to end the call.

***

Eva was lying on the bed, half watching the television when she heard the husky cough. She jerked forward. Her eyes shot to the door.

All was quiet. She glanced about the room, her gaze resting on the untouched carrier bag of food on the table in the corner. There it was again. The same grating cough. It came from the corridor.

Eva rose and tiptoed slowly across the room, pressing her hands, fingers splayed, onto the door, leaning her right ear against it. She heard someone fumbling with a door lock, the squeak of an open door…

She exhaled with relief, cursing her shattered nerves. Was this her life now?

She turned and rested her back on the door. Tears blurred her eyes. Eva was angry. Angry with Jules for putting her into this situation, angry with Naomi for dying, angry with whoever it was that was after her, angry with the police for leaving her here, alone.

She squeezed her eyes together. There was something else. She was also riddled with guilt. Maybe she shouldn't have shared the whole story with the detective. Maybe she should have missed out the part where they'd discovered the packages in the door panels. But she was tired. Tired of running.

Memories of driving through the official pillbox of passport control at Calais, snaking the route to the ferry and riding its ramp, crowded her mind. Passing the port staff in fluorescents, she'd half expected dogs to come running, an arm to whip out and pull her over.

Eva recalled the palpable relief when the ferry crossing

drew to an end and she glimpsed the white cliffs of Dover. She didn't dare look at Naomi as they drove off the ferry towards the British customs tunnel. She could see the copper, on the edge of the tunnel, as if he was standing in front of her right now, trussed in enough fluorescent for a dark night on a motorway. But she kept driving, her knuckles white on the steering wheel.

She remembered red brake lights flashing up in front of her, slowing to a crawl and seeing the customs officers in bright jackets, their beady eyes watching the vehicles in their path.

Eva had read somewhere that, unless they saw something suspicious, customs officers only stopped every twenty-fifth car. The odds were stacked in their favour. Naomi's trembling knee knocked against the door. They crawled along, leaving the officers behind. And then she saw it, just before the end of the tunnel, the arm stretched out.

A rush of adrenalin pumped her veins. This is it. Don't look guilty. She slowed more, tilted her head at the officer, but he shook his head and waved her on. It was the car behind her that he was interested in - the one visibly weighed down with five young men.

They left the tunnel and headed into Dover. Naomi sputtered out sobs, her whole body trembling, but Eva ignored her, pressing on through Dover town. Her fingers still glued to the steering wheel. She had to stay focused, to get as far away from the port as possible. Only then would she feel like they'd made it.

It wasn't until they left the town behind them and rose up into the hills that Eva had pulled over, pushed the door open, hung out her head and retched.

The sound of a door slamming in the car park outside brought Eva back to the present. Her thoughts turned to her mother. What would she think? Her daughter - the little girl she'd raised single-handedly in the early years after her first husband left her, when Eva was just a baby. They'd neither seen, nor heard from him since. The little girl she picked up when she had fallen, cleaned her grazed knees, sent to the best schools, worked extra hours to pay for driving lessons. Even when she left university her mother and stepfather supported her decision - after doing their best to talk her out of it. They just wanted her to find the right path, to be happy. An image of the newspaper stand in Glasgow flashed into her mind. She could imagine the headlines, her parents' disappointed faces. Eva shuddered.

And what good would it do? Naomi and Jules were dead. Neither could support nor deny her story. And worse still, she could face a charge or even prison. The thought made the dull ache in her head sear. Years ago she read a book called *Inside Out* about middle class college student, Rosie Johnston, who was given a custodial sentence in Holloway after being convicted of possession with intent to supply illegal drugs. Her description of the cold cell, the terror of prison inmates, the lack of dignity and freedom had stayed with Eva, terrifying her to this day.

But Eva had liked Detective Chief Inspector Lavery. She had an easy way about her. She came to meet her alone, without an entourage of panda cars or uniformed officers like they did in TV dramas. And somehow, sharing the story, her story, a story that had corroded her insides, slowly poisoning her over the past week had felt like a huge relief.

She slid down the door, into a seated position, teardrops spotting the pale pink carpet. How had she got herself into this? Two weeks ago, she was a normal twenty-three-year-old, down on her luck perhaps, working a job she hated with a bank balance that couldn't meet the rent. But she was safe. Now she was all of the above and her life was at risk. When the detective met her earlier she felt like a fish, stranded in a rockpool when the tide receded. Now she felt like the tide was rushing back in to meet her, but she wasn't sure what it was bringing with it.

Chapter Twenty-Seven

It was almost eight o'clock when Helen arrived home that evening. As she inserted the key, the door opened from the inside to reveal Robert's anxious face. Helen started. "Hi, you," she said. "Everything alright?" It had been many years since her boys had come to meet her at the door.

"Gran's sick," he said, moving aside to let her through.

"Oh dear." Helen crossed the threshold and dropped her briefcase below the coat stand. "How sick?"

"She's gone to bed with a bucket."

Helen pulled her coat off and threw it over an empty hook. "I'd better go check on her."

"I'm supposed to be at Jack's for a sleepover," he said, sheepishly.

"Oh. Where's Auntie Jo?"

"An old friend collected her. Won't be back until late."

"Right." She half recalled her mother mentioning something.

"Can you take me to Jack's?"

She rummaged through the pocket in her coat to retrieve her mobile before turning to face her youngest son. "I need to check on Gran."

Helen heard him huff as he slunk off into the lounge, and sighed. He was probably still smarting from their argument the night before. A heavily hormonal teenager was the last thing she needed at the moment.

She crossed to the kitchen and through a door into a small utility room. A pair of black shoes sat neatly beside the door. The stairs opposite led to Jane Lavery's adjoining flat.

Helen took the stairs two at a time. At the top they opened into her mother's front room. Black and white photos of the boys adorned the pale pink walls. The surface of the sideboard in the corner was barely visible through a collection of other framed photos, including a large one at the back of Helen in mortar board and gown. The pink and grey chintzy curtains behind the television were open, the grey two-seater sofa untouched and a vase of tired-looking yellow roses sat on the coffee table. Two white panelled doors led off the lounge - one led to the bathroom, the other the bedroom. The bedroom door was ajar.

"Mum?" Helen halted. No response. The air in the room was calm.

As Helen approached the bedroom she saw the curtains were only half drawn, allowing the soft evening moonlight to penetrate the room. Helen's mother lay on the near side of the bed, eyes closed, hands tucked beneath her chin. She looked peaceful. Helen drew nearer, bent down. Finally, she witnessed the gentle rise and fall of her chest and breathed an instant short sigh of relief.

Her mother had always been a strong and capable woman. It was easy to forget that she was a pensioner rapidly approaching seventy. Only at times like this, when her hair that was usually secured in a neat bun, lay straggled over her shoulders, her face was gaunt and ghostlike and the veins in her hands seemed to protrude more than usual, did Helen remember just how vulnerable she was. And how old…

Helen squatted beside the empty bucket at the side of the bed and stroked her mother's hair gently. Jane Lavery's eyelids flickered, then opened. She managed a weak smile, but didn't move.

"How are you feeling?" Helen asked.

"A bit better." She blinked wearily. "I think I just need to rest."

"Can I get you anything?"

Her mother shook her head once and blinked again.

"Okay, call me if you need anything." Helen pointed to Jane's mobile on her bedside table. "I'll just be downstairs."

Helen was almost at the door when she heard her mother's raspy words, "Robert has a sleepover."

She turned back. "He'll live."

Jane Lavery moved to lift her head. "He'll be disappointed."

It was just like her mother to be more concerned about the social diary of her grandson than her own health. "Mum, relax. Do you think you'll be okay for ten minutes?"

Jane smiled gratefully and followed up with a short nod.

"Then I'll take him. We can't have him being upset, can we?" But the sarcasm was lost on her mother, who'd closed her eyes and sunk back into oblivion.

***

Nate slowed as the lights turned to red. Switching to neutral, he glanced across to the passenger side, stretching out a hand to stroke the leather seat as if it were a hooker's thigh. He had loved Chilli's old BMW X5, but this Mercedes SLK 55 AMG was something else. 0-60 in less than five seconds, a specially designed exhaust making the engine growl, the sleek white, sports finish, the surround sound system… He fisted his hands and banged his knuckles together.

A car horn sounded behind him. The lights had changed. He flared his nostrils, raising his middle finger out of the open window before powering away. The spike of anger was replaced by a crooked smile as he sped up the road, passing the turn on the left that led home. He might as well take the beast for a run tonight.

Nate was buzzing. He'd been watching the doors for a couple of hours this evening before being called to the office. Chilli invited him in and introduced him to a tall, dark-haired detective. But he'd seen the face before. This was no police visit. The man eyed him warily as Chilli called Nate his 'Chief of Security'. Nate had nodded, but remained silent. Chilli waved his black book at the man threateningly. Nate had seen that book before.

"What sort of man would I be if I let this one go?" Chilli said. The man had swallowed, but said nothing. "I want the girl," Chilli added through gritted teeth.

"Can't you spare this one?" the man said, barely managing to keep the desperation out of his voice. It was pathetic.

Chilli gave a hard stare, shook his head vehemently and brandished the book again. "The code doesn't work like that. If I go down, you come with me. Get. Me. The. Girl."

The silence that followed was broken when Chilli calmly asked Nate to take the car home. He would join him later. This was the very first time he had trusted his pride and joy to Nate, alone.

'Chief of Security'... Nate felt a rush. He'd never had a title before. He'd always just been 'Nate' or 'my nephew'. Chilli promoted him, just like that, no discussion. But that was Chilli - a man of few words.

Nate raised the volume and bobbed his head to Eminem's 'Almost Famous'. He could feel the blood coursing through every vein in his body. The time was coming to step up. Chilli had no kids of his own and didn't bother much with the rest of the family. Soon *he* would be attending the meetings. They would be asking *his* opinion. And they would hang on his every word. He puffed out his chest. He was THE MAN...

As Nate approached the edge of Hampton, the roads grew quieter and the stench of cow dung filled his nostrils. Eyes fixed on the road he pressed his foot to the floor, cornering the bends. He felt like the cars in his video games whizzing around the track, trying to make the best time. The faint purr of the engine was still audible beneath the heavy sound of rap.

Even when its lights started flashing, Nate didn't notice the car on his tail. It wasn't until the sirens howled that it caught his attention.

Nate ground his teeth as his eyes flashed across the dashboard. He was over eighty in a fifty zone. They'd take great pleasure in doing him for speeding, a young lad in his uncle's posh car.

His mind raced through his options. Chilli didn't court the attention of cops, in fact he did everything possible to keep them out of his hair. He'd be angry. But there was another reason he couldn't pull over. They'd search him, and the car, and he couldn't allow that to happen.

He floored the accelerator. The purr of the engine became urgent as the cold country air rushed into the car. He glimpsed his rear-view, the police car was battling to keep up. They'd know by now who the car belonged to. He would have to think up something good to get out of this one.

His eyes flicked back to the road just in time to see the bend. His reaction was visceral; he turned the wheel without jerking. It rounded the corner quickly. The back end swerved to take it. Years of gaming paid off. He saw the sign for the next bend and slowed to keep control. Another shot in his rear view. The car behind him was losing speed.

Another bend, sharper than expected. He overcompensated, the rear end fishtailed, but kept on course. He couldn't see the police car. He'd lost them. He was just congratulating himself, when the next bend came out of nowhere, followed by another sharp one. He slammed the brakes. Dust rose as the tyres scraped the asphalt sounding like a flock of screeching gulls, the force so massive they lost contact with the ground. The car tumbled, his body walloped the side. He felt a suffocating sensation. The world swirled around him as he lost all orientation. The vehicle teetered for a few moments, before resting on its side.

He was aware of people moving around, somebody trying to get into the car, a body in the distance. He heard his uncle's voice calling him urgently.

He wanted to respond, to explain, to apologise. The suffocating airbag was starting to deflate. He saw a face at the open window. But it wasn't Chilli. An agonising pain seared vertically through his chest, up into his throat, choking him. He opened his mouth to speak, but coughed words were drowned by spluttering blood. Then darkness descended.

Chapter Twenty-Eight

Back home, Helen checked on the sleeping patient, replenished the glass of water at her bedside and withdrew to the kitchen. A growl from her stomach reminded her she hadn't eaten. Lacking the energy to cook, she opened a tin of baked beans and placed some bread under the grill. As she moved around the kitchen she became aware of the silence around her. Her mother was indisposed, Jo out, Robert on a sleepover and Matthew at camp. For the first time in years, the house adopted a quiet stillness akin to an empty old church. It was disconcerting.

Her mind skimmed over Dean's 'family crisis' as she sat at the table and ate. "You know teenagers," he had said. Although Helen had never met his daughter, Lucy, she knew that she was about the same age as Matthew. And over the past twelve months Matthew had flexed his muscles. Only a few months ago he'd been suspended from school for smoking cannabis, arrived home from a friend's party in a drunken stupor. Yes, she could definitely relate to teenage problems. She wondered if girls were more of a worry than boys. Was that who he'd been arguing with in the cafe the other night? Was it the reason for all those unanswered messages in the pub? But why ignore them? It didn't make sense.

Her phone buzzed twice and she clicked to read the

message. It was from Dean. *Call me.* The very idea that they both thought of each other at the same time made her stomach roll. What if his family crisis wasn't really a teenage daughter problem? What if it was with his wife? She slouched back in her chair. For a brief moment she'd wondered whether the old feelings were returning, whether this time they might have a chance of a future. The reality check made her curse out loud. First he double-crossed her at work. Now this. She had no time for mind games.

She fleetingly thought about calling Eva, then changed her mind. She wasn't expecting contact before the morning and Helen didn't wish to alarm her. Anyway, if there was a problem, Eva would ring.

Pemberton had asked her who had allocated Dean to the case. The comment confused her. During her meeting with Jenkins, when she was removed from the case, he had told her the order had come from above. She thought back to her conversation with Dean. He had told her the assistant chief appointed him. But surely Dean came under regional funding. No wonder Sawford was annoyed. Her assistant chief didn't have jurisdiction to appoint Dean's team to clear up Naomi's case. Was he throwing his weight around to save Hampton's budget? But the victory would be claimed by MOCT. Surely Sawford would be pleased by this? It would certainly add weight to his securing funding for his team for another year.

Something didn't sit right. The fork scraped across the plate as Helen gathered up the last few beans. She glanced at the clock. It was after ten. Against her better judgement, Helen grabbed her phone and worked the keys quickly before she had time to change her mind.

Sawford answered on the third ring, "Helen?"

"My sergeant said you wanted to speak to me about Operation Aspen?"

"Yes. Just a few loose ends. We can meet in the morning."

The very idea that Sawford had already planned to travel down from Nottingham on a Sunday to discuss a solved homicide case rang alarm bells with Helen. "Of course," she said warily. "There's another development I would like to share with you now though."

"Oh?"

"We've traced Eva Carradine."

"You have?"

"Yes." Helen swallowed her pride and shared a brief update of the afternoon's events.

"That is interesting," Sawford said when she was done. "Certainly explains a few discrepancies."

Helen felt her stomach leap. "Discrepancies?" She fought to keep her voice even.

"Yes," Sawford's voice was equally cagey. "Were you on scene when Jules Paton's body was discovered?"

The question threw Helen for a moment. "No. DI Fitzpatrick's team were first on scene. I was searching Eva Carradine's house and thought it imprudent to attend."

"Of course."

The phone went silent. It was only for a split second, yet long enough to allow a seed of doubt to germinate in Helen's mind.

"Interesting… Helen, who took you off the case?" Sawford eventually asked.

His words threw her off balance.

"Jenkins advised me that Dean had offered to do the file for the coroner, as the two cases are linked. Part of the assistance with our gun crime figures."

"Jenkins. Are you sure?"

"I believe the order came from the assistant chief constable. He wanted my team to concentrate on the cold cases."

"I see."

"Pardon?"

Sawford ignored her. "Who was the pathologist on scene for the suicide?"

"Gooding, I believe."

"Have you seen the report?"

Helen's thoughts raced. She couldn't recall anything suspicious. If Jules' death had been murder, there would be signs of this detailed in Gooding's report. "Only briefly. It was passed to DI Fitzpatrick's team."

"Right. I'll have a word with the pathologist in the morning."

"Good idea," she replied.

"Right. Thanks for phoning me, Helen. Let's pick this up in the morning. We'll meet up in your office at, say nine o'clock? It sounds like we need to iron out a few things."

The line went dead. Helen chucked her phone on the table and scratched the back of her neck irritably. The call left her exhausted, yet her curiosity was piqued. Although thoughts of the tenacious Sawford as an ally made her physically cringe, it was heartening that another senior officer was looking at the case through her eyes. But why were his answers so circumspect? Was he going to suggest she took the case back from MOCT? That didn't make sense. Why not keep the case, gain a result? Or was he trying to punt it out, now that it wasn't all it seemed?

The clock on the wall chimed. Ten thirty. Helen raised her eyes to it and rested on the photo underneath of her two boys in a canoe, taken during their holiday in Scotland the previous year. They were laughing. A splash of water hid the scenery behind them. Suddenly the house felt too large and she yearned for the regular background hum of Robert with the TV, Matthew texting on his mobile, her mother sitting reading at the kitchen table.

Helen finished the last drops of tea and rubbed her forehead as a wave of nausea hit her so suddenly, that it took her by surprise. She closed her eyes, laying her head down on the table as a deep sleep quickly engulfed her.

***

Chilli Franks sat as still as a statue, dark eyes fixated in space. The empty house mirrored the hole in his hollow soul.

A car door slammed in the street beyond. Through the slice of light bestowed by the street lamp outside he could see the stained patch of carpet Nate had cleaned earlier. He swallowed the lump in his throat and clamped his teeth together to fight the tears brimming in his eyes.

Nate's face filled his mind. The young boy that had been so delighted to get his own room, so grateful of his uncle's basic care. Many an evening he had listened to him playing on his Xbox; they'd shared Indian takeaways, worked at the club together. A simple soul. One that had become close to his own. One that he could trust. The only one he could trust. All that he held precious, gone in the course of one evening.

His chest heated, sending a fireball rushing through his veins. Chilli stood. He flexed his fists then grabbed an empty mug and, with all his might, threw it against the far wall. He didn't stop to watch the smash. He kicked the coffee table repeatedly until it upturned and one of the legs broke off. He ran his hand along the mantle. Ashtrays, empty beer bottles, used coffee mugs all crashed to the floor.

Chilli didn't feel the cut on his wrist. Blood dripped to the floor. Sweat coursed down his back as he kicked and punched, casting aside everything in his way. Photographs scattered across the floor as the sideboard fell forward.

The sight of a single photo halted him. He swayed, clutched the side of the sideboard, panting. His eyes fell on Nate in the boxing ring, pressing his gloved hands together, a rare smile on his face. At that moment the fireball burst into Chilli's lungs. He held his head back, took a deep breath and let out a bloodcurdling roar.

Chapter Twenty-Nine

Helen sensed a light touch on her shoulder. A pain shot through her neck as she jerked round to see the face of her mother.

"Oh, it's you."

Jane Lavery smiled pleasantly. She had secured her grey hair in a knot at the nape of her neck and wore a white dressing gown with grey mule slippers, but her face was still pale and drawn.

Helen's eyes moved around the room. She'd fallen asleep at the kitchen table. Dried bean juice marked the empty plate next to her. The morning light seeped in through the French doors. "What time is it?" she asked as she massaged her neck.

"Almost seven. Have you been here all night?"

Helen nodded. "You feeling better?"

"A little," she replied. "Just wish somebody would tell my stomach."

"Still sore?"

Jane Lavery nodded.

"Fancy a coffee?"

"No, thank you. Can't quite face it yet. Think I'll just take some paracetamol." Helen watched her mother cross to the corner cupboard in the kitchen and retrieve a box of tablets from the shelf.

"I didn't hear Jo come in," Helen said, puzzled.

"Oh no, dear. Sorry, forgot to say that she phoned and was sleeping at her friends. They were hitting the town, apparently."

Helen raised her eyebrows. "Poor Hampton."

Jane Lavery smiled. "Can you manage Robert this morning? I think I might go back to bed. Give this stuff time to work its magic."

Helen's eyes felt dry and heavy. "Sure. Jack's parents are taking them both to football. I'll drop out from work and bring Robert back here afterwards. Can I get you anything else?"

Jane Lavery clutched her stomach. "No, thank you. I'm not feeling so good again."

Helen watched her mother retreat to her flat and rolled her shoulders. She wasn't looking forward to this morning's meeting one bit.

***

Eva replaced the handset and edged out of bed. At the window, she lowered her eyes to the car park where a man in casual slacks and sweater was wheeling a suitcase across the tarmac. He stopped beside a black Toyota. The boot lifted automatically. She watched him lower the case into the boot, close it and pull a phone out of his pocket.

Eva had just spoken with Detective Chief Inspector Lavery, who'd asked her whether she'd had a comfortable night. She'd spent the night listening to the wind whispering in the nearby trees, watching shadows of car headlights passing on the road outside spin around the room and jumping at every distant sound. But she didn't share this with the detective.

Helen had gone on to explain that room service had been ordered and she was asked to check outside the door to see if it was there, while the call was still connected. Eva looked across at the food on the table: a bowl of cornflakes, a jug of milk, a covered plate that she suspected contained a cooked breakfast, something wrapped in a serviette next to a tiny selection of jam pots and a sachet of butter, alongside a teapot, cup and saucer. She didn't feel like touching any of it, although she knew she had to eat something.

The detective hadn't sounded concerned. She told Eva to stay in the room, that they were having a meeting this morning and she would ring her again before lunchtime. She assured her of her safety. But Eva didn't feel very safe.

The man in the car park lifted the phone to his ear and spoke into it. He leant against the side of his car, his free arm raised as he ran his fingers through waves of dark hair. Watching him from behind the curtain, she suddenly felt as though she was peering into another world. A world where she no longer played a part.

At this moment Eva felt like a spectator, watching the lives of others, while her own life was placed on hold.

***

Helen arrived at work just after eight thirty. As she entered the car park somebody pricked the rainclouds that had been hovering in the sky and they burst their contents over Hampton. Helen pulled her coat up over her head, battling to carry her briefcase and bag, as she exited the car and ran to the entrance.

Pemberton was standing just inside the door as she passed through, depositing a pack of Embassy cigarettes back into his pocket. "Morning Sean," she said. "Everything alright?"

He looked solemn. "Sawford phoned a couple of minutes ago. He's stuck in traffic."

"Do we know how long he's going to be?"

"No idea. A lorry crossed the central reservation on the

M1." A loud drumming noise caused him to hesitate and gaze out into the car park. The rain was coming down hard now. "Could be a while."

"What about Inspector Fitzpatrick?"

"No sign yet."

"Great!" Frustration chipped her tone.

"Big news from last night is that Chilli Franks' nephew was killed in a police chase," Pemberton said, changing the subject as they walked together towards the stairs.

Helen paused and whipped around to face him. "Nate?"

Pemberton nodded.

A picture of Nate entered her head: the dirty blond number two hair cut, the acne riddled face, the dark eyes that always looked frighteningly intense. He couldn't have been much more than eighteen. For the first time in her life she felt a marginal amount of pity for Chilli Franks.

***

Helen was pleased to see the rain had cleared as she turned into the small car park beside Weston Park school. It was packed as friends, parents and supporters had turned out to watch the football game. She parked on the grass at the far end, desperately hoping the ground wasn't too waterlogged. She didn't relish the prospect of being hauled out of the mud. As she left the car and headed towards the pitch she noticed how quiet it was. She checked her watch. Just after ten. The boys should have just started the second half. Normally there would be calls from the pitch, cheers from the crowd, words of encouragement from coaches, the shrill sound of the referee's whistle.

She trudged around the back of the building to the field. It was empty. That explains the lack of noise, she thought. Usually the game didn't finish until ten thirty. She was just wondering if she had the wrong location when she entered the clubhouse at the far end of the pitch and was met with the muddy, sweaty aroma of a football team.

Helen glanced up at the notice board. Pictures of lads beamed back at her: a formal shot of them all in smart club kit, the coach at their side, then numerous other photos of the team on events, in training, partying, paintballing. The boys varied in age from around ten to fifteen. Robert loved football, playing in Hampton's junior league every Sunday morning during season. Suddenly, she was struck by the difference between her boys. Matthew showed no interest in rugby or football, preferring athletics, water sports and climbing whereas for Robert it had always been football. He'd pushed a ball around the lounge before he could walk.

Helen felt a pang in her heart. Her boys were growing up fast. It seemed like only a few years ago that she was persuading them to take a shower, change their underwear and clean their teeth. Now they both spent hours in the bathroom. Razors sat next to toothbrushes in the holder, a couple of bottles of hair gel and aftershave were added to the shower gel, shampoo and conditioner on the shelf.

A distant noise made her turn towards the windowed doors where she could see a group of boys marching towards the clubhouse. She felt a mild nudge on her arm and turned to see Jack, Robert's friend, beaming at her.

"Hello Mrs Lavery."

She smiled back at him. "Helen," she corrected.

He gave her a cheeky smile. Jack was a stocky lad, with clumps of brown hair that stuck out in all directions and ruddy cheeks. "You missed a great game."

"I was hoping to catch the end."

"Oh, we started at eight today. Special fixture. Did you not get the email?"

Helen formed her lips into a smile. "Must have missed

that. What a shame."

"We won the Stars Cup!" He beamed at her, exposing a wide gap between his front teeth.

"Well, I guess congratulations are in order then. Well done!"

"Three - two. Robert scored the winning goal."

"That's great!" Helen became distracted by a group of boys exiting the changing room with bags slung over their shoulders, chatting noisily. She looked back at Jack. "Where is Robert?" she asked.

"He got a lift back with your friend. Dave, Den... No, Dean, that's it, isn't it? The tall guy. Jack placed his hand above his head to indicate height. "Good of him to come and watch the second half. He cheered all the way through."

"Dean was here?" Helen felt a rush of blood to her head.

"Yeah. Anyway, coach took us all for a milkshake to celebrate and Robert got a lift back with him."

Jack turned towards the door. "There's my dad. Gotta go. See you soon, Mrs Lavery and tell Robert I'll text him!" His final words were muffled as he disappeared into the changing room. She became aware that Jack's dad was standing next to her and turned, politely thanking him for Robert's sleepover last night, before turning out into the air.

As she made her way to the car, confusion consumed Helen. What was Dean doing here?

She was just sliding into the driver's seat when a torch shone inside her head, reminding her of their conversation on Wednesday evening. He'd expressed an interest in going to the match. But she'd been against it. Anger flared inside her. Reaching out to her through Robert was a very low ball. A very low ball indeed.

***

Helen rested her head on the steering wheel. That certainly explained Dean's absence from the station this morning. But where was he now? And more to the point, where was Robert? She tried their mobiles. Both switched to voicemail and she left urgent messages to call her immediately.

As she raised her head she noticed that the rain had started falling again, soft droplets dancing on the windscreen, blurring her vision. She called Pemberton who confirmed that Dean hadn't returned to the station. Then, chewing the side of her lip, she called home.

"Hello?"

The sound of Jo's voice threw her off balance and she paused momentarily. "Oh, hi. I wasn't expecting to get you. Thought you'd still be recovering from your night out."

"Didn't drink."

Helen didn't miss the pithiness in her tone. "Oh."

"I'm with child, remember?"

"I didn't mean that. It's just that you didn't come home last night."

"Couldn't get a lift until this morning."

Helen was starting to feel frustrated. The last thing she needed right now was an argument with a grown adult over their social life. "Is Robert with you?"

"I haven't seen him. I thought you were picking him up?"

Ignoring the question, Helen ploughed on, "Is my mum up?"

"She came down briefly for some water. Still looks like a ghost… " The line crackled. "Helen, what's up? You don't sound yourself."

"Nothing. Really. Just Robert's not here. Must have met a friend, forgotten I was picking him up."

"Is he okay?"

"Yes, I'm sure he is. Do me a favour though, will you?"

"Sure."

"Call me if he gets back before I see him."

Helen rang off. Where are they? Her brain offered a practical explanation. They were at Hayes cafe, Robert tucking into a chocolate ice cream sundae, reliving the final winning goal of the match. But why the mystery? She didn't like this. She didn't like this at all.

Chapter **Thirty**

Helen drove up and down the streets of Hampton's town centre, desperately searching for Robert's red hoody, the navy sports bag slung over his shoulder. Finally she reached the high street and parked outside Hayes cafe. She jumped out of the car and ran to the entrance, but even before she was through the door, her hopes had trickled down the nearest drain. Through the glass fronted coffee house she could see perfectly well that neither Robert nor Dean were there.

Unrelenting, she pushed open the door and rushed up to the bar. Apart from a young couple huddled together on one of the sofas by the window, the place was empty. The waitress looked up and gave her a familiar smile as she approached. "Latte?"

"No, sorry. You haven't had my son in this morning, have you? A young lad, thirteen, may be in a sports kit." Her words were running together, mingling with her quick breaths.

"No." The waitress looked alarmed, shaking her head. "We've been dead all morning. Is everything okay?"

Helen raised a hand. "My son. I think he's gone off with a friend." She reached into her pocket and pulled out her card. "Please give me a call if you do see him?"

As soon as Helen was out of the door she whirled around. Where to next? Dean's bed and breakfast flashed into her mind. She headed down the road in a half run, flinging herself around the corner. The hotel sign was still lit up, even though it was now mid-morning. Helen rushed through the entrance. A rich, musty smell welcomed her into the hallway she'd seen two days earlier. She grabbed the small gold bell and rang it hard.

It took several minutes and two more rings before she heard footsteps and saw feet emerging from the stairs. As the body came into view, Helen witnessed a dumpy woman in her early fifties with hair thinning at the front. She had on a loose navy skirt and a cream jumper that was bobbled across the chest.

"What's going on?" The woman's voice croaked as she spoke. A strong smell of nicotine followed her.

Helen flashed her identity card. "I need to see Mr Fitzpatrick," she said.

"I was just doing the rooms on the top floor," the woman answered. "I haven't seen Mr Fitzpatrick this morning. He didn't come down for breakfast."

"And you are?"

"Vera Little, proprietor."

"May I take a look in his room?"

The woman looked surprised momentarily, but didn't argue. She pulled a book off the table beside her. "Now which room is he in… "

Helen ignored her, and headed upstairs to room four. She tried the handle, but it was locked. She started banging her fist on the door as Vera's heavy footsteps grew louder, followed by short, raspy breaths.

"Hey! Wait a minute," she said, as she unlocked the door.

It opened to reveal a room veiled in darkness. Helen blinked, allowing her vision to adjust. The curtains were closed and it smelt dirty, as if the bedclothes needed a good wash. It had seemed larger to Helen on her last visit, more spacious, tidy, glamorous. Or maybe that was the drink talking.

The empty room injected a sick feeling into the pit of her

stomach. Helen turned, pausing briefly to lock eyes with Vera and press a business card into her hand, before she ran down the stairs.

Outside the guest house, Helen's mind reeled. Where else? She dug into the depths of her memory. A Chinese restaurant in Roxten pounced into her mind. They were open all day Sunday with a buffet. Dean frequented it regularly when he stayed in Hampton. He'd suggested taking her there for a late breakfast once, but the thought of eating Chinese in the morning had made her stomach turn. But Robert wasn't so discerning. And he loved Chinese.

She raced back to her car and headed out of the city centre. In less than ten minutes she was turning into the small car park at the front of the bank of shops, of which the Chinese restaurant, 'Wok Up', was on the end. She parked hastily and jumped out of the car. The windows of the restaurant were steamed up, obscuring her view, but she could see that there were several bodies milling around inside.

Two middle aged men, plates loaded with food, turned from the buffet bar as she burst through the door. The rush of thick heat beat her cheeks. She scanned the tables. One at the far end was surrounded by a group of dishevelled teenagers who looked like they hadn't slept since the day before. A man sat alone at a small table beside the window. Two waitresses stood behind the counter and watched as a waiter approached her. But she didn't stop to speak to him, merely turned and left the shop.

The sick feeling in her stomach started to churn her insides. She put her hand up against the brick wall to steady herself. Where were they and why hadn't they answered her messages?

At that moment, Helen saw a hint of colour disappear around the side of the building. It looked familiar. She followed it. Nothing. She walked around to the back of the restaurant, past a bank of dustbins overflowing with cartons, paper and food scraps. A clicking noise caught her attention. She whizzed around. Another movement. Again Helen followed it, back onto the side street, past a block of two storey flats. It led to a dead end, a pedestrian alley the only outlet into the rest of the estate. She continued down the alley, into another street lined with houses on either side. There it was again in the distance, just for a split second before it turned off. She tried to call out, but her lungs sucked the last breaths from her mouth.

Helen ran down the road, her feet pounding the pavement, and turned at the next corner, unsure of where she was heading. She passed a teenager dressed in a black hoody and jeans, texting on his phone. He looked up briefly, but didn't meet her gaze. Helen headed through another alley and whizzed around. She was in the heart of the rabbit warren now. She didn't recognise her surroundings. The streets were bare. She reached into her pocket for her mobile. It was missing. It must have fallen out. She was desperately trying to recall when she last used it when she saw something out of the corner of her vision. He was on his mobile. She sped towards him. Almost as she reached him, he disappeared around a corner and up the side of a house.

She turned the corner. Helen heard a thump and felt a simultaneous sharp pain penetrate her skull just as the world turned black.

***

Pemberton was starting to feel edgy. He checked his watch again. It was now after one. Sawford had reached the station before twelve and called several times enquiring after Helen. He wanted to meet urgently. But where was the DCI? She said she'd be back by eleven.

She wasn't answering her mobile. He'd left several

messages. Dean hadn't shown up either. The word around the station was that he was sorting out family problems, but nobody could reach him. Had they met up? But surely she would ring. It was out of character for her not to be available on the end of her phone.

He made his way out towards the car park and was just pulling the external door open when he heard Sawford's monotone voice, "Sean, any news on the DCI?"

Pemberton cringed inwardly and stood for a split second to regain his composure before turning to face him. "Not yet. She'll be back soon."

"So you said, an hour ago." Sawford stared up at him, a file tucked beneath his arm.

"She's obviously been delayed."

Pemberton had seen that look before, the scrutinizing look that examines your face and body language searching for the truth. He'd used it himself on many an occasion. But he remained silent, refusing to be drawn.

"Problem is, sergeant, this won't wait. And, as she's not answering her phone, we'll have to start without her."

Sawford turned on his feet and Pemberton reluctantly followed him into a meeting room. Sawford placed the file he'd been hugging on the small round table in the middle, sat back in his chair and folded his hands together.

Pemberton sat opposite him.

"I'd like to hear more about the DCI's relationship with Dean Fitzpatrick," Sawford said.

"I told you yesterday… "

"I heard what you said, yesterday," Sawford cut in. "But I want to know the truth. Are they involved?"

Pemberton stared at him in disbelief, careful not to narrow his eyes or react in any way. When he spoke, his voice was impassive. "In truth, I've no idea. They are old friends. That's all I know."

"Oh, come on, Sean. You work very closely with the DCI. She must talk about her home life, partners?"

Pemberton eyed him warily. "Not really. Occasionally she mentions her kids, her mother, but generally she's quite private about her personal life."

"It's a coincidence that they have disappeared together, don't you think? And my sources have been watching them. They've worked on this case together, tied up all the evidence."

Pemberton stared at him, trying to work out exactly what he was implying. "Helen didn't believe the case was solved," he responded. "She thought there was more to it, worked hard to keep it. She pressed Jenkins because she didn't feel the evidence tied up."

"Did she? Are you sure? Or did she just say that to keep herself in the clear?"

Pemberton's head was spinning. He'd worked closely with the DCI. She was passionate about making a difference, just like her father.

Sawford leaned forward, leafing through the folder. "I've spoken to Gooding," he continued. "There was further bruising on Paton's neck, inconsistent with the ligature we found. It's possible he may have been killed first, and hung later to make it look like suicide."

"That's practically what Helen thought, yet there was nothing in his report."

"No, because he was told to ignore it. He was told that the evidence against Paton was compelling and there was no need to pry further."

"By who?"

"DCI Lavery. He still has the email in his inbox."

"That doesn't make sense. What about Eva Carradine? Helen worked hard to locate her, put her in a safe location."

"To draw her in." Sawford said, leaning forward. "Don't you see? She's bait. Eva is the smear on this case and without her it'll get tied up nicely, the hype will die down." A short silence ensued.

Pemberton tried to recall the events Helen had relayed from Eva. They were sketchy at best. But then, this wasn't her case to investigate. And why would she call him if she was luring Eva into some kind of trap. A trap for whom? He tried to question Sawford on the wider picture, the motive, but Sawford wouldn't reveal anymore. Pemberton chewed the inside of his mouth. The email he couldn't explain…

"I'm sorry, I know you've worked closely with the DCI, but I think you've been used."

For the first time in all his service Pemberton was starting to question his own judgement. His gut instinct refused to believe the allegations against the DCI. Yet a relationship between Helen and Dean muddied the waters. And the last call he'd received from her, was her looking for Dean. When she was supposed to be there.

"I think you'd better take it from the top, sergeant," Sawford said sharply. "And don't leave anything out."

Chapter **Thirty-One**

Helen stared at the mildew creeping up the walls around her and shivered. She shifted position on the concrete floor, curling her nose at the smell around her. Her left shoe was missing and there were grazes on her knees and ankles where they'd brushed the rough walls as she'd been carried here.

As her eyes grew accustomed to the semi-darkness, Helen followed the path of damp up the wall, resting on a small rectangular window at the top that had been painted black. The tiniest glint of daylight slid in through a gap at the side where the frame had corroded; the only light in this dank, empty cellar.

It was still daylight outside. She had no idea what time it was. Helen cast her mind back. It must have been around eleven when she had seen Dean and blacked out. She raised a hand and rubbed a lump on the back of her head that felt like a camel's hump.

Did Dean do that? Why? Thoughts of his elusiveness over the past twenty-four hours snuck into her head. The phone calls, unanswered messages over the last few days. But then... He had family problems.

Flashbacks shot into her mind: Dean's face in his office on the afternoon Paton's body was discovered, his anger at The Angel Tavern.

Her hands turned clammy. Dean, a bent cop? No way. She would have known.

She wrenched the ideas from her mind, failing to comprehend the incomprehensible just as George Sawford's presence slid into her brain. Formerly with PPSU. Formerly, or still? Him asking how she found Dean.

The urgency in Dean's voice when she told him she'd located Eva Carradine sliced through her thoughts.

She raised a hand to her forehead. Dean's problems weren't his teenage daughter, weren't his wife. He was involved with the very group Eva was running from

And Dean was the last person to be seen with Robert.

Her throat constricted. Helen clutched her knees into her chest. She racked her brains. She'd left work to collect Robert, phoned home when he wasn't there. Work would be expecting her back. Her mother would be expecting Robert. Surely somebody would come looking? But looking where? Where was she? Her mobile had disappeared. For a split second she hoped that it was left on - the police could locate her through it. Then her heart sunk. She remembered leaving the guest house, searching her pockets. It was missing. It could be in the guest house, in the coffee house, a gutter, anywhere.

Helen closed her eyes, concentrated her senses. All she could smell and taste was damp soil. She heard no traffic, just the soft movement of footfalls on the boards above. No possible clues to her location.

Helen adjusted position and winced as the graze on her ankle caught the floor. Nobody knew she was here. Nobody suspected something was wrong. Nobody was coming to save her.

***

Eva was starting to feel deserted. It was after two and the DCI still hadn't called. She'd spent the past half an hour pacing the room, but working her options only made her feel like a dog chasing its tail.

In desperation she picked up her mobile. She knew she shouldn't, it went against all the advice the DCI had given her. But nobody was playing by the rules now, and she needed to know where she stood.

The phone fired up, the screen lit. Her heart jumped as she saw a message, number unknown. She clicked on it and gulped. *We've got the detective and her son. Contact us now, or they die. Then we'll come for you.*

***

Pemberton reached Helen's silver Honda by mid afternoon. He'd pulled some strings and had her mobile located, drawing him here. He didn't know what to believe when it came to Helen's behaviour, but until he spoke to her, face to face, he wasn't going to give up just yet.

Helen had been under a lot of pressure. He figured she'd taken herself off somewhere to think. Maybe she'd taken Robert with her? Nobody had raised an alarm for either of them, as yet, so Pemberton decided to search for her himself initially. Jenkins wouldn't have wanted the instant response team involved. It could cause an embarrassing situation, especially if the press got hold of it. But Pemberton wasn't concerned about any potential embarrassment. Right now his thoughts were consumed with his colleague and friend. Right now all he could think about was saving Helen.

He scouted around the outside, carefully checking for scratches and dents, a sign of a collision. When he found none, he tried the door. Surprised to find it unlocked, he moved inside. Helen kept a fairly clean car, no crisp wrappers on the floor, barely any dust to speak of. With no evidence of an altercation, Pemberton was confounded. He now knew that she had been gone for a minimum of four hours. Why would she rush off and leave the car unlocked? Where was she now?

Pemberton sat back in the driver's seat and thought hard. Rather than phone Helen's home and alarm her mother, he'd driven by her house earlier and checked for her car. It wasn't there. He knew she'd left work to collect Robert. Had they argued? Pemberton was aware of problems with Helen's eldest son, Matthew, taking drugs last year... Nothing with Robert. This wasn't surprising though given that she didn't share a great deal of her personal life with her colleagues.

He considered Robert. He had met him briefly a few months back in town with his mother. Pemberton guessed he was about eleven or twelve, but then he wasn't very good at ages, his two girls now all grown up had left home and had families of their own. He recalled the photo of Robert in a football kit on Helen's desk. Maybe he had got tied up with his mates and lost track of time?

Perhaps she drove to Roxten, thought she saw Robert, parked swiftly in the first available space and rushed after him? But why didn't she return? And where was she now? Her family hadn't reported them missing which led him to assume that they believed nothing was untoward. Had she dropped Robert and gone to meet Dean?

A tingling in his back made him sit forward. He turned and glimpsed her mobile phone. A feeling of dread clawed at him. Helen was now missing without means to contact anyone.

A trace of déjà vu wafted over him. As a rookie in the police, his sergeant had disappeared in a police car on night shift. An arduous search ensued. The location of the car was eventually discovered by a farmer on a rural byway on the outskirts of Hampton. The gate to the byway had been left open and the cows that occupied the field beside were roaming the nearby roads. Pemberton was first on the scene.

Initially, he thought his colleague was asleep in the car. Then he spotted the hose taped to the exhaust pipe leading into a small gap in his side window, sealed around the edges with duct tape.

Pemberton cast his mind back. Sergeant Backley was his name, or 'Backers' at the station. An investigation revealed that earlier the same day he discovered his wife was having an affair. A revelation not mentioned when he came to work that evening and briefed his team as normal, before taking the car to meet his fate. Pemberton drew a breath. Whatever troubles Helen faced, he wasn't about to let history repeat itself.

He grabbed the phone and stroked the screen. The voice on the other end of the line cracked with panic. "Helen?"

"No. This is… "

The line cut off. Pemberton hastily accessed the call register for the last call. It wasn't recognised. The number looked oddly familiar, although he couldn't think why. He tried to call back. There was a short delay before the phone rang out. One, two, three, four… then dead again.

Pemberton pinched the top of his nose with his thumb and forefinger. He desperately needed to find out who was on this call. He searched Helen's contacts from bottom to top - a habit adopted by an old colleague who discovered that many criminals stored close associations at the end of their call register, convinced that people wouldn't be bothered to search that far. School, Robert, Pemberton, Mum, Matthew… There were other names he didn't recognise. He drew the screen down further. Nothing.

Pemberton reached for his own phone out of his pocket and punched in the numbers carefully. He needed to get this right.

Chapter Thirty-Two

"Well, well, well if it's not James Lavery's daughter. Didn't we strike gold?" The hiss in Chilli Franks' voice reminded Helen of a snake.

Chilli Franks stood in front of her. The man who'd held a grudge against the Lavery family since her father worked so voraciously to put him away, over twenty years earlier.

In normal circumstances, a man of Chilli's experience and intelligence would realise that kidnapping a cop meant instant ruin. Helen's colleagues would pull out all the stops. But one glance at Chilli Franks – his unnaturally wide eyes, his glassy gaze, his dark expression – told her he wasn't acting rationally as he stood there clutching a small handgun in one hand, a bottle of Budweiser in the other.

Chilli didn't blink, "I believe you have something I want."

"I don't know what you mean."

"Like father, like daughter," he hissed.

Helen said nothing.

"I'm waiting." He cast a wide glance around the bleak cellar walls.

She wetted her lips. "You'll have to help me out here, Stephen. I really don't know."

The use of his real name pulled his glare back to her. He flicked the safety catch off the side of his gun.

Helen battled to hold her reserve. If it was Eva he was after, he wouldn't kill her. Not before he reached his prize.

"Where's my son?" she asked defiantly.

"He's quite safe. For the moment."

Her worst fears were confirmed. Dean hadn't only betrayed her. He'd betrayed her entire family. She recoiled, crushing a whimper. "What have you done with him?"

"He'll be fine, as long as you help us."

Her mind reeled. "I don't know what you mean."

Suddenly, tears of anger swelled his eyes. "Believe me, you don't want to play games. Not right now."

Helen felt her throat constrict.

"Where is she?" He spat the words out, a line of spittle sticking to the side of his cheek.

"I don't know what… "

The crash of the bottle hitting the floor cut her words, making her jump back. A small pool of liquid merged with the splinters of glass scattered over the concrete floor, glinting under the naked bulb.

"I'll ask you again… Where is Eva Carradine?"

Giving up Eva went against every principle, every ounce of integrity that clung to Helen's fragile soul. Yet he'd been clever. He'd taken her son too. Robert, barely a teenager. With his bony body, he'd always been small for his age. She couldn't lose him. He hadn't had a chance to grow, flourish, show the world what he was really made of. She wouldn't.

"Let me see Robert," she said.

Chilli paused. For a moment his face adopted a strange softness as if he recalled a distant memory. But just when she thought she'd penetrated his thick skin, his eyes glazed over. And when they turned back to her they were harder and blacker than before.

"Why should I?"

"He's just a boy."

"Like Nate. Your lot didn't think of that when they killed him."

"He crashed his car," she said. "It was an accident."

"Yeah? Like it was an accident when your dad hunted me down all those years ago? When he worked around the clock to pull my life from beneath me?"

"You maimed somebody."

Chilli sneered. "I've seen that look in your eye. So self-righteous. In reality, you're no different from me. We both teach people lessons. We just go about it differently. But taking my boy…" He shook his head. "You've gone too far this time."

Chilli's threats against her family all those years earlier crashed into her mind. 'Shallow thoughts of a condemned man,' her father had called them. But they hadn't been shallow. They had grown and festered like a cancer in Chilli's mind. Until now.

"Let Robert go, please, it has nothing to do with him."

"He's a Lavery, isn't he? It has everything to do with him."

"I'm sure we can sort this out, you and I."

"Spare me your police bullshit."

"I'm serious. Let me make some calls."

The shrill cackle of his laughter was evil itself. When he finally spoke, his voice was barbed. "We can sort this out." His face hardened. "Give me the address."

Helen could feel the battle slipping away. "Let go of Robert and I'll tell you," she said, biting back her conscience.

"The boy stays. And if you don't tell me, I'll kill him now."

Thoughts raced through her mind. She needed to find a way to save Robert. "She's at Cross Keys police station waiting to be interviewed." The words spilled out of her mouth, rushing into one another.

Chilli said nothing. He turned, the metal Blakeys on his heels clicking the bare wood as he climbed the stairs. She heard the door slam, the sound of locks, the flick of a switch. Once again she was immersed in darkness.

Helen swallowed as realisation set into her bones. Dean had sold his soul to the devil. Chilli Franks had no intention of allowing her to leave this room alive.

***

Eva's chest burned as she held her breath. First they tried to contact her using Naomi's mobile phone, then they answered the DCI's. When the phone rang again, Eva jumped and stared at it, as if it was a ticking bomb. An unknown number flashed on the screen. Should she answer it? A wave of nausea hit her. She picked up the phone and clicked it off.

Her head pounded. She rushed to the bathroom, splashed water over her scarlet face. That's when she heard the rustling noise.

***

Pemberton studied his phone. Was that Eva? He was just considering having the call traced when his own mobile rang again. It was Spencer. Back at the station, they were all starting to get edgy. Spencer had been monitoring control room calls for any sign of the DCI when a strange call caught his attention. A woman was searching the industrial estate in Roxten for her missing cat when she'd spotted a female being lifted out of the boot of a car and carried into the empty warehouse beyond. Suspicion raised, she called Hampton Police.

Pemberton sighed loudly. "Control room would have allocated despatch."

"No, you don't understand," Spencer said. "The woman had long dark hair and wore a beige overcoat. The informant crouched behind a car, doesn't think they saw her."

The hairs on the back of Pemberton's neck sprung up. "What's the address?"

"32 Ceaser Place, Roxten."

"Chilli Franks has just bought that property," he said. "Plans to turn it into a gym, I believe." He turned on his heels. "Cancel the despatch. I'm only five minutes away."

Chapter Thirty-Three

Helen blinked as the glaring light suddenly illuminated the room once again. Footsteps clicked against the stairs. She watched as Chilli's faded jeans, black shirt, shoulders then gaunt face appeared at the bottom. The same handgun was in his right hand, a kettle clutched in his left, the loose cord wound around his hand. "That your idea of a joke?" he snarled.

Helen shrank back. She'd had to think fast to come up with a fake location for Eva. It seemed like a logical explanation that she'd be at Cross Keys police station waiting to be interviewed. A location where Chilli would need Helen to negotiate some kind of access. Perhaps in his twisted mental state he might have even thought she could pull some strings and get Eva released. But Helen wasn't really thinking about herself anymore. Her mind was consumed with her youngest son. If Chilli needed Helen, he wouldn't harm Robert, not yet. Her one hope, her only hope, was that she could raise the alarm and he could be saved. But it could only have been minutes since he'd left the cellar. How could he have discovered her lie so quickly? "I don't… "

"Save it!" He crossed to a table at the far side and lifted the kettle onto it, plugging it into the single socket behind. "Looks like you need some persuasion."

Helen's eyes slid across to the kettle. Her heart thumped.

More than anybody, she knew what he was capable of.

Another set of footsteps. Heavier this time. The face that finally appeared answered her question by its very presence: Dean Fitzpatrick.

Dean said nothing, made no gesture. He stood uncomfortably, his head bent forward to avoid the low ceiling, gaze averted. 'I've missed you so much.' Those simple whispered words entered her head, stinging her ears.

Chilli caught her gaze. He looked across at Dean and back to her. "Bet you thought he was one of yours, didn't you?"

Helen bent forward, said nothing. The kettle started to gurgle as the water began to heat.

Chilli drew a deep breath. His eyes didn't leave her. "He's got black blood. Just like us." His face hardened. "Just like Nate."

Chilli's eyes were fixed upon her, as if deep in thought. It was now or never. She pulled a deep breath. "Let Robert go. Keep me if you want, but let him go. Please. He's just a kid."

Chilli darted forward, raised his hand and slapped the side of her head. Helen crashed across the floor. The room blurred for a second. She raised a hand to her face as pain seared through her cheekbone. Defiantly, she flickered her eyes towards Chilli.

"Like Nate." Chilli's expression remained unchanged. The sound of the water heating rose and mingled with the dampness in the room. It felt uncomfortably eerie.

"The right address this time?" he said. The kettle started bubbling merrily.

Helen looked from Chilli to the kettle and back. "Please," she said. "I'll tell you if you let Robert go."

Chilli snorted. "You're lucky he's still alive. If you don't tell me now we'll bring him in here and you can watch me pour the boiling water over his feet. Then we'll move up his body, nice and slowly."

Helen flinched. Steam rose into the air. The kettle switch flicked off. A sharp pain sliced through her like the blade of a knife.

Chilli turned to Dean. "Go get him."

"No!" Helen leant forward.

"Well?"

She reeled off the address of Eva's hotel, praying inwardly that Pemberton would have raised suspicions back at the station over her disappearance and be there with her now.

Chilli's lip curled into a sneer, as if he'd just won a ton of cash in a game of poker. This time he knew she was telling the truth. He raised his pistol.

Helen blanched. For a split second nobody moved.

Finally, Chilli blinked. "Oh, I'm not going to kill you," he said with perfect calmness. He flicked his glance to Dean. "He is." Dean's body flinched slightly but he kept his eyes buried in the floor. And with that, Chilli Franks flashed her one more contemptuous gaze, and disappeared up the stairs.

Helen could taste bile rising in her throat. Dean stood perfectly still. She could just make out beads of sweat collecting on his upper lip. The light bulb flickered. The walls felt like they were closing in on them. And then she saw his gun.

Helen was no marksman. She knew handguns were notoriously inaccurate, but at what range? She thought hard, wondering whether Dean had ever pulled a trigger before.

"What have you done with Robert?" she said.

Dean finally met her gaze. His eyes were unexpectedly soft, almost apologetic. "Don't worry, he's safe. I made sure of it."

"Where?"

"I can't tell you that."

"Can't or won't?" He didn't answer. "Why not? I'm going to die anyway. Can't you at least save my son? He's just a boy, Dean. I trusted you." Again, he didn't answer.

Anger like no other infused Helen's limbs. "Safe? I don't know what you owe Chilli Franks, but kidnapping Robert… " Her voice faltered. The audacity of his words grabbed her and at that moment a ball of maternal rage exploded within her, sparks of anger ricocheting through her torso.

"Where is he?" She flew at Dean, grabbing the wrist of the hand holding the gun, pushing it away with all her might. Every tendon in her body struggled against his overpowering weight. He pushed her back, evenly at first, then brutally as she persisted.

Helen clawed into Dean's face, her free hand slicing through the flesh. She elbowed him in the stomach, the other hand still clasped firmly around the wrist holding the gun.

Hard as she tried, Helen could feel her strength starting to wane. The gun moved towards her. She couldn't stop it, her muscles were weakening. Using every inch of energy in her body, she lifted her knee to his groin.

He folded instantly, butting her forehead as he did so. Her eyes blurred. Pain seared through her brain. Then she heard the crack slice through the air.

***

Eva turned off the tap and froze. All was quiet. She swung round, hands still wet and approached the bathroom door, hardly daring to breathe.

Slowly, tentatively, she peered around the gap. The room was still. She pulled the door open slowly and strained her ears. Nothing. Eva approached the room's main entrance and looked through the peephole, closing one eye to sharpen the other. Wet hands pressed on the door. The corridor looked empty.

She let out a shallow breath. She definitely heard something. And it wasn't followed up by the sound of a door opening and closing - this wasn't a neighbour on the move again. Her fingers moved across the locks, checking each individually.

Standing very still, bare feet sinking into the carpet, Eva collected her thoughts. The DCI said somebody was trying to trace her. Surely the noise didn't come from within the room? Her blood chilled. She turned quickly. How could they get in? And where would they hide?

Her eyes rested on the wardrobe. Taking a deep breath, she stepped forward and slid the door back. A few stray hangers wobbled on the rail. She exhaled sharply. But something didn't feel right.

She recalled how, as a child, she was always scared that a monster would be in her room, wait for her in the shadows, ready to attack when she slept. She remembered even into her teenage years, checking her wardrobe, underneath her bed, every corner and every space, no matter how tiny, to satisfy her mind that it was empty.

And she regressed back now, leaning down to look beneath the bed, poking the long curtains. Finally satisfied she was alone, Eva sat on the edge of the bed, head in hands.

The soft sounds of footsteps on carpet caught her attention. Her ears pricked. There were more. This time she wasn't mistaken.

Eva gripped the end of the bed tight, waiting for the sound of a neighbouring door to close.

The bang that followed shook the whole room like an earthquake.

***

Helen became aware of voices mumbling around her. She felt like she was lying in a warm bath, the heat of the water pressing down on her. Her mind drifted. She was in the park with the boys, although they were much younger, Robert barely a toddler. They were on the seesaw, Matthew bouncing his feet hard as they touched the ground, sending them higher and higher. She opened her mouth to tell them to slow down but her voice was mute. She raised her hand desperately, glancing anxiously from one son to another. They ignored her, chuckling merrily, enjoying the thrill.

The image changed. Helen was sat at her mother's kitchen table in her old house. Her father was there grinning, his eyes shining as they always did when he relayed an anecdote.

Somebody was calling her name in the distance, breaking the image. She strained her ears. Part of her wanted to reach out towards them, yet it felt cold, distant. Helen returned to the warmth of her memories and the voices slowly hushed, as if someone had turned the volume right down.

Chapter Thirty-Four

Pemberton stared across the table at Chilli Franks. "What were you doing at the hotel today?"

Chilli didn't answer. He sat perfectly still.

Pemberton tilted his head. "Why break into the girl's room? What did you want with her?"

Nothing.

It had been several hours since, following Pemberton's alert, Sawford had organised an armed team to evacuate Eva's hotel, removing her and laying in wait for her pursuers. Later, Chilli had arrived with three henchmen, surprisingly unarmed. They weren't expecting Sawford's team.

"I'm guessing it was something pretty important since you took your guys with you. And you created quite a fuss when you met the police, didn't you?" Pemberton snorted. "I heard they had to use the stun gun to calm you down."

Pemberton paused as his colleague's pen scratched the pad beside him. He'd been in the custody suite when Chilli was brought in. Later he'd watched Sawford pace the room, his face pallid, fingers fidgeting on the hands clasped behind his back with every step, as he listened remotely to the dull silence his own detectives faced from their interviewees. He was two officers down and every one of his suspects refused to comment.

As time passed, Pemberton had watched the sea of tired, hollow faces grow around him in the custody area. Attacks on cops were rare, but when they reared their ugly head they pulled every rank and file out of the woodwork. Nobody could rest until they had some answers.

Finally, he'd pleaded with Sawford to let him have a shot at interviewing Chilli. Pemberton and Chilli were old adversaries, after all. Their paths had crossed many a time over the years. If anyone could get through, he believed he could. Although half an hour later in the interview room, he was beginning to wonder.

Pemberton rested his hands on the table between them. He decided to change tack. "What can you tell me about the cops attacked in the cellar of your warehouse?"

A chair squeaked on the floor as David Easton, Chilli's solicitor, shifted in his seat next to him.

"Come on, Chilli. You can't deny you've been there today. I saw you leaving the premises myself."

A faint flicker of alarm rippled across Chilli's face.

"You didn't know I was there, did you?" Pemberton asked. "I parked behind the garages next door."

Easton cleared his throat. "My client acquired that warehouse for conversion," he said. "There's no reason why he shouldn't spend some time there."

Pemberton ignored him. "I've been in that cellar, Chilli. I saw what you did this afternoon. And I also saw the holdall containing used Glocks and Baikal guns, the stash of cocaine in the warehouse. There must be at least half a kilo there. You're not going to deny they're yours too, are you?"

Easton cast his client a sideways glance, but said nothing.

"You forget, Chilli, we've got Eva Carradine," Pemberton continued. "We know about the holiday she took to Milan with Naomi Spence. We know how they smuggled drugs back in the lining of the Mini for Jules Paton. And now Naomi Spence and

Jules Paton are dead, killed by somebody pursuing something missing from that car. We also know Eva was being hunted down by the same people, this time using her dead friend's mobile phone. Tell me - why was that phone found on your person when you were arrested?"

"This is ridiculous." Easton heaved a sigh. "Jules Paton committed suicide."

Pemberton shook his head. He didn't take his eyes off Chilli. "On the contrary, new evidence has come to light that indicates he was murdered."

Easton heaved himself forward. "Is my client a suspect in the murder of Jules Paton?"

Pemberton ignored the solicitor, leant in closer to Chilli. "What was missing from that car? What was so important it meant attacking so many people, including cops?"

Easton shifted uncomfortably in his seat.

Pemberton sighed. "We also know that your boy, Nate, killed them."

A single muscle flexed in Chilli's jawline, but he maintained his steely reserve.

Pemberton eased back. "Oh, he worked hard to make it look like Naomi Spence knew her killer, planned it well. But he left footprints in the snow in her neighbour's garden, footprints that matched the shoes he was wearing when he died. He wore her watch, the engraved Rolex her parents bought her for her eighteenth birthday. Jules Paton's mobile phone was found in his pocket."

Easton put his pen down. "That means nothing."

Pemberton cast him a cursory glance and turned straight back to Chilli. "No, not on its own. But the samples of their hair found on his person does. We also found more hair samples folded amongst the clothes in his bedroom. Who do those belong to, Chilli?"

Wolf-like eyes met his gaze. "How dare you plant evidence

on my dead nephew."

Pemberton felt a pulse of adrenalin. He rushed to keep up the momentum. "Thought you'd got it all tied up, didn't you? But Eva was your scorpion, the sting in her tail holding the capacity to bring down the whole operation. You couldn't let her live, could you? That's why you abducted Chief Inspector Lavery, to find out her location. That's why you broke into Eva's room at the hotel today, isn't it?"

Chilli snorted. Shook his head.

Pemberton sat back in his chair. Nate's young face filled his head. The boy who'd revered his uncle, been nurtured into the same murky world. He shared Chilli's dark eyes, the same eyes that stared back at him now. Pemberton lowered his tone and when he spoke his voice was grave, "Why Chilli? You could have given Nate anything, found him an apprenticeship, kept him away from the club and the criminal underworld. But instead you got him to do your dirty work. You used him."

Chilli bolted forward. His solicitor shot a guarded hand to his arm.

"Careful Chilli," Pemberton said, belligerently. He glanced at the clock. The tension in the room was mounting. Pemberton's frustration grew by the second. "I've been speaking to you now for thirty-five minutes, Chilli," he finally said. "My colleague interviewed you before, for over an hour. You won't talk about DCI Lavery. Why?"

Chilli's stare was accompanied by thick silence.

"Okay, let's talk about Dean Fitzpatrick."

"Get Fitzpatrick in here," Chilli suddenly said.

Pemberton continued to return his stare. He allowed the silence to hang in the air for a moment before he responded, "Not possible." He shook his head, began gathering his papers.

"Get Inspector Fitzpatrick in here now!" Chilli's hand thumped the table in front of him. A biro scattered off the table, hit the floor and rolled in circles.

Pemberton watched it a moment, then stared back at Chilli. “Not possible. Unless you can raise him from the grave?”

A tick formed beneath Chilli’s eye as comprehension spread slowly across his face.

“We know about Dean Fitzpatrick, too. We found your black book in the safe at Black Cats. The book containing coded details of all your debtors. We know he was into you for over £70,000. What was it, gambling debts?”

Chilli shook his head. “I don’t know what you mean.”

“Oh, come on, Chilli. If you’re gonna use codes, you need to be a bit more cryptic. Breaking those was child’s play.”

Chilli’s eye twitched again.

Pemberton stood. “You can’t wield the power in those codes anymore, Chilli. The inspector isn’t here to mask your dirty secrets. And neither is Nate.” He bent forward, squared his hands on the table. “You’re finished.”

The whole station heard the chair crash to the floor as a fireball of temper erupted from Chilli Franks.

Chapter Thirty-Five

Spasms of pain pricked the back of Helen's eyes as they peeped through narrow slits.

Slowly, she scanned the room. It was a small box with bare magnolia walls. Peach curtains covered the window. Her watch lay on the cream cabinet beside her bed. A chair was positioned on the opposite side.

Helen glanced back at the grey cushioned chair where the consultant had sat this morning and explained that she'd suffered concussion as a result of blows to the front and rear of her head. She'd been dizzy on admission yesterday, floating in and out of consciousness. She'd heard someone mention cracked ribs, head injuries, a concern about internal bleeding. A CT scan showed no clots, but ophthalmology tests revealed the retina behind her right eye had become detached with the blow, making her eyes oversensitive to light; an injury that would take four to six weeks to heal.

As soon as she woke, thoughts of Robert spiked her brain. In desperation, she'd rung for the nurse who reassured her that he was home and well and would be visiting later. Helen felt impelled to question further, but the nauseating heaviness in her head forced her to close her eyes and fall back into her slumber.

Whispers in the corridor woke her. Gingerly, she adjusted position. She recognised Pemberton's voice and persuaded the nurses she felt well enough to receive her colleague. She could see him now, sitting at her bedside. Pemberton, the most reserved person she knew, pressing his hand on hers.

"Jenkins was here earlier," Pemberton said. Helen tried to raise her eyebrows, but said nothing. She couldn't imagine Jenkins sitting beside her bed. "Got called back to the station, but sends his best regards. He'll be in tomorrow."

"Well, come on. Fill me in," Helen urged.

Pemberton sat forward and relayed the series of events following her disappearance. He started with the meeting with Sawford where he felt that Helen's integrity was questioned as flaws were pointed out in Operation Aspen. How Sawford implied that the evidence had been manufactured to solve the case and that Dean and Helen were mixed up together in something untoward. When he mentioned the email, allegedly sent by Helen to Gooding, Helen gasped. Only this morning had Pemberton managed to get the station techies to prove her account was compromised and the email was sent by a third party, probably Dean.

He explained how he'd searched for her. How he'd located her through the control room call, arriving just as Chilli Franks and his associates exited the building.

He described the scene when he reached the cellar: Fitzpatrick and Helen lying in a pool of blood. Initially, he thought them both dead. But a trace of pulse in Helen's wrist motivated him to wrench Dean's dead body away. The bullet had pierced Dean's heart, killing him instantly. He'd inadvertently butted Helen on his fall, causing her to lose consciousness. They both lay in a pool of his blood, her body trapped beneath his.

Helen listened silently as he explained the events that followed.

Finally, he said, "Chilli's associates heard the commotion in the interview and started to talk. Apparently, Chilli's been teetering for a couple of years, paranoid that people around him, some within his own organisation considered him past his best and were pushing for his retirement."

"They weren't specific, probably too scared of the legal repercussions, but they didn't need to be," Pemberton said. "What they alluded to just confirmed our suspicions. Black Cats has been a front for organised crime for years – drugs, prostitution, firearms – Chilli was just too clever to let us get close. He kept it well under wraps. They did mention that those boys Leon Stratton and Kieran Harvey that were shot last year were from the 'East Side Boys', runners and suppliers for Chilli's rivals. Their deaths could have been Chilli's idea of a message if this war has been raging for some time. I'm guessing that whatever it was that disappeared from the latest shipment was arranged by the East Side lot too. And Chilli could see them closing in.

"When Nate died, Chilli's world was literally ripped apart at the seams. He raised that lad the only way he knew how: as a torturer and a killer, his perfect ally. Without him, he could trust no-one."

The events played on Helen's mind well after Pemberton had left her to rest. What was missing from the Mini? What motivated Chilli? What caused Nate to plan out these murders so meticulously? She recalled Dean's presentation to them when they arrived in Hampton, "Many of the guns are smuggled in from the Baltics." The girls had travelled to Milan. Surely they wouldn't need to travel that far for a shipment of heroin or cocaine? But Italy bordered the Adriatic Sea, close to the Baltics. The police would no doubt try to trace the car, but it was most likely emptied out, cleaned and sold on. They would probably never know for sure.

She thought about Sawford. She guessed he had received intelligence on Dean, suggesting a link to Chilli. And when Dean became involved on this case, he came down to take a closer look. Maybe he'd been watching him for some time, his move to become his boss engineered in an attempt to bring him closer. Sawford was a pedantic investigator, with political allegiances to forward his own career. But, at this moment, Helen was grateful for his presence, without which none of this may ever have come to light and she may have died in that cellar.

And Dean. Pemberton had told her about the debtor's book they'd found in the safe at Black Cats, which indicated regular loans to Dean over the past nine months. They'd matched the dates with a private card game Chilli had run with some of his associates. Helen was astounded. What drove an apparently honourable man like Dean to gamble with the likes of Chilli Franks, and eventually become tangled into a web of organised crime? She could just imagine Chilli's delight at having a senior detective in his pocket.

Outwardly, Dean had appeared calm, his usual congenial self, but inwardly, it seemed he tussled with the strains of servicing a debt that multiplied daily. And yet there were no giveaway signs – no chewed fingernails, nervous twitches, mood swings – all habits and mannerisms they were taught, as detectives, to notice. Perhaps his years in the force helped him to mask his own troubles. But eventually they'd eaten away at him, consuming his honesty and integrity, until there was nothing left. Chilli and Dean: an unlikely alliance. It was ironic that the one person who didn't succumb to Dean's charms, brought about his downfall.

But there was one small thread of conscience left in Dean. Instead of taking Robert, kidnapping and securing him as Chilli intended, he'd borrowed the boy's mobile phone and dropped him within an hour of home - far enough that he'd have to walk and Helen couldn't reach him and close enough to keep him safe. Chilli trusted Dean's loyalty that he'd secured him. Yet all the time he was safe at home. Although he tracked Helen through her GPS, hunted her down for Chilli, Dean's refusal to involve her youngest son in the debacle that followed was significant to her. Did Dean know this was the end? She would never know.

There had been a time when Helen wondered if he had engineered the move into organised crime, the assistance to Hamptonshire force in their hour of need, to be close to her. She had been flattered by it. Helen thought about the dingy guest house where he was staying, where she had stayed with him. She could see him, smell him, feel the tender touch of his hand, the softness of his eyes upon her. But really he was settling his debts. And he was willing to sacrifice her in pursuit of this goal. This thought sickened her mind.

Now he was dead. The image of him standing in front of her, gun in hand made her stomach cramp. He used her. Thick droplets gathered in her eyes. Right now, she felt like a glass, knocked off the table and smashed into a million broken pieces.

As she quietly sobbed, she considered her fate. She had achieved the same as her father, caught the same dangerous man, brought down an empire of organised crime. Yet right at this moment she didn't feel like much of a success.

Chapter Thirty-Six

Eva peered out of the car window. They passed a jogger in a fluorescent jacket, a woman struggling with a mobility scooter on the uneven tarmac and a group of teenagers, clumped together, laughing. It was a normal Monday, the rest of the world continuing about their business whilst her world had toppled and almost fallen apart.

She had just endured a police interview under caution. With no solicitor of her own, she chose the duty solicitor, Janine Rhyme: a tall, well built woman whose big teeth, long nose and ponytail of black wavy hair made her look distinctly horse-like. It only took twenty minutes alone with Janine for Eva to take her advice and elect to make 'no comment' when interviewed. 'The Crown Prosecution Service only prosecute a case where there is a reasonable chance of a conviction,' Janine had said. And with Jules and Naomi dead, unless the police were able to trace the vehicle, she was confident there would be insufficient evidence to build a case against Eva.

When the interview was over, the detective advised that her parents were waiting for her. For the first time in what felt like forever, Eva felt a jolt of relief. The walk down the corridor to meet them seemed to take twice as long, anticipating the look of sadness on her mother's face, the disappointment on her stepfather's. They weren't due back for another week.

Her heart felt like it had been clamped as she opened the door. The rest was a blur. Arms wrapped around her, larger arms encased them all. For a moment she was packaged in human bodies. A firm kiss was planted on her forehead. She looked up to see her stepfather's worried face staring back at her.

The meeting seemed like a whirl, almost an out-of-body experience. Eva was racked with guilt, the shame she had brought on the family, the disaster of her own making. They were more concerned for her wellbeing, the tortuous events she had faced alone.

It wasn't until later, when Detective Dark brought them coffee, did Eva discover that the detective had updated them in advance of the frightening incidents Eva had encountered over the last ten days.

But one question still puzzled her: how did they find out? Eva's mother explained that they switched their phone on to call and check on her a couple of days ago and received a message from DC Dark, asking them to ring urgently. Dark had obtained their mobile number from the Spences'. What caught Eva were her mother's words, "Your stepfather booked us on the next flight home."

Her stepfather, the man she always disappointed, the man who said she needed to grow up and make some real decisions; he'd said this?

From the back seat, Eva twisted her head to view him. He reached his left hand down to change gear, then back up to the steering wheel, concentrating on the road as any advanced motorist would. She could see the side of his face, the patch at the back of his head where his blond hair was thinning. Her mother reached her hand across and patted his knee affectionately.

He'd been married to her mother for almost sixteen years and Eva certainly hadn't made it easy for him. She'd refused to take his surname at her mother's request, stayed out until the early hours as a teenager, flunked out of university when he'd paid the fees. Yet, he still drove her to youth club all those years, picked her up from the school disco, rushed back home to help in her hour of need, insisted that she go stay with them for a few days to rest.

And it wasn't his fault two of her friends were murdered and she'd been interviewed for alleged drugs trafficking. He wasn't even in the country. This one was down to her. Until now, her body had felt numbed by the tragic events she'd faced over the past week. Suddenly, a warm feeling trickled into her veins. This was like being given a second chance at life, her life. There were a lot of issues she needed to resolve. And she would start by making it up to him. This time she wouldn't mess up.

***

The door opened and Helen managed a feeble smile as her mother, Matthew and Robert filed into the hospital room.

Jane Lavery approached the bed and stroked the back of her folded fingers across her daughter's cheek. "How are you feeling, darling?"

"Like a boxer's punchbag." Helen recognised the shock and concern that her mother attempted to conceal and forged another smile. It caught the split in her lip, causing her to flinch and suck it into her mouth.

She turned to Matthew, who dug his hands into his jean pockets and hunched his shoulders uncomfortably. "How was your weekend?"

"Good, thanks." He looked away, as if he felt guilty for enjoying himself.

Robert stepped forward. "You okay, Mum?"

His tiny frame almost always made him appear younger than his years and this time his facial expression followed suit. The relief at seeing him alive and well was palpable. She was desperate to grab him, hug him and never let go. Yet she didn't want to make a fuss or alarm him anymore right now.

Helen suddenly realised how the bruises on her face, the split in her lip, the darkness in the room must be frightening for her boys. "I'm fine, really," she said, easing her expression. "It looks a lot worse than it is. The doctor said I'll be able to come home tomorrow."

An uneasy silence descended upon them. Helen searched her mother's face. There it was: the terror behind the eyes. Worse still, she could see the same terror both in Matthew and Robert. It wasn't right. They were too young for this.

Helen had felt the same terror herself as she mentally fought against Matthew joining the Air Cadets, putting himself in danger, possibly being taken from her in a flying accident, just like his father. And thoughts of the amiable Robert being kidnapped, in danger, possibly dead, had plunged her heart into a freezer these past twenty-four hours. She was both a mother and father to her boys. Yet, through this job she consistently placed her own life in danger.

Maybe it was time to change positions. Take a desk job, a safe bet for her family. But did it have to be work or family? She had gained her own passions from her father's career. An event like this was unlikely to ever occur again, not even in her line of work. She glanced from face to face, considering how to address the elephant in the room when the door swung open and Jo burst in.

"Hi, Helen. God! You look awful!" Helen struggled to keep the split in her lip together as she smiled. "There are hoards of reporters out there," Jo continued, oblivious to the atmosphere she'd interrupted. "You're front page news. Always thought there was something shifty about that Fitzpatrick." She sniffed.

Jo rambled on but her mere presence in the room lightened the mood.

"Well, boys," Jo eventually said. "I bet you're really proud. Your mum's a hero."

Helen shot her mother an awkward glance.

"Yes, she is," Jane Lavery said, her face impassive. "A hero… "

Interview with the **Author**

When and why did you start writing?

Although I've always had an interest in writing, it was a diary that my husband and I kept during a gap year to travel the world, some years back, that prompted me to take it up seriously. While photos held memories, the words conjured up the essence of each and every place we visited and encouraged me to enrol on a creative writing course on my return.

Initially I studied non-fiction and did some freelance work for newspapers and magazines, then later started the fiction side of the course and fell in love. I wrote a few short stories and eventually decided to try my hand at a novel. I wasn't even sure whether I'd manage to complete a whole book but as soon as I finished *An Unfamiliar Murder* I started *The Truth Will Out*, and am already working on a third, a new crime thriller set in Stratford-upon-Avon.

I love the psychological element of putting ordinary people in extraordinary situations and watching their characters evolve alongside a criminal investigation, so I guess I was always going to write in the mystery/thriller genre. An avid crime reader for many years and a fascination with police investigations and criminal elements, it seemed the right decision to write books I like to read myself.

The character DCI Helen Lavery is both strong and vulnerable. How did you come up with the character, and do you see any aspects of yourself in her?

I knew from the beginning I wanted to avoid the tired, divorced alcoholic detective who lives alone (a role done brilliantly over the years by other authors) and do something different with Helen. I decided to make her realistic, a regular person like you or I, so that we feel her journey. It didn't take long to establish that a single parent managing the most difficult job in the police force whilst raising teenage boys is not unrealistic in modern day policing.

What makes Helen special is that she has little interest in the statistics, politics and resourcing issues that dominate the senior echelons of the police force. She raced through the ranks to follow in her late father's footsteps into this 'hands on' role to make a difference and put away the 'really bad guys'. Leading the murder squad is her ultimate ambition forcing her to occasionally adopt unorthodox methods in pursuit of a killer.

It always makes me chuckle when people ask if Helen is like me. Her personal side is made up of fragments of people I know, acquaintances, and a lady I passed by in a café in London. (It's incredible how a chance encounter can have such an impact!)

I have great admiration for Helen and I'm sure if she was real we'd be friends, but that's where the similarities end. Helen likes to investigate murders; I prefer to write about them.

How did you research the police and forensic procedures referred to in the book?

I'm quite fascinated by forensic developments, the work of detectives and the techniques they employ to solve a case. I think it is important to reflect the police procedural side as accurately as possible in order to keep the novel authentic. There is nothing worse than reading a story and thinking - that would never happen!

I probably spend as much time researching as I do writing a novel and although I do read books and research online, I do prefer the personal approach. I'm very fortunate to have built up lots of contacts throughout the police force and related organisations that are willing to talk through the reality of potential scenarios, although it should be said that real police investigations are actually very methodical and quite laborious in pursuit of the truth, so fiction tends to focus on the more exciting elements.

How do you feel Helen's husband's death has shaped her character?

Losing her husband plunged Helen into life as a single parent. She feels the weight of being both a mother and father to her boys whilst pursuing her passions in her job, but it does have its disadvantages in the unsociable hours and demands it places on her personal life, hence the need for her mother to help out with childcare. Whilst being very protective over her boys, she's also forced to make choices between her personal and professional life and constantly wondering whether she has got the balance right.

I think many people, for whatever reason, find themselves in situations these days where they have to juggle both home and work life. A lot of working parents diligently manage their time between their children and fulfilling the demands of a challenging job and question whether they are doing both well.

What would you have done in Eva's position if you had witnessed your friend being attacked?

Ah! The thousand million dollar question.

The natural reaction would be to call the police, an ambulance and rush to Naomi's side, but then I have nothing to hide.

What fascinates me is that the decisions we make as individuals are often coloured by external circumstances beyond our control. There are times in all our lives when we are required to make quick decisions and judgement calls, which can have wide-reaching consequences.

Eva is essentially a nice girl, she wants to do the right thing, but her secret leaves her cornered: she can't contact the police and she can't go to Naomi as she fears she may be next, so she goes on the run. It was interesting to watch her own character develop as she pushed her life aside and tried to disappear, and how later she dealt with the truth and turned things around.

The novel approaches sensitive subjects including police corruption, drug trafficking and domestic abuse. How important was it to you that these topics were covered accurately?

I think it's important for books to emulate the world in which we live and touch on subjects that exist in the murky underworld of society, but it can be challenging to research and reflect them accurately.

I admit after spending so much time in the company of police officers, I did find it difficult to write about the dark world of police corruption. It makes for exciting fiction, but we should remember that it's extremely rare. It seems police officers rarely receive the praise they deserve. I have nothing but respect for their bravery, integrity and the fact that they put their own lives in danger every day to keep us all safe.

Although domestic violence is quite a small part of the book, I found it very upsetting to research something that is very real and has wide-reaching ramifications for anybody who has ever been affected by it.

When it comes to drugs trafficking and organised crime, what interests me are the motivations behind the actions. Aside from the obvious money and power, what makes a formerly upstanding individual become involved with the criminal fraternity? And more to the point, what makes a serial killer? With this in mind for Nate's character, I consulted a psychologist to help me with his background profile to ensure that his motivations and actions were believable.

Your first novel *An Unfamiliar Murder* was published in the USA, how do you feel about publishing in your home country for the first time?

With improvements in communications, it's so much easier to carry out business across the globe. Although my first publisher was in America, we shared lots of Skype meetings in order to maintain that personal touch and, as the book was also released on Amazon UK and stocked in my local bookshops, it was also available in this country which meant that I could still carry out lots of events to celebrate its release.

That said, it was lovely to work with Legend Press on *The Truth Will Out*. Based within an hour of my home, I was able to travel to London to meet the team and discuss the book and schedule with my editor, which made the process feel more exciting and special.

Who are your favourite crime writers?

From an early age I was captivated by Conan Doyle's enigmatic Sherlock Holmes, his relationship with Moriarty and his powers of deduction. I also enjoyed the mysteries of Agatha Christie and used to love to sit and watch Poirot and Miss Marple with the family, trying to guess 'whodunit'.

In recent years I've enjoyed the twists and turns of Jeffery Deaver, the police procedurals of Peter James and the psychological suspense of Linda Castillo and Elizabeth Haynes.

Come and visit us at
www.legendpress.co.uk

Follow us
@legend_press

Visit Jane's website at
www.janeisaac.co.uk

Follow Jane
@JaneIsaacAuthor